Peace-Lord
of the Red Planet
Steven H. Wilson

PEACE LORD OF THE RED PLANET

This is a work of fiction. All the characters and events portrayed in this book are fictitious, and any resemblance to real people or events is purely coincidental.

Published by
Firebringer Press
6101 Hunt Club Road
Elkridge, MD 20175

ISBN: 9780977385126

July, 2010

Cover Design by Ethan Wilson

Printed in the United States of America

ONE

The farmer's fist hit my face for a third time, and now I fell to the ground. Blood clouded my vision, and a piece of one of my teeth lay loose on my tongue. As I tried to stand, a boot impacted my head. I screamed despite myself and opened my eyes, squinting against the bright sun in the Virginia sky. Through a red haze I saw what must have been the same boot, raised, about to stomp on my face. I inhaled, feeling broken ribs, and willed myself to roll out of its path.

"Leave him," said a voice.

"Leave him?" demanded another. I decided it belonged to the owner of the foot. "I'm gone kill the sumbitch!"

There was a scuffle as my assailant was pulled away. He protested with much enthusiasm and vulgarity.

"We're gone kill him all right," said the owner of the first voice, "but let's leave him so's he knows it's happenin'."

I was hauled to my feet by two men who turned me to face the mob which had descended upon me. To my surprise, the first face I saw was that of a woman, red and inflamed with rage. She stepped forward.

"In Harrisonburg," she said, "they's women that asked to form their own regiment to fight them that done this to us. If women can fight, what's wrong with you?"

My lips were swollen from the blows. I was moved to vomit by the taste of my own blood, but I managed to croak, "Our Lord commanded us to love our neighbor as ourself."

She spit in my face and turned away.

"String 'em up!" shouted a man behind me. They marched me toward a tree.

A week ago, I had been in Baltimore, at the home of Philip Meigs, childhood playmate and member of the Society of Friends. I traveled frequently to Maryland. The Fairfax Meeting, in which I'd been a member since birth, was a part of the Baltimore Yearly Meeting, and Meigs lived in the city, where he was an investor in Hopkins and Brothers. Philip had attended school with me, also training as a physician, but had not found success in medicine. I attributed this to his apparent lack of interest in the suffering of his fellow human beings. I had always assumed him to have a good heart, and I suppose one always assumes one's childhood friends do, but he hid it well. His lack of tenderness did not prevent him amassing a small fortune as a businessman.

This October of 1864, however, had brought hardship on the business of Johns Hopkins and his brothers. Purveyors of "Hopkins Best" whiskey – although Johns was a Quaker, and most southern Quakers detested the use of spirits – they purchased their stock in the rich Shenandoah Valley. Dealing in various wares from wagons, they accepted corn whiskey in trade. This he re-bottled and sold in Baltimore. His trade led to his expulsion from the Meeting, but he maintained it was legitimate business, even though his own uncle accused him of "selling souls into perdition."

Perdition on earth, however, was where his suppliers had recently found themselves. The Shenandoah, in the wake of the Union's General Sheridan, was a smoldering ruin. Over 2000 farms had been burned to the ground, all the crops destroyed, the livestock seized or killed.

"It's a damned frustrating setback for our business," Philip said as he cut into his steak, stopping briefly to ask his butler to reprimand the cook on its temperature. "Those bastards drank, stole or drained all the whiskey, and left the cornfields a black smear on the earth. I doubt our suppliers will be able to rebuild. I don't know where we're expected to find another source of stock."

"Nor where your former suppliers are to find a new source of income?" I asked pleasantly.

He shrugged. "Hardly my concern, is it?"

I felt my jaw tighten. Philip's attitudes often infuriated me. When I lost my temper with him, as I had often over the course of our relationship, he never failed to make sport of me. I'd learned to control my outbursts, more or less.

"They are fellow human beings, Philip," I said.

"Obviously they are. And it's unfortunate that they happened to live in an area of such strategic importance that it had to be routed by the Union forces. But what else was the army to do, eh? The Shenandoah was used repeatedly as a staging ground for attacks on Washington and Maryland. They had no choice – "

"Christians always have a choice," I said, too loudly. "Making war is never necessary."

"The majority of the nation – two nations, if the rebels are to be believed – is not in agreement with you, Shep."

"With us," I corrected him. "They are not in agreement with us."

Again he shrugged. "I suppose. Though I don't see how we're to break the South of slavery, other than through war."

"Do you believe this war will break slavery?" I asked.

"It cannot help but, if the North wins. They will not allow the South to continue this practice which gives them such an economic advantage."

"Philip, it irritates me how you speak of the evil of man against man – brother against brother – as if its only consequences were financial ones."

"One must be practical, Shep – " He threw down his fork. "I cannot eat this damned steak!" He exclaimed to his butler. "Take it away and ask the silly woman if there is something she does know how to prepare in a state that a human might consume!" He turned to me. "Though how one's digestion is to function in the presence of Dr. Autrey and his oozing emotions is beyond me," he said scathingly.

"I'm only asking you to show some compassion, Philip. As a physician, and a Quaker, one would think you'd have a little."

He sighed. "You do make me tired, Shep. I am merely considering how the events around us affect me and my livelihood. Is that wrong?"

"Only insofar as you fail to see how you might be contributing to the suffering of others."

"And how am I doing that?" he asked.

"By failing to join your brethren in combating the evils of both war and slavery. Before this conflict erupted, you did nothing to help bring about a peaceable end to what the Southerners call their 'peculiar institution.'"

"You mean I didn't endanger my household by taking in fugitives," he said sourly.

He knew that I had sequestered four Negroes who had escaped their masters in my own home, and seen them move safely on to the North in a quest for their freedom.

"My household was in little danger, I assure you. But better that I, a single man, be in danger, than leave the burden to fall to a family with children."

"You live in the country," he said. "I do not. It's far more difficult to hide an escaped slave in a crowded neighborhood such as mine."

"Nor have you offered any medical aid to the casualties of this war," I pressed on. "As so many of our fellow doctors, and our fellow Friends, have done."

"I am not a practicing physician, Shepherd."

"I wonder if you are a practicing Christian, " I said.

He threw down his napkin. "Ah! I see. Now I am to be threatened with expulsion, like Mr. Hopkins, because I do not meet your standards of piety?"

"I would not move to have you expelled," I said.

"You damned well better not! Were I to lose my standing with the Friends, my business would suffer!"

"Oh, in the name of God, is that all you can think of?" I shouted, flinging my own napkin across the table. Philip swallowed, taken aback for once by the violence of my tone.

Embarrassed by my outburst, I stood to leave. I began to make my apologies, however insincere, for my breech of etiquette.

Philip raised his hands in a calming gesture. "Now, Shep. Let us not allow our tempers to color our friendship. I understand that you feel strongly about what is happening in our land. I... simply do not... show my feelings as easily as you do."

I sighed heavily. "With that I would agree."

"Please sit down. We'll have some sherry. I have a fine amontillado in the cellars, I believe. It will calm you."

He called for the delivery of the spirits while I composed myself. When we were alone again, I said, "Philip, please forgive my outburst. It's just that you seem so... indifferent to human suffering."

"It's just that there's so much of it," he countered. "What can one man do?"

"One man can do what he can," I replied. "Your... associates in the Valley. You could show them some Christian charity. I have no doubt that they are hungry, homeless. In such conditions, disease flourishes, and more violence."

"And what would you do to stem the tide?" he asked quietly.

"Many Friends have set up hospitals and shelters," I said. "Offering comfort to the wounded, the dying, the bereft. You could go there – "

"I would be shot by the Union troops were I to go near the Shenandoah!"

"Unlikely," I said. "Safe passage can be arranged, especially for doctors. And Quaker neutrality is... grudgingly accepted."

He shook his head. "You are having sport with me, Shep. You do not believe for a moment I could go and – "

"I do!" I insisted. "I believe any man of conscience would go and offer aid – "

His face lit up with interest. There was no good intent in him then, I was sure. "Would you go yourself?"

"Of course!"

"To the Shenandoah? Tomorrow?"

"I – yes. As soon as I could make preparations – "

"I do not believe it."

I met and held his gaze. "You think my convictions so shallow, after all these years?"

"I believe even you are too practical to walk into such danger."

"I will prove you wrong, then," I said. I started, once again, to stand and leave.

Philip smiled his most predatory smile. "I do believe you're serious!"

"I am."

"Well then... perhaps we could discuss... a small wager?"

Of course, laying money on a proposition – any proposition – was enough to secure Philip's interest. Those of my faith do not believe in gambling. It inflames the lust for profit which distracts us from the more noble impulses which our Lord called upon us to follow. In this case, however, I felt moved to accept Philip's wager. If a small sin on my part would draw my errant comrade into a moral venture, was it really a sin?

Because of course, Philip would not take my word where money was concerned. Once I had agreed that I would pay him a sum of fifty dollars were I to fail to go to the Valley and spend full two weeks there, aiding the afflicted, there was no way he would remain home and take me upon my word that I had fulfilled my part of the bargain. No, with money on the line, he was willing to travel with me.

So it was, days later, that we had arrived in Virginia and joined in relief efforts near the ruined town of Winchester, where one of the few standing homes had been converted to a makeshift hospital. Here wounded soldiers were treated. Here, also, those left homeless as Sheridan had cut his fiery swath through the Valley came in search of food and shelter.

On our second day there, a woman arrived with six children, the oldest being a fourteen-year-old boy who looked about ten. He was thin and small for his age, not malnourished, just slower than average in his physical development. The father, I was told, was a soldier in the Confederate Army. He had gone off to war six months previous, and they'd had but one letter from him. The smaller children proudly told me that Daddy was a brave soldier, gone to Washington to kill Abe Lincoln, but the eyes of the mother and the oldest boy told me that they believed Daddy was dead and buried in an unmarked grave somewhere.

Their home, like so many others, was gone. Burned to the ground. They had only the clothes on their backs, and those not much to speak of. But the mother, herself a Quaker like so many in the Valley, fell in with me.

She nursed the wounded and helped find beds and floor space for the refugees. The boy likewise attempted to help, but was largely occupied with supervision of his young siblings. I find that the young have a natural proclivity to be helpful to their fellows, and no such natural understanding or kinship with the practice of organized violence. Strike out when they consider themselves injured they certainly will. But plan and execute a campaign of murder and mayhem? No, that is adult foolishness only. With children, the injuries are forgotten as quickly as the temper is lost.

It was near sunset on our sixth day that a group of men rode up to the house on horseback. They were a ragtag collection, one carrying a tattered Confederate battle flag, their leader dressed in most of a gray Confederate uniform. They made their business clear immediately – they were recruiting to raise a regiment. As physicians, Meigs and I were overlooked for their purposes, it being clear that our services were needed here. I was not to evade their notice for long, however.

While their leader made his way through sick beds, surveying for bodies able enough to accompany him, one of his lieutenants came into the ward, literally dragging young Joseph, the fourteen-year-old, by the scruff of his neck.

"Put me down!" the boy screamed. "I got to stay with my sisters!"

"Women can see to the children," said the fellow carrying him. "Women and those men as aren't fit for manly work," he raked his eyes, burning with hatred, over me.

The man in uniform said, "Little puny, ain't he?"

"Says 'e's fourteen," said the other.

"Well then. Guess you're goin' to war, soldier."

The boy's eyes widened. At this point, his mother charged into the room.

"What do you think you're doing?" she demanded.

"None of your concern, woman," said the officer.

"It certainly is my concern," said she. "The boy is my son."

"Then you should let him be a man," he replied.

"I've had little choice," she said bitterly, "since you drafted my husband. Now he's all I have to help me care for his sisters. You can't take him! Have you no compassion?"

"We're at war," said the man coldly. "There's little room for compassion."

I could keep silent no longer. "See here, friend," I said. "This lad may be of age, in your eyes, but... look at him! He's not fit for battle."

The stranger scowled at me and gestured toward the windows of the room. "Have you seen my men, Doctor? Which of us would you say is fit for combat? But what are we to do, when the Yankee dogs burn our homes to the ground, and leave our children to starve?"

"We are to act as our savior would have us act; to aid our brethren; to have the same compassion that Christ himself had for us. Would He have seen children dragged from their mothers– ?"

He rolled his eyes. "Je-sus Christ! I've had my fill of you Quaker cunts and your love-thy-neighbor preachin'! I loved my neighbor jest fine – until the moment a Northern bayonet went through 'is eye and killed him!"

I swallowed, shaken both by the violence depicted and by his taking of the Lord's name in vain. "God have mercy on you friend, and may His mighty hand heal your wounds. But do not extend your sufferings to this innocent child – "

"It's time for you to shut up," he said. He reached across and took hold of Joseph's arm, pulling hard to draw the boy to his side. Joseph winced in pain as his shoulder was wrenched, but said nothing. His captor drew a knife from his belt and jabbed the tip of it against the soft, white flesh of the child's throat.

"Now," said the officer. "You can come with me, boy, or I can let your mama watch you die here and now. What do you say?"

Joseph's eyes, alive with terror, met mine. I shook my head, not knowing what to say. Were I to tell the officer my opinion of his cowardly behavior, he would surely kill the child for spite.

"Please!" shrieked Joseph's mother. "Don't hurt him!"

The knife remained where it was. "Make your choice, boy."

"I - I'll go," Joseph squeaked out.

The officer, satisfied, shoved him back toward his original captor. "Knife to yer throat kinda puts things in perspective, don't it, Doc?" he sneered.

"For the young," I said. "I wouldn't expect a boy to have the courage to die for his convictions."

"Izzat a fact? So, I s'pose you woulda just let me cut yer fool throat?"

I wondered if my mouth had gotten me in trouble. It often did. "Before I'd agree to kill other children of God, yes, I would."

"Yer lyin'," he spat. "Yer a coward. All ya'll Quakers is."

"Hardly," I said. "It takes true courage to resist violence."

"You callin' me a coward?" he demanded.

"Doctor Autrey, please," the woman begged silently.

"Let him answer!" my opponent barked.

"If the shoe fits," I said.

His face went red. "We'll jest see who's a coward!" He nodded to the other man, who came from behind me and seized my arms in a vise grip. "Take him out there to that tree by the road," his superior continued. "String him up – "

"No!" called the woman.

The officer ignored her and went on. "But give 'im a chance to beg for his life, 'fore he dies. I wager he'll be ridin' outta here with us."

Meigs came into the room just as they were leading me away. "Shep, what in the world?" he demanded.

The officer pointed at me. "Friend o' yours?"

Philip was silent.

"He is a physician, come to help the needy," I said. "He's done you no harm."

The officer strode over to Philip and looked him in the eye. "You a Quaker too, pansy?"

Philip swallowed. "I - I am. I am here with a writ of safe passage – " he reached into his coat.

The officer knocked his hand away, and drew his gun, leveling it at Philip's head. "Passage is what yer gonna get all right. We're gonna string you up next to your friend."

They led us outside, and to a tree, as promised. When we arrived, ropes had already been cast over the sturdiest of the lower branches, nooses tied on the end.

The strangers crowded around to watch the execution, as did some of the children, herded there by soldiers. At the edge of the circle of faces, I saw Joseph, weeping openly.

"Please," I said to my captors, "I am prepared to die. The Lord will protect me. But may I be allowed to pray with the boy?"

"Good god, Shep, don't make things worse!" cried Philip. I feared he was becoming hysterical.

I ignored him and looked at the officer. "Please," I said. "In the name of Christian charity – "

He drew back and drove his fist into my mouth, loosening the first of my teeth. Then he grabbed my hair, spun me around, and held me out before the assembled mob.

"Anybody care to show him what we think of those what won't fight for their freedom?" he asked. The mob advanced.

And now, here we were, beaten, bloodied, about to be hanged. Three men lifted me bodily and deposited me on the back of a horse. Next to me, Philip, one of his eyes so swollen that, were we to live past this hour, he might surely lose it, was similarly mounted. While the horses were held in place by one man, another, mounted on the shoulders of a third, slipped the nooses around our necks and tightened them.

"Oh god," moaned Philip. "Please..."

"Your friend is about to put on a show for us, I think," said the officer. "You gonna sing, too?"

I shook my head. "I trust in the Lord."

This statement was met with guffaws. "Maybe the Lord'll break the rope for ye!" someone called out.

"Shep, they're going to kill us!" Philip wept.

"Yes," I agreed. "They are." I hoped I sounded calm. I felt sick to my stomach. I was grateful not to be expected to stand, for my knees were weak. I prayed to God to be given the strength to meet death with courage, as Jesus had met His on the cross. "Pray for strength, Philip," I said quietly. "It will be over soon."

But, instead of praying, Philip called out to our attackers, casting his face about, as I think he was blind. "Don't listen to him!" he shrieked. "We aren't ready to die! We'll do whatever you ask!"

"Philip!" I hissed, but someone struck me in the gut with the butt of a rifle.

"Please," Philip went on. "We'll join your army!"

"Will ya?" asked the officer. "Will ya come and kill the yanks with us?"

"Yes," said Philip, trying in vain to nod, despite the rope around his neck. "I'll kill them all! Filthy, Yankee pigs!"

I shut my eyes and began to pray, silently, for my friend's immortal soul.

"Well that's different," said the officer. "If you're willin' t'join us – "

"I am!"

"Then I better put it to a vote!" He turned to the throng about him. "Whaddya say? Should I let 'im live?"

The blood lust was upon them, however. They'd been promised two deaths, and they believed, somehow, that those deaths would ease the pain of their recent losses. It is a foolish belief, but such foolishness is common. As one, they cried out that we should die.

The officer shrugged. "Sorry, friend. It's outta my hands."

"But," Philip protested. "You said – "

"What can I tell ya, friend? War makes animals of us all." Then he threw back his head and laughed, and motioned to the handlers to release the horses and whip them forward.

I closed my eyes again. I heard Philip dissolve into sobs beside me, and smelled ammonia as, in his fear, he lost control of his bladder. I distanced myself from all of this and looked inward, toward the light. Within me, as within each of us, was that spark of divine fire. I sought it out.

I had a great deal of experience at this kind of inward-looking prayer. In addition to the accepted practice of quiet worship in the Friends' meeting house, I had read works describing the Eastern Buddhist religion, and its practice of meditation. Although Buddhists did not personalize the light, as we did, they did seek it, or a state of being much like communion with it.

Today, this last day of my life, during these final moments, I finally found myself achieving that state of peace, of exclusivity from the outside world, which had so long been my goal. I heard, but did not register the cursing and jeering of the crowd. The smell of the horse on which I sat, the leather of its saddle, did not touch my nose. The coarse fibers of the rope about my neck did not chafe my flesh. I was spirit alone, drifting down, inward, toward a pinnacle of light on the horizon.

The world was balanced. Everything was as it should be. I was at peace. Vaguely I knew I was going to die, but I knew with utter certainty that the author of the universe was pleased with me, and that I was under His care. This death, this little, petty end to my little, petty travels on the corrupt world of my birth, was but a trifle. It was a branch on the pathway, to be noted, stepped over, and forgotten. The true journey lay ahead.

From somewhere far off, I heard a snap, a clatter of hooves, a creak of a branch, as it was weighed down, a sickly, gurgling sound. Someone was being hanged. Was it me? Was it Philip? I thought of Philip, of his fear, his failed dignity, his body, swinging at the end of a rope, his expensive trousers, sodden with his own wastes, even before death had finally relaxed the body's muscles...

I prayed for Philip. I had no concern for myself. It was not that I didn't think of myself – I did – but I had no fear for my own soul. Philip, on the other hand, was frightened, discouraged, a sinner who did not know how to put his sins aside and stand before the Lord. I prayed for him.

Reach out to him, Lord, I called into the light. Take his hand, gather him to Your bosom. Comfort him, as You have comforted me. He is unworthy of Your love, even as I am. Yet show him compassion.

I wondered what would happen next. Would God himself appear to me, or Jesus? Was I to be welcomed into the arms of the Savior and the Father? The light brightened. It bathed me. I was sure I felt its heat upon my face. All threat to my physical body, all pain from my wounds, was forgotten. I was traveling home, to the Glory of God.

The light overtook me, and then began to fade...

⸻

I landed on my back with a thud. Beside me, I heard groaning. I looked to see Philip, stunned and, like myself, sprawled face up. The mob was gone. The horses were gone. The trees were gone. There were no ropes about our necks, nor was there a stitch of clothing on our bodies. I wriggled and pulled a medium-sized rock from between my shoulder blades. Heaven had a sandy, rocky surface, and the soil was tinged red, like blood. The sky was purplish gray.

To my right, there was a sudden clamor. I turned as quickly as I could, and saw hundreds, no, thousands of men bearing down on us. Some were on foot. Some rode unbelievable contraptions of metal, which moved through the air without support. All were near as naked as we, and all carried weapons of some kind. These they fired or swung, striking the bodies of others similarly clad and armed. Blood spattered the already red sands, and men fell, wounded, even dead, to the ground.

There was war in heaven.

TWO

I roused Philip and helped him stand.

"Where are we?" he demanded, though his thick and battered lips muffled his speech.

"Dead, I'd gather," I said.

"If I'm dead, why does everything hurt?" he asked me. "And what in the world – ?"

He turned and took in the scene of the battle which was inching our way at a generous pace. "Who are those people?" He looked down. "What happened to our clothes? In the name of god, Shep – !"

"Try to stay calm, Philip," I said, feeling silly for saying.

"Calm! We're – !" He spread his arms and gestured at the alien landscape. "And there are – " He pointed at the encroaching warriors. "And – "

"I don't know," I said. "I don't know anything more than you do. But, given our state of... undress. I'd suggest we move away from this conflict, and – "

I was interrupted by a whizzing at my ear. Philip screamed and, dropping to his feet, covered his head with his arms. Beyond him landed what was obviously the source of the whizzing noise, a spear. Curious, I moved to collect it. It was not an ordinary spear of wood and stone. Its tip glowed, as if it were heated metal. Gingerly, I moved my hand close to it. There was no heat. I brushed the backs of my fingers over its brilliant surface, and received a strong static shock.

Surprised, I pulled my hand away.

"What is it?" wondered Philip.

The warriors were on top of us now, bearing down. Whether they wished to claim the weapon, or simply thought us more of their number, I did not know. Seizing the spear by its inert shaft, I pulled Philip by the shoulder and exhorted him to run, keeping an eye on the throng behind us. Ahead were hills, red and rocky, like some enormous red velvet cake. There might be shelter.

Behind me, a scream sounded, high-pitched and terrified. I spun and saw a boy, no more than seventeen, sprawled on the ground, one hand raised in pitiful defense. Over him stood a burly man with a pistol. The gun was like none I'd ever seen, but its intended use was clear. The brute aimed it at the boy's face.

"Come on!" urged Philip.

I could not continue. This boy did not belong on the field of battle, any more than Joseph had. As one of the Society of Friends, I believed no one belonged in battle, of course; but there were degrees of wrong. Grown, competent adults at least were equipped to face their own sin. This was but a spindly boy, his limbs not fully formed, his skin a milky white. I wondered if he was even healthy.

I could not allow this callous murder of an innocent. I sprung forward and seized the enormous man's wrist with both my hands. His natural strength was greater than mine, but I had the advantage of surprise. I also was the youngest of four brothers, and knew well how to resist a larger opponent for a time. As I dug my fingers into hard flesh, attempting to force the brute's fingers to open, the boy scrambled away.

My opponent was gaining ground on me. With the boy gone, he shot his free hand to my throat and began to squeeze. The pain of my compressing windpipe let me know that I must still be alive. I feared that I would not be for much longer. I would never know the means of my deliverance to this unlikely place of battle.

And then, as quickly as he had grasped my throat, the warrior released it. Over his shoulder, I registered a flash of light. I smelled a sickly stench of burning flesh. The brute dropped his weapon and reached to clutch his back. Immediately, he pitched forward on his face, and revealed a horrid, gaping wound, edged with burned flesh, which exposed his spine. He coughed once, ejecting blackish blood on the sand, and then was still.

I looked to see the author of this violence, whom I must also call savior, I supposed. A man of my own years, perhaps a few more, strode forward. He was cloaked, but barely clothed otherwise, save for a belt with scabbards and holsters to hold his weapons. In his hand was a pistol, much like that my opponent had brandished. I reasoned that it was this which had killed the big man.

"Are you all right, Hylas?" my rescuer asked in unaccented English. It did not occur to me at the time that it was English, but it must have been, for I spoke no other language.

The boy stepped forward. "I am well, father." He looked to me. "The stranger saved me."

His father nodded. "I saw. You are a brave warrior, my friend, and you have my thanks."

"I am no warrior," I said. "My name is Shepherd Autrey, and I am a stranger here, as your son says."

"That is obvious," the father agreed. "Come, Shepherdautrey. Our part in this battle is done, now that my son is safe again." He looked me over. "You have seen much battle today. You and your companion. I will have your wounds looked to."

———

His name was Scorpius, and he was the king, for lack of a better word, of his people. The battle we had fallen into the midst of had erupted when foreign agents had kidnapped his son, Hylas, the boy I had saved. They'd hoped to ransom him but, when the battle did not go well, had thought it better to kill him. I'd prevented this senseless brutality, and, apparently, won the favor of a powerful family. All this Scorpius told me as he led me back to his home.

They lived in a city they called Aspar, and I'd never seen its like. Buildings towered above its streets, touching the sky. I wondered how they had attained such height without collapsing. I'd read that advancements in engineering would allow taller and taller buildings. In Washington, an obelisk honoring President George Washington had been under construction for sixteen years, and was promised to scale 600 feet, though only 200 had been achieved before money ran out. I doubted it would ever be finished.

And the mode of transportation to the city! I'd first noticed the things when I'd found myself here on this red landscape. With shapes vaguely like the body of a horse, they were made of polished metal, and floated – floated! – above the ground at the same height a horse might. But I learned they were capable of far greater heights when young Hylas strapped me on the back saddle of his – they were designed to hold two – and shot hundreds of feet into the air, laughing happily at my wide eyes, and the screams of Philip, who rode the back of his father's mount.

I tried to ask what manner of device this was, but the rushing wind resulting from our flight prevented conversation. That was made to wait until we reached the spires of Aspar. Fortunate it was, too, for I knew Scorpius would have questions for me, and I had no idea how I should answer them. Should I tell the truth, and say that I was about to be hanged, and then awoke here, believing I was in Heaven? Anyone telling such a story would certainly be locked away as a madman.

Or would he? What if – God help me! – this really was Heaven? What if the afterlife really were this absurd parody of the world I grew up in? Was God that much of a trickster, as some ancients had believed? What other explanation was there? That I had been transported to some other world?

Before I was ready, the time came. I was in Scorpius's apartments, atop one of the frightful towers, looking down hundreds of feet on the city below. We were so high up it was impossible, looking through the enormous windows, to distinguish any recognizable features of the people below. After indulging in the novelty of looking down from such a height, I stepped away from the windows. The sheer scope of the distance unnerved me.

Philip was still with the Doctor. His eye was badly bruised, and the cornea scratched, the Doctor said. I was amazed at the confidence of the man that he could do anything but minimize the pain of such an injury, but there were wonders aplenty this day.

Scorpius had invited me to have "some lunch." His modest offerings included two complete roast... I suppose they were pigs; a selection of interesting fruits; breads and pastries more elaborate, surely than any a Paris bakery might produce; and wine, or its equivalent, and much of it. This I attempted to decline, having always believed in moderation. There was precious little else to drink, however, and even young Hylas was having his fill.

Reclining on his couch as three beautiful (and naked) maidens attended us, Scorpius asked, "Now tell me your story, Shepherdautrey. How did you come to our city? You're clearly foreign."

"I – yes," I acknowledged. In my distraction, I sloshed wine from my goblet on my bare thigh. One of the maidens immediately came to dry it with a napkin. Her nearness, her heat, and our mutual lack of clothing conspired against my decorum. I reached for a blanket which was artistically draped over the arm of my sofa, and artistically draped it over myself.

"Are you cold?" asked Hylas innocently.

"I... cold. Yes."

"One of the servants will warm you," he said solicitously. My comfort was clearly of concern. The boy began to gesture to one of the young women.

I shot up my hand. "The blanket is fine! I... This is fine." I adjusted my covering yet again. Hylas and his father, still nearly naked, sat, unashamed and... un-flustered... by the presence of so much feminine beauty. I suppose they were accustomed to it.

"What gave me away as a foreigner?" I asked, desperate to change the subject.

Scorpius laughed. My question was apparently absurd. "Your accent. You didn't think I had noticed it?"

"Of course not – " I began.

"Don't be insulted, my friend. Most foreigners are incapable of learning the Asparian language." He gestured at the girls. "They barely understand a word of it, poor, stupid things. But your command is quite good, if heavily accented. You're from Equatoria, I gather? Your coloring suggests it."

"I... yes. My coloring." He clearly assumed I was from a southern clime, where I was exposed to sunlight. My skin is rather dark, for a white man. Father was descended from pure English Quaker stock, but Mother, who'd joined the Friends as a child, was half Cherokee. My skin and eyes bespoke her heritage.

Scorpius and Hylas were pale – more pale than I was accustomed to. At first, I'd assumed the boy was sickly, and had not had sufficient exercise in the outdoors. Now that I observed him more closely, I saw that he was well-formed, if thin. The years would correct his thinness, I had no doubt. It seemed that the near-albino coloring of the skin was a common trait, but these people were not albinos.   Hylas had deep green eyes, the color of new grass. His father's were steely gray. Neither had the white-blond hair of the albino. I'd never heard of their like on earth. They were paler even than Scandinavians.

"You've traveled a long way," said Hylas quietly. The boy, like so many his age, seemed shy around a stranger, and yet exceedingly eager to be noticed and included. It was apparent he wanted to stand with the men, not the children.

"Not... under my own power," I said truthfully. "I had a... disagreement with quite a number of unsavory characters. They... transported Dr. Meigs and myself here."

"It seems you stood up for yourself," Scorpius observed, nodding to my many bruises. "Such evidence of battle is not seen on a coward. Not a living one, anyway."

"Shepherdautrey said he's not a warrior, Father," said Hylas.

"Don't be ridiculous," said Scorpius, "all men are warriors, who are not slaves."

"Actually," I said, "where I come from, not all men are warriors. I am not one.   I am a doctor."   I added, "And my name is actually two – Shepherd Autrey. Please call me Shepherd, or Shep."

"Two names?" wondered Hylas. "What do you do with two names?" I laughed. "The second one indicates my family," I said.

Scorpius gave a thoughtful grimace. "Very different customs they have in Equatoria. We've not seen it in my lifetime, I'm sorry to say. Since the quakes during my father's reign, there's been little wealth there to plunder. It seems that's changing."

"My land is faced with conflicts of its own," I said, amazed at how easy it was to tell the full truth, yet have the end result of telling a lie. Was that a sin? If so, I begged my Heavenly Father for forgiveness, but I did not think it wise to tell the whole truth until I knew where I was.

"Still and all," said Scorpius. "Your bravery is evidenced by the fact that you came through a battle with a greater number of enemies – and what cowardice they displayed, to attack you en masse!"

"They certainly were driven by fear," I said.

"And your courage is more directly spoken by your actions in saving my only son," he nodded at Hylas.

"I could not just walk away when I saw him threatened," I said. "War is bad enough, without it threatening those who have yet to experience life."

"War is life," Scorpius said carefully through a frown.

I did not respond immediately. I silently asked myself how Christ would have responded to such an absurd remark, without completely ending discourse with he who uttered it. I had no wish to be ungrateful for the hospitality I'd been shown. I decided my best tact was to try and learn more about this strange world into which I'd fallen.

"Tell me about those who kidnapped you, Hylas. Your father said they wanted ransom?"

"Indeed they did," Scorpius answered. "It is a common custom this, taking the heir to a people's throne. Some cities fill their public coffers entirely on ransom paid by others. Close to your own country, I believe there are cities with hostage exchange programs, where sons – and, amazingly, daughters – are sent to live with the enemy, to ensure that treaties are followed."

"But that fellow was going to kill Hylas, I am sure," I said. "Where is the portion in that?"

The older man snorted. "There is none. They are barbarian fools, the Amal hordes. They think of strategy and profit only as long as the battle goes in their favor. If they fear they might lose, they become brutal and vindictive, killing anything that moves. Sometimes, in their rage, they kill their own comrades. Idiots! It's no wonder they do not rule themselves."

"Who rules them?" I asked.

"The Jentana, our greatest rivals. They send the Amal as their advance guard, to do the hard labor and the dangerous work."

"I would think that kidnapping would require subtlety," I said.

"It does," agreed Scorpius. "But kidnapping my son is dangerous. The Jentana don't trade their lives easily. They enjoy them too much." He sounded contemptuous.

"You sound as though you disapprove of enjoying life, Scorpius."

He chuckled and pinched one of the servant girls on her exposed posterior. "I take my pleasure from it. We do believe in our comforts." His face darkened. "But my people understand that a man is judged in the afterlife on his bravery, his ambition and his leadership. Those who value their lives too highly will not be looked on with favor by the gods."

There was a point of interest to me. He believed in god. Or gods. Clearly, he believed in primitive war gods, but still. Perhaps I could parley that belief into an opening to witness to him of the True Way, the path of Christ. There would be time enough, I hoped, to explore that possibility. Still, I was baffled. How could those who worshiped primitive idols of war have accomplished the technological wonders I saw about me?

I asked, "Wouldn't the gods also be impressed by what you have done in this very city? These beautiful towers? We have nothing like them in my land. And I pride myself on coming from an advanced, civilized land, but your physicians are aware of medicine I've never encountered. My friend Meigs would have lost his eye, had I been left to treat him. But your doctors tell me they can save it. Your engines of flight are true marvels. Do you tell me that all these things which celebrate and enhance life would be looked on indifferently by the gods?"

"Why would the gods be impressed by that which they have wrought?" he asked.

"I don't follow you."

He spread his hands to indicate all that was around us. "Our city, our medicine, our hoversteeds – all of these were given to us by the gods. They are not our accomplishments. They are tools that we are to use in striving against our enemies, to the glory of the gods."

At least they understood the source of all gifts, I thought, even if they mistakenly assumed that there was more than one, true God.

"Your humility does you credit," I said. "Only a man of true faith ascribes all his glory to God."

Scorpius nodded. "As I surely do. It is because my men fight bravely and have proven themselves worthy time and again that Aspar is favored by the gods. No other city is so blessed with godly gifts." He rolled his eyes and took a swig of wine before adding, ruefully, "Except the damnable Jentana."

"They are... similarly blessed?" I asked.

"More so, it pains me to admit. Their gods have greater resources than ours."

"They have... different gods?" I wondered, incredulous.

"To be sure. Their cursed Mother Goddess and her whoring followers cast out the warrior prince Raxes, son of her own brother the god of War. Raxes is rightful heir to the throne of the gods, but the great whore and her traitorous fellows overthrew their King long ago. The Mother Goddess, as she calls herself, took it for herself, killed her brother, and denied his child his rightful heritage."

My head spun. Scorpius's religion was structured like a serial novel.

"So... your gods... are at war?"

"Of course! It has been so since they created the New World for us!"

"New World?"

Scorpius shook his head and laughed. "Equatoria must be in a sad state, for so noble a one as you to be so poorly educated," he said. "Surely you knew that there was an earth before this one? Where the first three kings of the gods ruled?"

"I... I certainly was aware that this was a different world," I said honestly.

"Well, there you have it. Did your teachers not also tell you that it was after the rebellion of the Mother Goddess, when she joined her father's enemies and deposed him, that she quit old earth, and brought us all here, to the red planet, to begin a new age? And that Raxes, once he came of age, broke out from under her control, and swore to claim this world for himself and his favored ones?"

Red planet? I wondered aloud, "Then... this is Mars?"

Hylas giggled.

"You are confused, but you obviously were taught something of the old stories. Mars was what some called the brother world to our old world, earth. But this is not Mars. The gods, with their phenomenal powers, brought us across the vault of heaven to this new planet! New Earth!"

My mind reeled, and not only from the wine. This was too much to take in. Was it possible that I was on another world? Another heavenly body? That the sun which burned in the purple sky was not the one which warmed the world of my birth? And that these people... really were descended from people of my own earth?

"I... fear my knowledge is lacking," I admitted. I grinned and nodded to Hylas. "And my young friend laughs at me."

The boy looked down, shyly. "I meant no offense."

"And I have taken none, Hylas. I hope you will assist me in filling the gaps in my educaton."

His face colored. "Me? Teach... you?"

I laughed. "Why not? We all can learn from each other."

He cast his eyes downward again. "I had... been hoping... that is, I mean to ask you... if you would teach me?"

Scorpius looked at his son with evident pride as he said this.

Confused by the gravity with which they both credited this request, I shrugged. "Whatever I know, my young friend."

Hylas colored even deeper, but grinned back at me hesitantly. "I am honored... Shep."

From the boy's awkwardness, and the glances passing between father and son, I gathered that to teach must be an honorable pastime among their people. I did not understand their near-solemnity, nor did I want to reveal too much of my ignorance. I let the moment pass, trusting that all would be revealed, in time.

"Well," I said, "I'm glad in any event that the Jentana did not succeed in their campaign, and that you are out of danger, Hylas. If we cannot all be spared the horrors of war, at the very least, the young should be kept from the battlefield."

"Your beliefs are strange," said Scorpius carefully. "We see things differently. The Amal seized Hylas before he had completed his warrior training. That is why his life was in such danger. In a few months' time, we will launch an attack on the Jentana capitol, in retaliation for this attempted kidnapping. Hylas will lead a squadron in that attack."

"Will he?" I asked guardedly.

"It is only fitting," said Scorpius. "If he is worthy, he will smite his opponents."

Hylas smiled wickedly and said, "I will show them no mercy."

"Won't you?" I asked.

"Of course not, once you have trained me in the arts of war!"

I nearly choked. "I – the arts of war?"

"Of course," said Hylas. "You said you would teach me." His eyes grew wide, and he was suddenly animated. "You wouldn't break your promise!"

I reached out a hand and took his shoulder. "I said I would teach you what I knew, Hylas. I'm afraid I don't know the arts of war."

"But – " Hylas began.

"Do not trouble yourself, my son," Scorpius said with confidence. "Shep is merely being modest. Doctors are like that. You and I have seen his courage. And I sense he is a man of his word."

"Well..." I said, hoping to make a quick exit and give myself time to think. "I... really need to check on my friend."

"Hylas will lead you to him," said Scorpius. "He is in his rooms now, and rooms have also been prepared for you."

"That's very generous of you."

There was surprise – almost disapproval – in Scorpius's eye as he asserted, "It is not generosity. I owe you my son's life. I pay my debts."

———

Hylas took me to visit Philip in his lavish apartment. He was either drunk or medicated. I don't know which, but he was being tended by two of the omnipresent young women who never spoke. I was astounded to see his eye – bruised and puffy, yes – but healing. I could see now that he was in no danger of losing it, but he had been. Of that I was sure. I must learn more of their medicine, I told myself.

And then, tired and bewildered, I followed Hylas to my own luxurious apartment: a suite of two rooms and bathing facilities to put the finest hotel in Paris or New York to shame. The furnishings were strange to me. They were not any style I recognized, but their functions were obvious. They seemed to serve them well. Hylas showed me all necessaries and comforts – including a fantastic device, similar in concept to a telegraph, but capable of carrying the sound of a voice, presumably over wires, from one remote location to another. I could use it, he explained, to communicate with the household staff if I was in need of any sort of assistance.

"Amazing," I said. "I've heard of devices which can convert sound into written symbol – the phonoautograph, I believe it's called, but – "

"You do not even have speakers in your land?" Hylas asked dubiously.

"Not even," said I. "We can send messages via wire, but not reproduce sound in this way."

"Listen to this." He fiddled with buttons and knobs on the small box which controlled this amazing invention, and, suddenly, the music of a wind instrument came forth, no doubt the playing of a set of pipes. It evoked images of shepherds, my namesakes, playing flutes in the field.

"But where is the one playing the music?" I asked.

"Nowhere," Hylas explained. "It's transcribed and stored. Would you prefer live musicians? I could have them brought here – "

"No need," I said. "I don't need music at all, I'm so tired. But your city and home are fascinating."

He looked expectantly at me. I wasn't sure what was on his mind. Clearly, he was not ready to leave me. Finally he said, "Thank you, for saving me."

"It was the right thing to do."

"Nevertheless, I am in your debt. As is my father. You shall not want for anything, as long as you live."

"That's hardly necessary," I said, "but thank you. You've already been extremely hospitable."

"Shep?" he asked, as I shuffled about with the bed clothes, hoping to gently suggest that I really was ready to go to sleep.

"Yes?"

"You will keep your promise? To be my teacher?"

"I wasn't aware I'd made a promise – "

"In Aspar, a word is a promise."

"It is the same with my people," I said. "We do not swear oaths, but let our yea be yea and our nay be nay. Our affirmation is always binding."

"Good. I will be honored to be your protégé."

"I'll do my best," I said, still not sure I knew what it was the boy expected of me. If he wanted a teacher in the arts of war, he was in for a sore disappointment. "Now, Hylas, I don't mean to hurt your feelings, but... aren't you tired?"

"I am, a little," he admitted. "But it's my duty to see to it that you have everything you need."

"You have done so," I said. "And now all I need is to go to sleep. In the morning, you can tell me more about what I don't know, and I'll try to tell you... whatever it is that I can."

"All right. You know how to call, if you need anything. And I'll send a girl around, to see to you."

"That's not necessary," I said.

"I would be a poor host, if I didn't," he said sincerely.

"Very well then," I agreed.

He came forward stiffly, and embraced me. It was a far more familiar gesture than I was accustomed to in an acquaintance of only a few hours, but they seemed to be a passionate people, the Aspar. I had saved his life, I reasoned. I enclosed him firmly in my arms and gave him a fatherly hug, receiving as I did an affectionate kiss on the side of my face. And then he bid me good night.

A few minutes later, just as I had crawled beneath the sheets of my bed, a girl did, indeed, enter the room, a pretty, young redhead, as pale-skinned as the rest of them. She spoke no English – or Asparian, if that was what I was somehow speaking – but I managed to convey to her that I needed no aid. I tried also to convince her that she was free to go, but it apparently did not work. The farthest she would retreat was to a chair near the door. I assumed that she was under orders, then, to stay and attend me. I had no desire to put her into displeasure with her masters, nor to insult my hosts. I resigned myself that she would stay.

The poor child attempted to assist me in getting under the covers, and looked hurt when I gently refused her assistance. I smiled and assured her, stupidly in a language she did not understand, that she was doing her job well and I was satisfied. She retreated again to the chair by the door. For some time I kept one eye on her, uncomfortable attempting to sleep, unchaperoned, in the presence of a young woman.

I was chained... stone against my back. Hadn't I been in... where? Birds circled above me, and the sun beat down. Was this where I'd almost... what? Where the mob had... who?

I was free. Almost. There was a weight pulling me back when I tried to walk. There were chains, still, but now only about my ankles. I looked down at their dull iron gray color as they encircled my flesh, bronzed from all those days in the sun... The sun... how it felt on my flesh... The sun... the fire... to be so near to the fire in the sky...

The scars were healing nicely. I traced their lines on my abdomen with my fingers. So many cuts. So much pain. Over now, and done; but the scars remained. They reminded me of what I'd endured, what I had chosen to endure. I could have ended the pain so easily by simply telling my tormentor the name he wanted to hear.

It had not suited my purpose.

She stepped before me, gray and beautiful. What about her was gray? I'm not sure, but the gray lady was beautiful.

"Tell me," she said in that lovely voice, so filled with wisdom, "what is the destiny of your children?"

I had waited so long for that question. I knew she would be the one to change everything. I couldn't act until she asked me that question.

"One day," I said, "they will ascend to the heavens and stand as god."

She nodded, smiling.

"And the name? Tell me the name of the one who will end God's reign and allow them to go to the heavens."

I told her the name. The beautiful name. The name of the Firechild.

He had yet to be born.

"What must I do?" she asked.

"Free me," I said.

She removed the manacles from my legs, opening the lock sealed with the voice of a mute, the hearing of a deaf child, and the vision of a blind man. None was as clever as the Gray Lady.

And I walked free in the sun on the mountaintop. And God looked down and saw his enemy walking free. And God was angry. And He cried out, "Who has done this?"

And the Gray Lady said, "It was I."

I awoke. I was not on stone. I was not at the base of the hanging tree. I was... yes, I remembered... in the bedchamber in the palace in the city of Aspar. I'd been asleep, dreaming. I was someone else, someone with scars on his abdomen. I had accepted the scars in the dream as old wounds, but I had no such scars myself.

The dream... so vivid... from whence had it come? The Gray Lady, and talk of casting God out of Heaven? And I believed I was the Enemy who would lead such an effort? Lord... had I dreamt I was Satan? Why would I be burdened with such a dream?

The Gray Lady... her eyes haunted me. Her sweet voice... "It was I!" ... defying God. An evil creature, surely, and yet, her beauty left me so... God help me, the only word for it was aroused.

And I was aroused. Carnally aroused, I am hesitant to admit, for it's not my way to openly discuss such things. But – pardon me for being so plain and vulgar – there was a stirring in my loins.

Groggily, I came awake, and realized from the warmth between my legs that my young redhead had left her chair, and was beneath my bedclothes, performing a service with her mouth of which I'd heard tales from the coarser companions of my youth, but which I had never personally experienced.

The Apostle Paul warned strongly against surrendering to the sins of the flesh. He advocated marriage for Christians, reminding them that it is better to marry than to burn. Presumably he meant that it is better to enter a sacred and sanctified union with another Christian soul than to burn with lust. It can also be argued that he meant that it is better to marry, and seek sexual gratification in the manner approved by the Lord, than to burn in hell. Either way, I was not married to this young lady who could not speak. The Apostle, it would seem, had left me no leeway in this matter.

But I was half asleep, I had had much wine (not entirely of my own accord... I think), the Apostle Paul was not in this bed with me... and there was no stopping what the dream and the touch of this girl's lips on my flesh had begun. Came it from Satan or not, it had come all the same.

I surrendered to the inevitable.

I must admit, it was more satisfying than my surrender to the lynch mob, only a handful of hours before.

THREE

I awoke and gathered from the dull if persistent light, that it must be some hours past dawn. My bed companion had again left me but, when I returned from attending my immediate needs, I found her kneeling by the bed.

"Good morning," I said tentatively.

She looked at me, expectation in her eyes.

"Ah," I stammered, "I... appreciate your... service... last night. I... must also beg your forgiveness. I know your customs may be different, but among my people... uh... "

She stood, then draped herself across my bed on her back. I assumed she wanted to resume the activities of the previous night.

"Oh, no!" I protested. "No, I... mustn't... presume any further."

She cocked her head, puzzled.

"It wouldn't be right," I said lamely.

After staring at me for a moment, she pointed at the opposite wall. I looked. I saw nothing significant, other than the trappings I would expect of a martial society – there were symbols which I assumed were some sort of family crests, and the usual swords mounted on clips.

"Is... someone coming?"

Finally, realizing I wasn't going to take whatever action it was she expected me to take, the girl got up again, and crossed to the wall. She removed one of the swords from its clip and brought it to me, placing it firmly in my hands. Then, as calmly as if she were sitting down to breakfast, she resumed her place on my bed, and gestured to the sword, and then to her own perfect throat.

I felt a wrenching coldness in my stomach. Was I interpreting her message correctly? Was the girl actually asking me to take the blade to her throat? To kill her? What madness had I fallen into when I fell from the tree with a rope around my neck? I had decided yesterday that this was not Heaven. Had I somehow fallen short of God's mercy, and instead arrived in Hell?

The door opened, and Scorpius came in. I expected that he, too would be surprised by the spectacle which greeted him. I was not disappointed. He looked to me with amused puzzlement. "Good morning, my friend. Did you not sleep well?"

"I... slept fine," I said, wondering how he could make small talk when confronted with such a scenario. "Apart from some... interruptions. But never mind that, this girl – "

"Yes, I see," he said. "I know you were tired, but I must admit some surprise that you haven't cleaned up for the day. Surely customs are not so different in Equatoria that we do not finish our business with a female."

"I... I don't believe... that is... " I gestured mutely to the bed.

"Ah," said Scorpius pleasantly, "you're worried about the blood. Don't be. The staff takes care of that. Tonight, the room will be as clean as it was last evening. I have my standards," he assured me. "I'm well aware that there are some houses where the stains are simply left on the floor and tolerated. I've spent nights in rooms where my feet stuck to the very floor, but – "

"Wh – what are you saying?" I demanded.

Out of the corner of my eye, I saw that Hylas and a pair of Scorpius's palace guards had entered the room. They watched with interest.

Scorpius's gentle smile left him. "My friend," he said sharply, "I believe I have been tolerant enough of your quaint humor. My debt of gratitude to you excuses much, but there are some rules none of us may flaunt. Kill the girl, and let's go have breakfast."

"Kill?" I repeated in disbelief.

"Absolutely. You are through with her. She is no use to another, once her maidenhead is taken, and – "

I dropped the sword. "My god," I muttered. "Give me strength in the face of evil."

Scorpius raised an eyebrow. "Evil, you say?"

"Yes," I said, my voice quavering with indignation. "I do say. Bad enough you sent this... this poor child to... perform... but now – "

Hylas stepped forward, his distress growing as did his father's evident anger.

"Shep," he said quietly, "it's ... a good joke. Maybe in bad taste, but... " His eyes pleaded with me. "It's not funny anymore."

"I am not joking," I said firmly.

"Gods of the sky and thunder!" Scorpius exclaimed. He looked as though he might strike me.

Hylas rushed to stand between us, holding up a calming hand to his father's breast. "Father, Shep simply doesn't understand. Please... " He turned to me and spoke as reasonably as he could. "She," he said, pointing to the girl, who still patiently awaited death, "is an enemy. A captive. All of the maidens here are captives. They are conditioned to serve, until such time as a gift is made of them to an honored guest or warrior. At that time, they are conditioned to expect death."

"Conditioned?" I asked. "What do you mean?"

"It is a process of mental conditioning," said Hylas. "It... softens resistance. Removes the defiant impulses."

"Some sort of... hypnosis?"

"I don't know that word," the boy said. "But a series of punishments and rewards are used." Impatience clouded his face. "It doesn't matter!" he exclaimed. "It only matters that you know that the girl has been prepared for death. In some ways, she wants to die now. It is custom among our people that you kill her, since you have claimed her virginity. I guess you might want to know that her own people would also kill her, if we released her, because she's been taken by a man."

"You're telling me that this girl was... tortured... to become a slave. And now she is to be executed?"

"If she does not die today," said Scorpius coldly, "her conditioning will begin to weaken. She will become wild and dangerous. If you feel compassion for her, you should also know that those who do outlive conditioning go mad at the memory of what has happened to them."

"You have to kill her," Hylas said quietly. He picked up the sword, and held it out to me with both hands.

I took the weapon gently from him, and cast it to the other side of the room. "I shall do nothing of the kind. I am a child of God, bathed in the blood of his son, Jesus Christ. He is my savior. For His sake, I must not – will not – sin."

Scorpius shook his head. "You're a fool."

"Perhaps. But I will not kill. I cannot."

"To allow a condemned enemy to live is treason," said Scorpius.

"So be it," I said quietly.

"Father, no!" protested Hylas. "He doesn't understand! His beliefs are different! Let me kill the girl on his behalf!"

"Out of the question," said Scorpius.

"Yes," I agreed. "Hylas, you will not kill in my name, nor will I stand by and allow this girl's death, any more than I allowed yours. Raise your hand to her, and I will resist you."

Words can inflict more pain than ever did hand, knife or gun. Hylas's face fell, and he gaped at me as though I had struck him the hardest blow he could imagine. He backed slowly away from me and covered his face.

Scorpius motioned to his guards. "Take him," he said quietly. "While I decide the manner of his execution." He faced me as they came forward and bound my hands behind me. I offered no resistance. "I will make it a quick death, and dignified," he promised. "I owe you that. But none who flouts our laws can be allowed to live. I am sorry."

They placed me in a cell, and I was left alone. It was the first time since we'd left for the Shenandoah that I had been alone, and I opened my prayers by thanking God for it. I needed to think. Even if I was to be executed within hours, which seemed more and more likely, I needed to try and understand what was happening to me. The mind, I believe, must keep functioning, keep questioning, keep striving to learn until it is silenced by the death of the body. Even then, my faith in Christ assures me, the mind will not be silenced. Perhaps it will be opened and allowed to learn even more. I liked to believe so.

I needed to believe so.

I had nearly died at the hands of an angry mob for daring to say that children should not fight in wars. Or had I died? It was possible I had. It was possible I was experiencing a nightmare, even as my body writhed in its death throes at the end of a rope in the Virginia sun. It was even possible the entire experience was a dream, and I was safely in my bed in Fairfax.

As far as I knew, however, I had seen the Light of the World in a vision as I came near death, and it had transported me here. "Here," according to Scorpius, was another world, apparently orbiting another sun, a different one than the one which had overlooked my birth on the distant world of earth. This was not completely unbelievable to me. I understood, as did every educated person living since the 16th Century, that the stars were suns like our own, and was aware of theories which speculated that many of them were also orbited by planets which might host intelligent life. Some Christians are uncomfortable with the thought that God did not create the earth, alone, to host life. I have never understood why it should bother them. Besides, the Aspar were not, so they claimed, alien life. They were people descended from the men and women of my own planet. Their story of being transplanted here by pagan gods was dubious and heretical, of course, but people believe all manner of foolish things.

And now, in this alien place, I stood again condemned to death for refusing to embrace a culture of death. Just as surely as the Virginians had wanted young Joseph sacrificed on the altar of War to dispel their fear and anguish after Sheridan's invasion, so did Scorpius want my bedmate slain to prove to his gods that he was worthy and a good warrior. Never mind the fact that only a coward of a man would slay a helpless, tortured girl whose mind was not even her own.

It seemed that, like many Quakers before me, I was to die for my principles. In the silence of my cell, I thanked God for giving me a glimpse of this fantastic world, for sparing my life even one day when I surely should have died in the Valley, and, if I was to die a martyr to Jesus Christ, I thanked Him for the opportunity to serve, and asked that he put me to whatever use He saw fit.

It was not that I wished to die, or that I have no spine or sense of self. I merely have utter faith that God moves in all lives for the best, and that the immediate needs of my body do not always serve the immediate needs of my soul. I do not know, short of having such faith, how one may endure this life.

My silence was interrupted sooner than I would have liked. A guard led Philip, now largely healed of his wounds, to my cell. He looked at me and shook his head.

"Can you not stay out of trouble for one moment, without my supervision?" he asked me.

I would not rise to his taunt. "It seems not."

"They say you committed treason."

"I refused to murder an innocent girl! A girl they sent to... have carnal knowledge of me."

He nodded. "They sent me two. I suppose they thought it would contribute to my healing."

"I've no doubt you enjoyed yourself," I said ruefully.

His face brightened. "In fact, I did. Oh, I'm still a bit sore, but – "

"Philip, have you no conscience? To submit to the sins of the flesh with heathen savages?"

"Oh, well, now, let's sort out just who's the pot and who's the kettle here, Shep! I didn't hear that you turned away your bedmate's attentions."

"She came upon me in my sleep," I said, but I knew he was right. I had no moral upper hand here.

"I see." He was clearly unconvinced.

"And were you required to kill the poor girls who serviced you?" I asked.

He shook his head and lifted one arm stiffly. "They could see I wasn't up to it. This arm was broken, and is still healing. I couldn't possibly lift a sword, even though their medical knowledge is astounding! Why – "

"What happened to the girls, then?" I interrupted. "I was told they'd turn wild if not killed?"

"Oh," he said nonchalantly, "one of the guards killed them for me." Then, seeing my look of revulsion, he added, "it was very quick and painless, I assure you."

My mouth hung open, and I stared in disbelief at my oldest friend. "Quick and painless? You just... stood there and watched? Two murders?"

"Two savages," he said mildly.

"Two of God's children!" I snapped.

"They don't believe in the god of Abraham, Shep."

"That makes no difference."

He sighed. "What would you have had me do? Jump between the girls and the blade? I would have been killed myself!"

"We're here because I jumped between Hylas and a pistol," I shot back.

"And don't think I'm not grateful," he replied. "But I thought you were crazy then, and I still do. The world has not been so kind to me that I am willing to die for strangers."

"I say again, Philip, they are children of God. And you are a Quaker."

He shrugged. "An accident of birth."

For a moment, I said nothing. Suddenly, I did not know this man before me. This was no friend of mine. "Leave me," I finally choked out.

"Shep, for heaven's sake, tell them you were still hung over from the wine! Scorpius will forgive you! Honestly, the old barbarian actually seems to like you. He just has to follow the rules. Tell him you're sorry – "

"And murder the girl?"

"Yes, of course."

"Get out of my sight, Philip."

"Shep! She's only a savage!"

"I said go!" I roared, advancing at the bars of the cell.

Philip took a step back. "They're going to kill you, Shep," he said quietly. "I don't want to see that happen. I'm – your friend – "

"No!" I cut him off. "No, you're not."

═══════════

The Aspar's treatment of prisoners was highly civilized. I was given a magnificent lunch, after which the guard informed me that the manner of my death was still to be determined. When they brought my dinner, the same guard informed me that I would be publicly beheaded upon its completion. It occurred to me not to eat, but I decided to show them that I was not phased. If nothing else, I would win the contest of wills. I ate.

As promised, as soon as I set down my empty goblet and my plate was clean, my hands were once again bound behind my back, and I was led to an assembly hall within the palace. Several hundred of the Aspar were seated, several hundred more were standing, all come to watch my execution.

The hall was laid out somewhat like a coliseum, with an open area in the center. I was bound to a pole at the center of that. I was tied at the arms and legs to the pole, and a strap was fastened about my forehead, presumably to hold my head still and make a cleaner job of my death. A party advanced on me, led by Scorpius. They were followed by two guards, each bearing an enormous broadsword, and rounded out by Philip and a weeping Hylas, who would not meet my eyes.

"Sentence has been passed," said Scorpius. "Do you ask for mercy?"

"None," I replied.

"Then before you die, there is something you need to witness." He nodded to someone outside my field of vision, and two guards dragged my young redhead paramour before me. Her arms and feet were bound. She struggled in her bonds now, and screamed. As they forced her to her knees before me, she bit the hand of one man. Blood spurted onto her face, and she smiled in satisfaction. His fellow cuffed her in the face, also drawing blood. She cursed at him in an unintelligible language.

"You see she has reverted to savagery, as I warned you," said Scorpius. "Now she is not prepared for her death. You have done her no mercy."

"Spare her," I said desperately. "She is innocent. She is a creature of God, just as – "

Scorpius waved an angry finger, interrupting me, and one of the girl's captors plunged his sword through her heart. He did it easily; there was little sound; and the poor child resisted not at all. She obediently stopped breathing, and lips which had so recently caressed and teased me trickled blood. Satisfied she was dead, he removed his sword, holding her body down with his foot to her face as he did so. He then came forward and wiped the blood from the sword against my chest. I felt bile rise in my throat. I suppressed the urge to vomit. I knew I was to die. I wanted, for the sake of my Lord, to do so with dignity. But this poor child...

"Her blood is on you," said Scorpius in disgust, "as it should be. And now you join her. Do you have anything to say before sentence is executed."

I swallowed and prayed for God's wisdom and peace. The words came easily: "I request that almighty God, the father, and his son, Christ Jesus, safeguard your souls, and turn you from your evil ways, that you might know his peace." Then, remembering the example of the Savior on the cross, I looked up to the sky and said, "Father, forgive them, for they know not what they do."

Philip shook his head. Hylas, still weeping, finally raised his eyes to mine. Scorpius swallowed.

"Please continue," I said. "I am ready. I go to my Lord with a clear conscience."

FOUR

The man who was to be my executioner hesitated. He was not clad in a black hood as an earthly practitioner of state-sanctioned murder would be. Since the Aspar did not practice that bit of hypocrisy, I could see his eyes, and I could see in them that my words had moved him. He looked back to his superior.

Even Scorpius's resolve seemed to have withered. He stared at me, and chewed his lip.

"Father," Hylas ventured meekly, "you cannot kill him this way. Not now. To sacrifice one so brave so foolishly would surely displease Raxes."

Scorpius nodded, his eyes never leaving mine. "My son is correct," he said. "You have broken our laws, but there is no shred of cowardice in you. You must not die like this." He jerked his head at the guards. "Take him to his cell. I must contemplate his fate."

═══════════

The Gray Lady stood before her accusers, her eyes flashing, her chin set firm. There was no fear in her. She would yield in body because she had no choice. In spirit, never. Never would her spirit yield! She might be bound in golden chains from Heaven's forge. She might be stripped of her raiments. Her dignity she would never shed.

"You were my favorite," said God, His massive voice sad. "I denied you nothing. See the tribute you have paid me."

"I pay tribute to the future," she said. "I lend my aid to those who will replace you. It is what is destined."

He shook His noble head. "Once you said you would have no man come before Me in your heart. I promised no other should have you. You have gone back on your word. I go back on mine."

Her muscles did not move. Her eyes did not blink. Her jaw did not quiver. She had been warned of what was to come. I had warned her, hadn't I? She faced it bravely.

"Who will have her?" called God to the hosts of heaven.

The assembled angels jostled one another, but one stepped forward, away from them all. He was tall and strong, not like an angel. There was fire in his eye and arrogance in his bearing.

I met the Gray Lady's eye. She hated this one. I knew she wanted to cry out, "No! Not him!" but she did not. I *had* warned her.

He claimed her and I watched. He took her there, in front of the assembled court of the Eternal Throne and I watched. Despite myself I was angry. I'd warned her of this, yet I was angry. I wanted to rip him from her. I wanted to cast him from the sky as once I'd been cast.

I wanted to kill him.

But I could not. This was what I knew was to happen. This was what I'd told her would happen and she had accepted it. This had to happen.

When he was finished his shameful business, he left her. They all left her, all but me. I never saw them go. They were suddenly gone. We were alone, she and I.

"It is done," she said. "It is begun. Take me from here."

And as she had removed my bonds, I removed hers. I spirited her away to a secret island.

In a hidden cave, I tended her. As the time came closer, she would lay before me, gaze in my eyes with her dazzling gray ones and say, "You are all I have left."

I would touch her swollen belly and murmur, "Soon there will be another." I would kiss her forehead. I would hold her as she slept.

She screamed. She screamed and her flashing eyes shot fire. Her whole body was aflame. She bucked and bit her lip and ichor flowed from the wound.

"Shhhh," I quieted her. "It will pass. He's almost here."

She said not a word. This was not the time for wisdom or rationality, and she had no words that were not such. She sobbed against me.

He came. Shrieking his anger at the world he had just discovered, he came.

His eyes, gray like his mother's, but still they burned in anger like his father's. He was bathed in flames of anger, redder than any newborn this world had known.

The Firechild. Just as I had told her. He came.

I cradled him. I would love him. He would be ours. I would love him as I now loved her.

I held his burning body against mine and reveled in the searing of the flames at my breast.

Another dream.

I woke and realized that's what it had been. It was morning in Aspar, and I was still in my cell. Was it this place that made me dream of the Gray Lady? Now, in my dreams, I delivered her child. I had delivered many children over the years. Never had I delivered one like this, this... Firechild. He wasn't human, surely. He was beautiful, though. In my dream, I'd loved him.

Loved him? How could I? Born in flame like a demon? The son of a blasphemer and a fallen angel? Or was the father, the arrogant one, the fallen angel? Had not I remembered, in my dream, being cast out of Heaven? Did I dream of being an angel? A fallen angel? The One cast out of Heaven?

God help me, did I dream of being Lucifer?

Was it this place that sent me the dreams? Or was it Satan himself who sent them?

===

I had spent another night and the better part of the following day in my cell. Philip did not return, and I was thankful. The fact that I had spent so many years' friendship on one whose character – if he could be said to have any character at all – was so far removed from my own concepts of morality, stung me. I felt ashamed and foolish for having defended him to others for so many years. I did not want his presence to remind me of my shame, even if it meant I had to die alone.

I was not completely alone, however. The three men who took shifts guarding me provided some companionship. During my first hours of captivity, they had been indifferent to me. Now, having faced death in their presence without flinching, I seemed to be something of a celebrity. Not only did they speak to me, but they did so in tones of respect and comradeship.

My morning-shift guard informed me, as he brought my breakfast, that Scorpius had proclaimed a challenge match for me. I suspected the meaning of this term, but asked further explanation.

"When a man of valor commits a crime," he told me, "it is not the same as it is for a common man. The gods grant courage only to those they favor. It would offend the gods to deal the same brand of justice to such men as we would deal to one unworthy. Our people would all pay the penalty for such sin. Great warriors, therefore, when they have broken the law, are not judged by mortal men. They must be judged by the gods."

"I see. And how do the gods make their will known?"

"As ever, through victory in combat. If the gods continue to favor you, despite your crime, you will survive tomorrow's battle."

"Whom am I to battle?" I did not bother to add that I would battle no one. The customs of this savage place fascinated me, in the way a venomous snake fascinates one who can observe it at a safe distance. One knows the snake is poisonous and deadly, but one cannot help but watch it for a time.

"There are always volunteers," he said. "Either brave men, out to prove themselves, or other accused criminals, who wish to commute their sentences. The lowest of the low, who defeated such as you, would be spared and granted high office in our ranks."

"What a promising opportunity for some poor unfortunate," I observed.

The guard grinned. "In your case, my friend, I'm sure someone of real courage will stand forth. No cowardly thief would face you, after yesterday."

I was embarrassed by his open admiration. I was not accustomed to such attention. "I did only what God led me to do," I said.

He nodded. "That is what bravery means. The coward flouts divine will."

I couldn't help but murmur, "Amen."

Tomorrow then, I thought, would bring me another chance to show the bravery visited by the Lord, in a repeat of yesterday's performance. For Scorpius's decision to change the manner of my death in his eyes, changed it not at all in fact. When my opponent confronted me tomorrow, he would kill me. I asked God, in advance, to forgive him his sin, and prayed that I might, in some way, serve as an example to this backward culture of the folly of violence.

But I also despaired in my heart, for my example, and that of so many of my fellow Quakers, had not prevented the hell-on-earth that was the War Between the States. I doubted it could work stronger medicine on this world.

———————

Hylas came to my cell that evening. He seemed subdued. The poor child had been through much in just a few days: his own near death, mine as well, and now this proposed combat. The boy was fond of me, I knew. I supposed he held out hope that I might fight and win tomorrow, but surely he also dreaded that I would finally die.

"It was good of you to come," I told him. "I hope you will not allow these events to weigh too heavily on you, Hylas. We are all subject to the forces of evil in this world. We often cannot escape them. We must remain resolute in our faith that God is with us, and that our souls are safe in His care."

He laughed ruefully. "My father is right about you. There is no braver man alive."

"I'm certain there are a few," I said.

"I have not met them."

"You are young," I reminded him. "And that is why you must try not to let my death discourage you. It is wrong, and the product of human sin, but I bear no ill will against your father – "

"You are *not* going to die," he said quietly.

"Has your father granted me pardon?" I asked. It did not seem likely.

"Pardon is never granted, except by the gods. Criminals triumph in battle, or they die."

"Then I am resigned to the fact of my pending death," I said.

He shook his head. "I will not allow it. I owe you a debt – "

"You cannot prevent it," I replied, the determination in my voice mirroring that in his. "And you must not try. You're too young yet to break the rules of your own society. Perhaps there will come a time. If my death has made you question the sinful nature of man, then God's purpose is served by it. He may be allowing my death so that you will become a leader in His cause – "

"I will become nothing," said Hylas. He took a breath, as if working up his nerve. "I will die tomorrow."

"What?" I demanded. He seemed so certain. Had his plea for leniency in my case so angered his father that he, too, was condemned?

"I have stepped forward for the combat," he went on. "I will be your opponent."

After a few moments spent recovering from the shock of this pronouncement, I saw it for what it was: a gallant gesture of impulsive youth. Scorpius would not let it stand. The Aspar were ruthless, yes; but surely they wanted to protect their young as much as any other people did.

"That is very noble of you, Hylas," I said. "I'm sure your father will agree with me, when you tell him, but – "

"I have told him," said the boy.

I stopped, processing this information. "You have? Well then... surely he has told you that he won't allow – "

"He has no choice. A volunteer for the combat cannot be rejected. It is the law."

"What if," – I grasped at straws, I knew – "what it another steps forward? Isn't one turned away?"

"No. If there are two volunteers, they battle for the privilege. The winner would fight you. But," he added, with a touch of arrogant pride, "I made my plea early, and before my father's guard. There is none in the city who would step forward now. It would be unseemly to compete with the heir to the throne for a battle he has chosen. I will be your opponent."

I sighed. "As always, the laws of war are foolish. Why would the heir be allowed to battle in such a duel? If you were to be killed, who would be next in line for the throne?"

"My opponent," he said, adding pointedly, "you, Shep. Tomorrow, when I am dead, you will be my father's heir."

I swallowed. I was resigned to my fate, but the actions of this youth brought further pain and tragedy to it. "I am sorry, Hylas. You have made a foolish decision. I will die tomorrow. I must. Now, it seems, it will have to be at your hand."

He jumped to his feet. "No! I won't do it! I won't kill you! I owe you my life! And I'm paying my debt! I'm giving you my life, so that you can live. You can't deny me this!" His face reddened, and he looked as if he might cry again.

I took his shoulders firmly in my hands and guided him back to his seat. I sat beside him, keeping one arm about him, hoping that the contact would soothe him while I tried to make him understand.

"I cannot kill, Hylas," I said gently. "God has commanded it. 'Thou shalt not kill,' he says plainly in the Bible, and – "

"What god?" he demanded in frustration. "I have not heard of a god who would say not to kill!"

"That is because you do not know the true God," I told him. "There is only one."

For a moment, anyway, I had distracted him from his pleas for death. "That's the stupidest thing I ever heard!" he blurted out. "How can there be only one god? It makes no sense!"

How could any person, even one generations gone from God's earth, be so alien in his beliefs? "It does make sense," I said quietly. "It is the only thing that does. One god, who always has been, and always will be. And He has commanded me not to kill. Even had He not, I could not take the life of an innocent child, even to save my own."

"I'm not a child," he protested.

"Of course you're not," I said. "But you have not lived as a man yet, either. You have years before you. I cannot take them from you, merely to assure that I will die of old age."

"And why do you say I'm innocent?" he pressed on. "No one is innocent!"

"You believe the doctrine of original sin," I said.

"Of course! When the Pretender rebelled – he's the one the Jentana call the Father of the gods – when he rebelled against the true Father, giving man the embers of heavenly fire, he passed sin to us all."

"The Pretender, eh?" I wondered. Perhaps their beliefs were not so alien. That account certainly sounded like Lucifer and his fall from Heaven. But had Lucifer established a cult of worshipers among these Jentana? Were they, then, Satanists? And the Aspar, like the ancient Israelites, clung to the practice of war and allowed themselves to be led into idolatry by the promises of false gods?

"There is no innocence," said Hylas firmly. "I am as sinful as you or anyone else, and I know it. The only favor I may find with the gods is by doing their will bravely. The gods have favored you. I will die for you, and my place in the field of warriors will be assured." He looked pleadingly into my eyes. "It must be this way, Shep. It will be so easy for you to kill me."

I grasped his shoulder more firmly in a sideways embrace. "You tell me there is no innocence, and then you offer your life for mine without a care, assured of your place in the afterlife." I shook my head in disbelief. "What more innocent expression of simple faith could there be? How can I let you murder me, and thus fall in sin?"

"Then you will fight for your life?" he asked, but his tone admitted the hopelessness of his question.

"I cannot kill."

"And I cannot let the man who saved me die for his bravery," Hylas replied. "It would be a breach of honor. I have to save you."

"Hylas, you cannot – "

"I have no choice, Shep. You saved my life. You made me your protégé. I cannot let you die before I give you the tribute you deserve. If I must defy my father, then so be it."

"No!" I insisted.

He stood, ignoring my argument. "I have to go and make arrangements. I'll be back at nightfall. Be prepared."

"Hylas – " I began.

But he had gone.

———

Well past midnight – or what I took for midnight, for I had learned nothing as yet of how the Aspar kept time – Hylas reappeared at my cell.

He wore a sword bound about his waist, at least two knives attached to his person, and he carried a pistol.

"Hurry," he said. "I have our escape route carefully planned."

I stood and made to follow him, asking, "Where are we going?"

"Out of the city," he explained. He opened my cell door (he had used his own key device for entry, as usual) and I followed him cautiously into the corridor beyond. My night guard was conspicuously absent.

"Isn't anyone about?" I asked.

"Pretty much no one but the guards awake in the palace," he said. "And I've paid them all for their absence, and their silence."

It was a bad business, and I didn't like that he had involved himself in it. I'm not so noble, however, that I resented the chance to live without being forced to kill.

"But what about you?" I asked as we ran through darkened corridors and streets, slowing occasionally, to look inconspicuous for passing servants. "You can't expect your father won't find out what you've done!"

He nodded. "I expect he'll know by morning."

"Then... you can't go back!"

"No. Even the son of the Warlord is condemned to die if he breaks the laws. I'd be given the chance to battle, because of my high birth, but..."

"Hylas, you can't do this for me!"

"I have done it, Shep, and don't be ridiculous. I am your protégé. I will do this and much more for you, in the years to come."

Again I had the sense that there was more to this apprenticeship to which the boy had pledged himself than I would know for some time to come. I told myself to be content in my ignorance. Perhaps it was God's will that I be saved to set an example on this warlike world, and Hylas was but God's instrument of my salvation.

The city was surrounded by a huge wall. Certainly the fliers the Aspar used had no trouble sailing over it, but I assumed it protected the residents from ground assault. I also gathered that there was weaponry, cannon of some sort, mounted on the turrets and the towers which scraped the sky, to take down enemy fliers, if there were such things.

At a small outbuilding near the city gate, Hylas stopped and retrieved two large packs, designed to be strapped to the back and carried. They were loaded with dry goods and drinking water, enough for some days, anyway.

"Are we going to walk?" I asked.

He nodded curtly, looking more like an experienced officer than a boy. "Best to stay low to the ground. Father's surveillance teams would notice and alert him immediately if we took to the air, and we'd be shot down before they knew it was us. Father takes no chances with uncleared fliers. We'll walk for about a day, and then I've made arrangements with a farmer I know, some distance from the City, to provide fliers for us."

"Don't you have horses?" I asked, stopping to secure the straps on his pack for him.

"What? What are horses?"

"Animals. Large ones you can ride. Surely – "

"Ah, I've never heard them called that. The Jentana still have some. They managed to save theirs, after the plague. It devastated – "

"Hold it there!" A voice snapped out from the darkness. Hylas and I spun. A soldier stepped out, wearing the regalia of the palace guard. He had a pistol leveled at us. I saw Hylas make a move for his, but he'd snapped it inside its holster before donning the pack. There was no way he could reach it before the guard shot him.

"Tanalios," Hylas said bitterly. "We had an agreement."

"So we did," he said sadly. "But you see, the stranger's absence has already been noted. I was speakered about it not five minutes ago. There's a reward for your capture. It's considerably more than you gave me, I'm afraid."

"I double what I paid you!" Hylas cried. "Please, let us – "

But the guard, Tanalios, shook his head. "At this point, I don't believe I'd have sufficient alibi if you escaped. Your father's so angry, he might kill even an innocent man for being nearby. No, my Prince. I'm afraid you're going to have to come with me."

He waved his gun to indicate we should move ahead of him. Hylas caught my eye, asking, I think, if I thought we could make a break for it. I have no doubt the lad thought that I might get away while the guard killed him. I shook my head.

We started walking, back toward captivity, and death.

FIVE

What happened next astounded me, I must admit. The guard, Tanalios, ushered us forward, his pistol in Hylas's back. I assume he guessed (correctly) that I would not start any trouble if the boy's life were in danger. The reverse might also have been true, but Hylas was young, impulsive and inexperienced. It was probably safer to train the weapon on him, and count on my cooperation.

It was as Tanalios lifted his wrist, to which was strapped one of the curious speakers by which the Aspar communicated, that I felt a sort of... snap. That's the best word I can come up with to describe the sensation. There is no perfect word to name it. I could not describe, say, a leg cramp, to someone who's never had a cramp. I cannot, then, describe this feeling in my brain to anyone who has not experienced the same feeling. To the best of my knowledge, I am the only earth human who has.

I remember that all of my thoughts were focused on escape. I fervently wished that Tanalios would trip and fall, or that something would distract him long enough for us to turn and run for the city gates. It was a more active desire to affect the outcome of a situation than I'd felt since... well, since Philip and I had been transported here, when I had wished so fervently for him to be delivered from his fear and his suffering. Now, it was because I knew that Hylas's life was forfeit as a result of his efforts to rescue me, that I wished so for, I suppose, divine intervention.

I did not feel this way when I was beaten by the mob in Winchester, nor when I stood to be hanged from the tree, nor even when the guard in the arena drew his sword and prepared to decapitate me. Apparently, danger to myself was not enough. When my life was threatened, I seemed to be focusing on those who threatened it. I don't think this is because I'm any sort of martyr, or utterly selfless, but because I have, for all of my adult life, felt at peace with the Lord. When one is at peace with the Lord, he is at peace with his fellow men and women, as well. So, when his fellows transgress in any way, his first thought is not of revenge, but of how those fellows might make themselves right in the eyes of God.

When the mob wanted to hang me, or the Aspar to cut off my head, my thoughts were on their actions – their *sins* – and how the Lord might lead them out of the ways of sin, and into the light. I suppose it's a natural extension of this impulse on my part that, when another is threatened, I worry both for his soul and for his bodily safety; and so it is then that my more worldly fears come into play.

Whatever the reasons, it happened that at that time I was wishing for a way to save Hylas from the tender mercies of his father. It happened that, just as my anguish became so powerful that I thought I might not bear it, I felt that snap in my brain, as if my mind were a railroad track, and the switch had flipped, to take the train onto another spur. It happened that, immediately following this queer sensation of mine, and immediately before he was able to signal for help, Tanalios froze in place.

When I say froze, of course, I do not mean literally that he became cold. The Red Planet, in every place that I visited it, was more temperate than much of earth. Few people had occasion to be cold there; but Tanalios stopped moving utterly, right where he stood. His wrist was still at his face, his lips, still poised to form the words that he had found the fugitives. Indeed, the person on the receiving end of his transmission called out to him, wondering why no one was speaking on the open channel. His legs and feet were locked rigidly in place. His eyes stared straight ahead. They still blinked. He still breathed, I noted, but he simply could not move.

"What happened?" wondered Hylas.

"I don't know, I think... is it possible...?"

"I don't know what's possible, Shep," said the boy, seizing my wrist and pulling me to follow him, "but I know we'd better run while we can. They'll come looking for him!"

Hylas was right. Time to ponder the unlikely coincidence of my odd sensation and the guard's immobility later. For now, I contented myself that God had blessed us with a chance to escape. It would have been ungrateful of us not to take it.

═══════

We made it out of the city, barely. It seems that, as we reached the gates, Tanalios was found by his comrades. They knew we were at large, and they knew we had done something inexplicable to him. Perhaps his strange immobility had even worn off as we left, allowing Tanalios to tell them which way we had gone. Perhaps the gate was just an obvious choice for any fugitive.

They caught up to us just beyond the wall, on the road leading out of the city. I wondered to what use they put roads, since they apparently had no horses. Spears flew at us, which we dodged. Then, our pace and our head start having put a distance between us and our pursuers which rendered spears useless, amber bolts of lightning began to flash and sizzle past us. I had seen them, briefly, during the battle – just two days ago? – during which I had saved Hylas's life. I had seen hard evidence that, whatever they were, they were as deadly as real lightning.

"Get down!" screamed Hylas as the night sky grew pale with the pistols' discharge. I fell to my belly and crawled, hoping to present a lesser target.

Hylas drew his own weapon, and aimed it at the oncoming party.

"You can't!" I called out.

"Would you rather die at their hands?" he asked me urgently.

In truth, I rather would; though I could not wish such a fate on my young charge. The thought of more bloodshed however...

Hylas aimed and fired his weapon. In the glow of battle, I saw the lead man in the party of guards fall. This galvanized me. I could not sit still for this violence. I seized the boy's arm. "You're giving them a clearer target," I said. "Let me try something."

"What?" he demanded, but he lowered his weapon.

I shut my eyes and, as I'd involuntarily reached out to God twice before, made a conscious effort to secure his attention now. I looked inside myself and sought the light within. I prayed for some way to halt the progress of our pursuers, yet not see them harmed.

"Look!" Hylas cried out.

I opened my eyes and saw the soldiers, their arms over their faces, attempting to ward off some sort of attack. "What?" I wondered aloud, but the answer came to me. A gentle wind had been blowing over the plains of Aspar when we exited the city. It had barely stirred the topmost grains of red sand on the ground. As I was in prayer, however, the wind had gusted, just enough, it seemed, to lift a larger portion of the sand and blow it towards the city gate. It was as if a hundred children stood before those dozen guards, and each expertly cast sand in the eyes of one of them. They were blinded. They fell to their knees at the onslaught, and knelt or sat on the plain, immobilized, but uninjured.

"That was fantastic!" Hylas cheered. "How – ?"

"Later," I snapped at him. "Do you know a safe place for us to go?"

He grinned, "I have it all planned. Follow me."

———————

"I played here as a little boy," Hylas said, throwing more dried grass on the small fire we had built. I'd tried to find dead wood, but there was little. There were few trees in this area. It reminded me a great deal of descriptions of the desert areas of North America or Africa. Perhaps more North America. Few trees, little greenery. Fortunately, the grass, which resembled sage brush, burned well when dry. Much of it was dry.

We were in a cave in the foothills. It had been some hours since our miraculous escape from the search party, and I saw telltale fingers of magenta stretching into the black of the sky at the horizon line. Dawn was about to break. We'd spent the intervening time busily setting up our camp, planning to sleep in shifts through the daylight hours, with one of us standing watch for intruders.

Now, relaxing back against the rock wall, passing between us a flask of wine which Hylas had thought to pack, we had an opportunity to reflect together on what had happened to us.

"How did you do it?" Hylas asked. "Make Tanalios stand so still, and stir up the wind?"

"I don't really know. Tanalios was an accident. With the others, I just... sort of concentrated."

"Will you teach me to do that?"

I smiled wearily. "I would if I could. Perhaps someday, if I can figure out what I did. If I'm ever able to do it again."

"You've never done anything like that before?"

I shook my head. "Just tonight." Then, thinking back, I added, "and maybe one other time, the day I first came here."

"Shep?" he asked, "where did you come from? I know it wasn't Equatoria, as you claimed."

"I didn't really claim anything. I just didn't contradict your father. I wanted to learn as much as I could, to figure out what I should say about my origins."

"Why? Why not just tell the truth? Are you a criminal in your land as well?"

"No. I suppose I was just afraid that telling the truth would get me locked up in an asylum."

"An... asylum?" he asked, as if he'd never heard the word before. And then I realized he had pronounced it phonetically, in English, not in... whatever language I'd somehow learned during my transit here.

"A... hospital, for the mentally ill. Surely you have them."

"What are the mentally ill?" he demanded. "You're either sick or your not. Your mind has nothing to do with it."

"Certainly it does. You mind itself can suffer illness, like the rest of your body. Surely you've seen someone who... whose perception of reality is compromised. Who imagines things that aren't there? Who hears voices, telling him to do evil things?"

"Oh, lunatics!" He nodded emphatically. "Yes, we have them. They're killed. Can't have disease spreading."

I kept forgetting what a ruthless place this was. "Madness is not – usually – a disease which spreads. Anyway, I can see I was doubly correct not to tell the truth."

"Why?" he asked, sitting up, and looking excited at the prospect of this insane secret. "What is the truth, that we would have thought you mad?"

"Promise not to run me through with your sword?"

He smiled. "I'd use the pistol, it's quicker and painless." Then he added, quietly, "But I'd sooner use it on myself than kill you, mad or not."

His affection for me was apparently as strong as it was sudden. I really didn't think I had earned it, but I would not hurt him by putting him off.

"I..." I hesitated. "Your father spoke of earth."

"Yes, what of it?"

"That's where I was born. Where I lived, all my life, until three days ago."

"You're telling me you're... from another planet?"

"I believe I must be."

"How did you get here, then? Only the gods can traverse between the stars."

"I would agree with you. I'm certain God had a hand in my coming here. You see, I was about to be executed. Hanged, by the neck."

His eyes went wide. "Then you are a criminal!"

"No. Well, maybe by the standards of your world. In mine, what I do – what my Friends and I do – is legal."

"What do you do?"

"We live by God's commandments. We do not kill, we do not steal, we do not covet that which belongs to others. We love our neighbors as we do ourselves. At least, we try to. We do not condone slavery. Most important of all, I suppose – or at least most noticed by others – we do not believe in war."

He gave a snort of disbelief. "Don't believe in war? That's like saying... you don't believe in air! Or in... I don't know... eating!"

"Many people on earth agree with you. When I... left, there was a great war occurring. Perhaps the worst my people have ever known, for it turned brother against brother. It would be as if your people in Aspar took to fighting and killing each other."

"That would not happen," Hylas said assuredly.

"We believed so in my country as well, for a long time."

"So, when this war came... you... did not fight?"

"No. The Society of Friends specifically forbids its members to fight."

"What did you do? Hang back with the women and gather flowers?"

"Hardly. Nor did the women gather flowers. I served as a doctor, treating the wounded and the dying. When I met up with the men who wanted to kill me, Philip and I were volunteering in a hospital, in one of the worst of the war-torn areas in our country."

He narrowed his eyes. "You... went where there was fighting?"

"Sometimes. Mostly where there recently had been fighting."

"You could have been killed, or injured," he said thoughtfully.

"I was injured, as you saw. So was Philip. We very nearly were killed." I then related to him the tale of my unusual transport to this world.

When I was finished, he looked down. "You faced death, and the gods saw fit to spare you. How they must favor you. I... am ashamed for suggesting you were a coward. Please forgive me."

I reached across and squeezed his hand. "Of course. As my savior has forgiven me, I forgive any who sin against me. But I don't think you've sinned against me, Hylas. You just don't understand my background."

"Your savior? Who's that?"

"Christ the Lord," I responded.

He looked at me blankly. The name meant nothing to him.

"Over a thousand years ago... uh... more than, um... half a million days – God sent His son to earth, as a human."

"Which god?" he asked.

"We only believe in the one."

"Right, you told me. What is he god of?"

"Everything. He... he's God. He created the earth, and each of us, and – "

"One god did all that?" Hylas asked.

"Of course he did. He's God! Don't you believe that your... gods... created you?"

He shrugged. "We were created by the Pretender, before he fell out of favor with the Old Father."

"The Pretender?" I asked incredulously, remembering his earlier tale of this fallen deity. "Are you saying that you believe Man was created by... Satan? The Devil?"

"He's not a devil, really. He doesn't do any wrong. It just angered the Old Father when he began giving gifts to us, and – "

"By the Old Father, I think you must mean my God," I suggested.

"You worship the dead god? You really must be from another world."

"I am. And no, my god isn't dead. But he is the Father of all."

"It's confusing," he said. "But I guess I understand. The Jentana worship the Mother Goddess, and we worship her rival, Raxes. I suppose some people might still worship the Old Father."

"If it's the same... person. But my God sent his son, Jesus Christ, to be born of a mortal woman. He lived among us, led a perfect life, and taught us of God's mercy."

"What happened to him?"

"He was executed."

"And you think my people are warlike?"

"I suppose mine aren't much better."

"So, you knew this... "

"Jesus. I know him."

"I thought you said he was dead."

"He rose again, after three days in the grave."

He took this in silently, considering it.

"And when did you meet him?"

"I've known him as long as I can remember. I learned about him in worship, and from my parents – "

"Yes, but when did you actually meet him? When did he save you?"

"When did he – ? Oh! No. He didn't literally save me. He saved all of mankind, when he died on the cross. He died so that our sins would be forgiven, and he rose again to prove that we are all immortal, through him."

"So... you... haven't actually met him?"

"No. No one living has. He ascended to heaven."

"In a flier?"

"No, he... Oh... Lord... how do I find the words?"

"I think I get it. He's your savior, and he told you you should forgive people when they sin."

"Yes."

"Then... I suppose I should try to do the same."

"Yes, you should."

"Because you're my savior, and I should follow you – "

"No! No, you shouldn't!"

He looked hurt.

"I mean... I mean, no, I'm not your savior."

"But you saved me!"

"Not... not the way Christ saves all. I saved your mortal life. He saves our souls."

"I don't understand. I don't see why the gods would forgive someone who displeases them. It only encourages people to displease them more."

"Maybe," I proposed, "we should talk about this again later."

He shrugged again, and took another swallow of wine. "All right."

"You started to tell me about the horses," I said, by way of changing the subject, "and a plague."

"Yes," he said. "It was long before I was born, but I learned about it in Agoge."

"Agoge?"

"It's where they teach young people."

"School."

"I guess."

"I see. Was it something native to the Red Planet that killed the horses, or – "

"Oh, no! It was a virus created by Aspar scientists. The killing of horses was merely a side-effect. It was meant primarily to kill the enemy Jentana, or leave them barren if they survived it. It was specifically engineered to be more virulent to women."

"My God!" I exclaimed. "Your people deliberately started a plague?"

"We have many times. This one killed many Jentana, before they found a cure. It killed some of our people too, and all of our horses. The Jentana, of course, never shared the cure with us. The plague was eliminated in Aspar, eventually, by the killing of all its victims – "

I held up my hand. "Please, Hylas. I can't listen to anymore right now."

"I'm sorry," he said meekly. "I didn't mean to upset you."

"It's just that... well, I suppose I can't say your people are more savage than mine have been, at times, but... It's just a matter of perspective."

He stared at me for a moment. "Are you really from earth?"

"I really am. Do you believe me?"

"I..." He considered it. "I think so. You're certainly not like any man I've ever met before."

"Then it doesn't bother you that I am not a warrior?"

"But you are!" he insisted.

"No, Hylas, I'm not."

"True warriors," he said firmly, "face death without flinching. They value the safety of their comrades above their own safety. They find the ways to defeat the greatest number of enemies at the least cost to themselves and their city. They carry the blessing of the gods with them."

He leveled his eyes at me in a probing glare. "Which of these does not apply to you?"

There seemed to be no shaking his admiration for me, alien as I was to everything he knew. It seemed he could only understand things in terms of his own culture, within the framework of militarism. Were we all so myopic in our views of the world?

"I am... flattered, that you find so much in me that is worthy," I said. "My gifts come from the Lord, of course."

"And I'm glad," he said solemnly, "that you chose me to be your protégé. Even with a whole city against us, I believe we can triumph. If we don't, our names shall be legend."

"Well," I sighed, "it's been a long night, and morning is upon us. We'd better get some rest."

I busied myself preparing a place to sleep. Hylas had packed bedrolls, along with the rest.

"Shep?" he said quietly, tentatively. "Before we sleep..."

"Yes, Hylas?"

"Will you... would you share your bravery with me now?"

"My bravery?"

"Yes. Your warrior essence. I'm your protégé. It's customary that I receive it."

I believed I understood. He referred to some ritual, no doubt, which was performed between members of a fraternal order like the Masons. It seemed natural that a warrior culture like his would indulge in such practices. An odd time to ask, I thought, but the boy was so intense, and the ceremonies and beliefs of his people held such meaning for him. A fitting quality for a prince, I thought.

"Remember that I am a stranger, Hylas. I... don't know how your people... share bravery."

He rose, and came to kneel beside me on my bedroll. He sat, cross-legged, and placed his hands on my knees.

"It's passed from the body of the mentor to the body of the protégé. The bodily essence carries with it the warrior spirit – the nobility – the bravery, the favor of the gods. It's an act prescribed by the gods themselves, so that great warriors may share with young warriors."

Passing bodily essence? I had heard of such things on earth, like the Indian practice of creating a blood bond between brothers. Each would cut his flesh, and the blood of the two would be allowed to flow together. The primitives believed that this sharing of blood created a true blood relation. It was a little silly, but I supposed it was harmless. Hylas's description sounded a bit one-sided, of course, since this practice allowed the blood of both to mingle, not merely the blood of one to enter the other. My only concern was that we were of different worlds, and what might not harm one in his own blood could be dangerous for another.

"I don't mean to be discouraging, Hylas," I said gently. "I can see this means a lot to you. It's just that, as a doctor, I know that the blood can carry certain impurities. If we mix our blood – "

"Oh, no! We don't mix blood." He smiled, amused. "You really don't know anything about our customs, do you? Even in Equatoria, they practice the sharing of bravery."

"I guess I don't – "

"*You*," he said, his patience waning, "put your essence into me. You know..." He gestured. He gestured between my legs.

It suddenly became clear to me what he meant. I went cold, and my mouth became so dry I could barely speak. "My..." I stammered. "Into your body?"

"Of course," he said. "It's not difficult. At least, I don't think it is. My friends have told me it only hurts a little. I've never done it, of course, because you don't do it with anyone but your mentor."

And then he maneuvered himself into a position which made his meaning all too plain.

"Dear God!" I exclaimed. I buried my face in my hands, and then I felt foolish. What a silly, melodramatic gesture that was! But I did not know how else to respond to this... absurdity. "You," I croaked out, "you want me to... *bugger* you?" I'm not given to the use of vulgar language, but this word seemed to fit the situation.

"Bugger? Is that what your people call it? It's kind of an ugly word."

"As well it should be!" I snapped at him.

His face fell. "You – you won't? I don't understand..." And then I saw anger and embarrassment rise red and hot in his face. "You promised! You swore!"

"I... I didn't know what you were asking, I – "

"Have you no honor?" he cried.

"Honor?" I demanded. "You believe there is honor in a man lying down with a boy in sordid relations?"

"Sordid? It is the purest, truest form of sacred love!"

"Of course," I said hotly, "you defile the love of man and woman! You take the innocence of virgin girls in your beds in the night, and slit their poor throats the next morning! The act of love as God intended it means nothing to you but a casual pleasure. What should be a love equivalent to that of Christ for the Church is instead a final, sadistic ploy in a game of murder! And yet you would have a man mount a boy and call it sacred! While both are drenched in the blood of innocents!" I was shaking in my outrage. I shouted at the ceiling of the cave, "To what den of iniquity hast Thou delivered me, oh Lord?" I looked to Hylas, "How many innocents have died at your hands, in these diseased orgies of yours?"

I'm not given to fits of temper. My anger quickly spent itself, but the damage was done. The face of the boy who had, until moments ago, looked on me with worshipful adoration, now distorted into a mask of rage and pain. Tears flooded his eyes and spilled down his cheeks, and he spoke in a voice tortured and raw.

"I have not killed anyone. A boy who is untrained by his mentor does not use women. I..." He could say no more. I took his meaning. The child was a virgin, and he had, by the customs of his people, set his heart on offering me the gift of his innocence. I suppose it made a twisted kind of sense, if one could see past the outrage one naturally felt at such sinful behavior. My anger abated, I now felt pity, and even guilt, for having hurt him.

"Hylas," I began.

He backed away from me. "Leave me alone," he said. He crawled over to his own bedroll, and sobbed himself to sleep.

SIX

Although I was exhausted I didn't sleep well. I don't remember any dreams, but I'm sure I had them, and they were troubled. I was awakened, somewhere in the late afternoon, by the sounds of wagons, horses, and the electric motors which drove the fliers so common on the Red Planet.

I sat up, wondering if the Aspar had found us. If so, why did I hear what sounded like horses?

Hylas was also awake, his face even paler than usual. "The Jentana!" he whispered urgently. "We have to get out of here!"

"Why?" I wondered. "We left no footsteps, and – "

"Just trust me!" he said, then added bitterly, "if you can."

Knowing a response would do more harm than good, I began gathering my bedroll and what few supplies were out and stuffing them into my bag. My work finished, I moved to help Hylas. He pulled away from me. "I can do it myself," he said sulkily.

I let it pass, and waited for him to finish. I heard footsteps near the mouth of the cave, followed by a woman's voice. "There are two," I heard it saying. Another woman, farther outside, said something I could not quite make out.

I pointed silently to the back of the cave, wondering if there were another way out. Hylas shook his head. I assumed he knew this place well, if it had been a childhood hideout. There was no exit, however, and so we drew into the darkness, hoping that, perhaps, we would be missed.

It didn't seem likely. The woman who was leading the party stepped into the cave. She was old, as I had gathered from her voice. Unlike the women I'd seen among the Aspar, she was clothed, her body almost completely enshrouded in a deep purple robe. She put me in mind of a witch, and for all I knew she was. Somehow, despite our careful precautions to obscure our presence, she had known we were here. I could think of no explanation for that knowledge, apart from a supernatural one.

She cast her gaze about, noting the extinguished fire. She gestured to her two companions, both male, clad in short tunics, and carrying both swords and pistols, as the Aspar did. They were unimpressive specimens, not heavily muscled, and with dull eyes which seemed to preclude strong intellect. Following the instructions of their mistress, they began combing the sides of the cave, moving toward us.

"If we run," I whispered as quietly as I could, "I doubt they could overtake us. I doubt they could hold us, either."

"Don't underestimate them," said Hylas. "They're Jentana. We can't escape."

I was dubious as to the accuracy of his statement, but I did not question it.

"Let me try something," he said, drawing his pistol. "When it's clear, run. Watch for the rest of their party. Head to the right at the cave mouth, and deeper into the hills."

"But you – " I began.

"I'll be right behind you," he assured me. He raised the pistol.

I grasped his wrist. "No killing."

"Not if I can help it."

Hylas leaped out of our hiding place, brandishing his pistol and shrieking something that sounded like an Indian War Cry. He leveled the gun at the woman, and instructed her and her companions to move away from the cave mouth.

"One false move," he said, "and I'll kill her!" He jerked his head toward the mouth, indicating that it was my time to run. Distressed as I was that he was threatening a woman, I emerged from the shadows and moved for the exit.

Suddenly, just as I passed them, one of the men panicked. "Protect the Oracle!" he shouted to the other. While his companion hurled himself between the old woman and Hylas, he launched himself at the boy, wrestling with him for the weapon.

I began to go to Hylas's aid, but he shouted, "Run!"

I did, looking over my shoulder as I went to see him easily peeling the Jentana male's hands from his weapon, and flipping that unfortunate bodily over his shoulder. The man landed hard on his back, the wind knocked out of him, and Hylas ran to follow me.

As he had instructed, I ran into the daylight and immediately to the right, where there was a sloping bank, covered in tangled vines. Hylas leaped onto the vines and seized them in his hands, using them almost as a ladder to scale the bank. I followed his example. As yet, I detected no sign of pursuit.

The rock wall of the bank was, perhaps, sixteen feet high. Hylas scrabbled forward as though he were born to it, which, I supposed, he was. I did my best to follow. The bank ended in what looked to be a horizontal ridge. I pushed forward, gained on Hylas, and we made the top. Together, we threw ourselves up onto the rock shelf, and took a moment to gather our breath.

"That was impressive," said a strong female voice behind us. I looked and saw a striking beauty, raven-haired, with a cruel mouth and black, unforgiving eyes. She was as tall as I, if not taller, and muscled like a panther. This I could plainly see, for the only clothing she wore was a short tunic of some tough, metallic-looking fabric. It had no sleeves, leaving her arms and legs exposed. Behind her were two more equally striking, and equally undressed, women. Clearly, the dark one was their commander.

"I forget," said the new arrival, "that here there are men with strength and stamina that approaches that of a woman."

I assumed these were more Jentana. I had no time for questions, however. Hylas reacted quickly, jumping to his feet, drawing his pistol and spinning in preparation to fire it at the women. I started to object, but quickly learned that my objections were unnecessary.

Even as Hylas took aim, one of the two warriors called out to her leader, "Escara! The whelp is armed!"

In a liquid blur of motion, the lead female Escara launched herself into the air, clearing the distance between my young Asparian companion and herself. Moving faster than the eye could easily perceive, she kicked her right foot high in a sweeping motion, her foot striking Hylas's hand and sending his weapon flying. Almost as her foot once again reached the ground, she drove her fist forward, catching the side of the boy's jaw. He went down hard.

I cried out and lunged forward to assist, but found myself quickly in the iron grip of the other two women. With little apparent effort, they pulled my arms behind my back and held me, kicking like a helpless infant. They were stronger than any man I had ever encountered. I couldn't have resisted even if I had thought it wise, and I did not think it wise.

Blood trickled from a wound on Hylas's forehead. Seeing it, the one called Escara smiled. She reached toward him.

"Please!" I called out. "Spare him. He's just a boy!"

Escara sneered, and I felt I'd never seen such contempt in any face, male or female. "He is a warrior. He should be prepared for death. Fortunately, unlike you, Aspar, we do not kill out of hand." She looked me up and down. "Though sometimes I doubt the wisdom of that practice. This world might be better off with a few less brutes like yourself."

She reached down to hook her hand under the heavy belt about Hylas's waist which held his weapons. She lifted him into the air by it, and threw him over her shoulder like a sack of potatoes.

"Bring him," she instructed her fellows, nodding to me. "We'll take them before Xhylanna."

They took us – actually carrying Hylas, for he did not quickly recover from Escara's blow – back down out of the hills, to an assembly of their people. Here were the horses I had heard outside – horses no different from those to which I was accustomed. Here also was a collection of mechanical fliers, including one much larger than those I'd seen among the Aspar. Where those were constructed to resemble horses, these were more like the carriage that a horse might pull. The size of a small buildings, but sleek and shaped to cut the air they moved through, they were ovoid in shape, and topped with a canopy of glass-like material. We approached the largest. I could see that inside were more of the robust women, like to those who had accosted us. As I came near it in the grasp of my captors, it lowered itself from the air, and sprouted metal legs from its sides, on which it proceeded to come to rest, leaving a fair clearance between its belly and the ground.

Below were more males like those we'd encountered in the cave, scrambling to care for the horses and take and clean the weapons of the returning females. None of them were pictures of physical perfection. I marveled at this alien dynamic – strong women, weak men. I wondered how such a thing could have come about.

Four of these meek creatures arranged rugs and a chair on the desert soil, in the shade beneath the strange craft. When this approximation of a queenly throne was established, all the assembled company came to attention and faced the port side of the airship, where a hatch was opening. A gangway, like that of a large boat's, was lowered, and an elegantly (if immodestly) garbed woman began to descend. Escara seized my hair and turned my head roughly to face the new arrival.

"You are in the presence of Xhylanna, Asparian. You will show respect."

The woman, Xhylanna, stepped down to where I could view her in full, and paused, looking us over. She really was the most beautiful woman I had ever seen. Hair the color of an autumn sunset showered down in ringlets to frame a delicate, ivory face, graced with arresting gray eyes and a graceful, full pair of lips. With these, Xhylanna smiled playfully, and asked, "What have we caught? Stray puppies, perhaps?"

"It was they the Oracle sensed in the cave, Priestess," Escara said. She had set Hylas to the ground, for he had regained his senses; but she still held his arm in an iron grip. "If I'm not mistaken, this one," she roughly turned his face towards her leader, "is the son of Scorpius."

Xhylanna descended the remainder of the gangway and stopped to make a brief curtsy. The gesture was mocking, but, for some reason, I could not be offended by the manner of this gentle creature. Tall and impressive she was, and her form left no doubts that she shared the strength of her sisters, and yet she was in no way unfeminine. I silently wished that I might be given some clothing, while in her presence.

"My good Prince Hylas," she observed. "We are honored. The gods smile upon us in bringing you here."

"Your gods, perhaps," said Hylas quietly.

She ignored his sarcasm, and came over to look at me. "And who is this, your companion?"

"He is... my mentor," said Hylas, with a trace of bitterness still in his voice.

Xhylanna nodded. "We are fortunate indeed, to stumble upon so August a pair of travelers. We go forth on a diplomatic venture to your city of Aspar. It bodes well that we are given the opportunity to rescue two leading citizens on the way. I hope that will open the Warlord's ears."

"You mean you hope to ransom us," Hylas corrected her. Escara cuffed him.

Xhylanna raised her hand in reprimand. "Please! We must treat our guests with kindness."

"The whelp needs discipline," the dark, cold beauty responded.

"Most Asparians do," Xhylanna agreed. "But we shall maintain our manners. The Prince is injured. Take him into the ship, and treat his wounds." Escara moved to obey, leading Hylas to the gangway. "And, Escara?"

The woman turned, her pose and expression carefully treading the line between deference and arrogance. "Priestess?"

"See to it that he collects no more wounds." Xhylanna smiled coldly.

The warrior woman nodded briskly and led Hylas away.

Xhylanna turned back to me. "He will not be harmed, I promise you. My soldiers can be... enthusiastic, but they never fail to follow my orders. I must confess they harbor little good will for your people." She stopped and looked me up and down again. "Or should I say, for Asparians? For they are clearly not your people."

"I am from Equatoria," I lied easily. Too easily. Dear Lord, was sin to become so familiar to me in this alien land?

"You are not," she said firmly, but not harshly. "But you thought it best to hide your background. That intrigues me." She gestured to the makeshift throne in the shade. "I always have some wine in the afternoon. Will you join me...?"

"Shepherd," I said. "My name is Shepherd Autrey. That's, uh, two names," I added, to avoid a repeat of the confusion I'd caused Scorpius.

"So I assumed," said Xhylanna, moving ahead of me to seat herself. My escorts maneuvered me to sit on the carpets at her feet. I didn't suppose I was in a position to argue the imposed humility. "There is nothing so odd about having two names," Xhylanna went on as she accepted a goblet from a male servant, and motioned him to offer one to me. "The Mother Goddess has two names."

"Does she?" I asked politely. I took the goblet proffered to me by the servant, and lifted it in salute to my hostess. I assumed I was to wait for her to drink first.

Xhylanna waved my guards away.

"Thank you," I said. "My arms were falling asleep."

She smiled. "I do not believe you could outrun me, though your physique is impressive."

I actually blushed as her gaze took in my naked body. Were I a cursing man, I would have cursed that there were no pillows or throws available for emergency covering. I begged for strength and chastity, at the same time apologizing to the Lord for the triviality of the request.

She raised her goblet and sipped it carefully. I matched the gesture, grateful for any liquid in my throat after sleeping away the hot day in the cave, and then running from her soldiers.

"Don't gulp it," she warned me. "Our wine is stronger than that of Aspar."

She hadn't needed to tell me. I nearly choked when the liquor hit the back of my throat, and sat coughing. She rushed to me, knelt beside me, and, taking the goblet, wrapped one elegant, soft-fleshed arm about my shoulders. I suppose it was good luck that I was too concerned about breathing for other involuntary reflexes to come into play.

"I should have warned you," she apologized. "And I should have remembered that you would be thirsty, after the chase. I'll send for some water."

"Thank you, I'm all right," I said. She dropped her arm, but sat back on her heels, looking at me with concern. "You're gracious to your enemies."

"Are we enemies?" she asked.

"I would like to think not," I admitted. "But my days among the Aspar have brought me the knowledge that they consider you enemies. You are Jentana, as Hylas surmised?"

She nodded. "I am. And what man in all the world would not know that?"

"Funny you should ask," I muttered.

She handed me back my goblet and returned to her place of honor. "Graciousness to enemies is the way of the Mother Goddess," she said.

"It is the way of my God, as well."

"Then you do not worship Raxes?"

"I'd never heard of Raxes, or your Mother Goddess, until mere days ago."

She shook her head in wonder. "Ignorance of the gods, and of the Jentana people. A name such as is not used in all the world. A claim to worship a God who shares the Mother Goddess's ways. Who are you, Shepherd?"

"You wouldn't believe me," I told her.

"No?" she seemed amused. "Fortunately, I have methods of divining the truth."

While my head filled with visions of torture and interrogation, Xhylanna gestured to someone behind me. The woman from the cave – the elderly one they'd called the Oracle, stepped forward and joined us.

"This is my Oracle," said Xhylanna.

"We've met," I said. "In the cave. I'm... glad my friend didn't injure you."

The old woman's face, shadowed by her hooded gown, was impassive. She didn't appear to care one way or another how I felt. She gazed at me from behind eyes that seemed, even in the broad daylight, to be forever hidden in shadow.

"He is not Aspar," she said, in a voice that sounded like the winter wind that blew up the driest leaves before the first snow. "He is not of the Red Planet."

Xhylanna raised an eyebrow. "Where is he from?" she asked with interest.

The Oracle nodded, as if confirming an unvoiced supposition. "He was born on the old world. He is from earth."

She said it as if the fact carried great significance, as I gathered from Xhylanna's expression of excitement that it did. "How did he come to be here?" she asked the Oracle. "Is he... the answer to the prophecy?"

The Oracle lowered her face, and was silent for a moment. Then she said, "Time will tell if he is the one whom prophecies have foretold. He was carried here by the gods. He has angered the Aspar. He flees death at their hands."

"Hylas told you that!" I protested. How else could she have known?

"One does not contradict the Oracle!" Xhylanna snapped. There was, in her tone, none of the softness or humor that had been there until that moment.

"Forgive me," I said reflexively.

"It is forgotten," said the Oracle. It seemed, in this at least, that she did not answer to the Priestess.

"Thank you, Oracle," said Xhylanna. The old woman nodded, and left us.

"Forgive my harshness," Xhylanna said when she was gone. "The

Oracle is the most respected of us. She speaks the words of the gods. We never contest her."

"Again, I apologize."

"You did not know. But I assure you, she did not learn your origins from Prince Hylas. The gods share with her far more than they share with you or me."

"But you are a priestess," I said.

"Yes, but a Priestess leads her people to do the will of the gods. She does not speak directly to the gods. Only the Oracle may do that, and she does not lead. She only speaks the truth."

"She is correct in my case," I said. "I am from earth, and the Aspar had sentenced me to die."

"For what crime?"

"I was... given a young woman... uh... "

"To bed?" she asked, amused.

I nodded, looking away from those flashing gray eyes.

"It is a common practice of theirs. Did you refuse her?"

"I... uh... she caught me by surprise. I was sleeping..."

Xhylanna chuckled.

"I wish I could find it funny," I said. "My people do not take physical love lightly."

"No?" she asked.

"No. It is to be practiced only within the bonds of marriage."

She looked at me in disbelief. "You may bed only your wives?"

"Wife," I corrected her. "A Christians man marries but one woman."

"My people abolished slavery," she said. "Long ago."

"Are you equating marriage and slavery?" I asked.

"Of course. They are the same. When there were marriages among the Jentana, long ago, the husbands dominated the wives."

"The man is the head of the household," I said, "as God ordains."

"That was the argument, I believe," she said. "And that is slavery."

"Not if the man respects the woman," I protested.

"And do you respect your wife?" she asked.

"I... do not have one," I admitted. "But I would honor the woman I took as a wife."

"You are not most men, then," she said. "For most men, I can't see that there would be any difference between taking a wife sexually and taking a slave sexually. Both are acts of conquest."

Again, I found myself blushing. "You speak very... plainly, Priestess."

"You would say that a woman should not speak so openly of sex? That is a slaver's view."

My face now grew hot with anger. What infuriated me most was that I could not completely refute her argument. "What of your men?" I asked defensively. "It would seem you dominate them. They appear weak, and servile."

I had expected to offend her. I did not. "They are weak," she agreed. "And suited to servitude. We do not enslave them. They are free to work for any mistress. They receive compensation for their work."

"Could a man lead your people? Be a priest, or an oracle?"

She laughed out loud. "How absurd! Of course not!"

"Why?" I asked.

"Because men are inferior to women!"

"And that is not a slaver's argument?" I asked.

"No," she explained patiently. "We do not hold a man's natural lack of gifts against him. On the contrary, we care for our men, protect them. We do what is best for them."

"As my people do their women," I said.

"You are from a strange culture indeed," she observed. "Your men do not despise women, as do the Aspar, but they deny their natural superiority. It would seem that, like Prince Hylas's people, yours are still barbarians."

"Well at least we don't send innocent girls to defile themselves with men, only to murder them when the atrocity is finished," I said bitterly.

Her expression became sad. Her eyes softened as they looked at me. "Is that what happened to you?"

"They expected me to slit the child's throat! As if I had not done her harm enough!" The guilt was welling up inside me, combined with the rage of what had happened to that poor girl.

"It is their practice," said Xhylanna quietly. "It is why we have been unable to find peace with them. They hold human life in contempt."

I sighed heavily, trying to collect myself. "I am sorry if I seem in ill humor, ma'am. It has been a difficult few days."

"And I am sorry if I have been too critical of your beliefs," she said. "It's not fitting a diplomat, is it? But I enjoy a good argument." She smiled at me and added, "With an intelligent companion, especially."

"Thank you," was all I could manage.

"You are very welcome. We will speak further. You intrigue me. Will you have dinner with me tonight?"

"Am I offered a choice?"

She chuckled. "I'll consider you a representative of a foreign power, and treat you completely as an equal, Shepherd Autrey."

"I don't know if I'm up to the task," I admitted.

"You are the only citizen of earth available to serve as ambassador, are you not?"

"That I am, Priestess."

"Good. Then dine with me this evening, as my equal."

"I would be honored."

She stood. "I must go and speak with the young Prince."

"Will you really ransom him?"

"I'll certainly consider it," she said. "Do you object?"

"It may be... inadvisable."

"Why? Certainly you kidnapped him to use for ransom?"

"I did not kidnap him."

"You mean," she asked incredulously, "that his story of being your protégé is true?"

"It is."

"Since when does an Asparian Prince take anyone but a noble of his own city as mentor?"

"Since I saved his life in battle," I explained. "The day I arrived here. Some of your people had apparently taken him – "

"That," she interrupted, "is the regrettable incident which led to my coming here. One of my... more impulsive generals conceived that plan, and hired the unpredictable Amal barbarians to carry it out."

"Was it that woman Escara, who captured me?" I asked.

Xhylanna grinned. "So it was. You are a quick study of people, aren't you? But then I suppose Escara is anything but subtle. She is a competent, even an excellent warrior. Her campaign, in this case, was a disaster."

"It did not portend to end well," I agreed. "One of the Amal was about to murder Hylas. I stopped him. In his gratitude, the poor child planned my escape from his father's custody. I would hate to see him ill-used, and I fear that his father might be as great a danger to him now as the Amal were."

"You turned the heir to Aspar against his father?" she asked, grinning at me. "I have greater reason, then to accept you as an equal, Shepherd. If you are not the man of earth of whom the prophecies tell, then I can't imagine what he will accomplish when he comes."

I have to say that, for captors, the Jentana made us very welcome, once Xhylanna had declared that we were not to be mistreated. I was given the run of the camp which they established in the foothills outside Aspar, with the firm understanding that I would be caught if I attempted to run.

I saw no need to run. The food was better here, the wine was better, and the Jentana had yet to ask me to murder any innocents. Pagan savages they still surely were, for no civilized person can worship such tempestuous, capricious gods as those the Aspar and Jentana told tales of; but they were infinitely preferable to Scorpius's people.

Nor could I pretend that the opportunity to look upon Xhylanna's beauty was one I did not relish.

I wanted to see Hylas. Things were not right between us, and the arrival of Xhylanna's expedition had interrupted any chance I might have to make my peace with him. I was still appalled by the request he had made of me, but I knew that he was but a product of his backward culture. He seemed a decent and noble soul, and I wished more than anything that I might be able to guide him to the truth. I could not do that if he felt I had betrayed him.

But when I asked one of the guards the whereabouts of my young companion, I was told that he was in audience with the High Priestess, and was not to be disturbed. I gathered, from stray comments, that the Oracle was with them as well.

It troubled me to hear the utter faith Xhylanna had in the old woman. Of course she was a fraud. No human being was a conduit to God. Each of us has moments in which we sense the infinite. Each of us carries that spark of the divine fire. Perhaps a few are more open to see the divine in the world around them, but that is all. No one man or woman speaks for the Almighty. That is why Friends do not ordain ministers, nor include the tiresome practice of preaching sermons in their worship.

But the Oracle did know my place of birth, the circumstances of my coming to the Red Planet (if poetically described), and my troubles with the Aspar. I had initially thought she had spoken to Hylas, but realized in contemplating the conversation later that she had not had time. How had she learned these things, then? Was it, like my own occasional abilities to influence outcomes, a factor of the Red Planet itself? And had I not attributed those events to God granting me special power, on a limited basis?

And if He could grant me such power, could He not do the same for the Oracle? But she did not believe in my God! She worshiped someone she called the Great Mother. Still, was not God sole parent to humanity? Mother and Father both? Was it not possible to speak of Him having some kind of feminine aspect? Did we worship the same god, and call Him/Her by different names? Or was I toying with blasphemy?

I joined Xhylanna for dinner that evening, never having had the opportunity to speak to Hylas. I must admit it was hard to think about my argument with the boy in the company of this engaging woman who apparently led a nation. But I did manage to ask what she might tell me of his audience with her.

"He believes his father will condemn him to death," she said.

"I am confident he is correct."

"I cannot understand how any parent could do such a thing to his child."

"Hylas has violated their most sacred law – that death must be given its due."

She smiled at me. "You do not approve of the Aspar, do you?"

"I do not approve of anyone who squanders God's gifts on making war."

"Then you do not approve of me, Shep?" She had taken to using my nickname affectionately. "I am a warrior."

"I thought you were a diplomat."

"A good diplomat is merely a warrior who has learned to minimize her losses," she observed.

"That's a rather cynical view," I said. "Peace should be sought because it is virtuous, not because it makes warfare more efficient."

She laughed. "Does your God really believe this?"

I shifted to recline into the soft cushions on which we had sat to eat dinner. We were in Xhylanna's cabin on the air ship. It occupied about half of the available space under the glass canopy. We had both had a considerable amount of the fine Jentana wine, I am shamed to admit, and were becoming sleepy and informal with each other.

"Well," I said carefully, "He sent his son Jesus to tell us that we were to love all others as we loved ourselves. Jesus instructed us that, if a man were to strike us, we were to turn the other cheek."

"And what would that accomplish?" she wondered.

"It would give him the opportunity to strike us again."

"That's silly!" she exclaimed.

"It also lets him know that his first blow did not cripple us," I said, "and that we believe we can survive another."

"That makes more sense. Was that why you stood so bravely at both of your executions?"

"I didn't tell you about my executions."

"Hylas did. He said you were the bravest man he'd ever met. He admires you deeply."

I sighed. "He's also very unhappy with me."

"Why?"

"I... I'd rather not talk about it right now. It's... upsetting." In fact, I was ashamed to tell a beautiful woman that this admiring young man had attempted to convince me to indulge in one of the most detestable of sins. It wasn't my sin, I knew, but the experience made me feel... tainted. Was there something about me that had suggested to the boy that I shared his perverse tastes?

"I didn't mean to upset you," she said, reaching out to stroke my hair. "I'll change the subject. You have not told me your God's name."

"Oh. We call Him God, mostly. The Bible – that's, uh, our holy book – sometimes refers to him as Jehovah."

"And Jehovah does not wish you to kill each other?"

"He has forbidden it outright."

"What will he do if you do?"

"If we do not repent of our sin, he will cast us into Hell."

"Where is Hell?"

"I don't know, really. Some believe it's under the earth, but... that strikes me as a bit superstitious. Anyway, it's a place of eternal torment."

"And great sinners go there?"

"All sinners go there," I corrected her, "unless they have repented their sins and asked Jesus Christ to be their personal savior."

"Where do good people go?" she wondered.

"All those who seek God's mercy through Jesus go to Heaven."

"Above the earth?"

"You've got the idea."

"But if a good person sins, and does not repent? What happens to her?"

"'The wages of sin is death,'" I quoted. "All humans sin. If they do not repent, all their goodness cannot wash away sin. Only God can do that."

"I don't understand. Your beliefs are so completely different from ours, or the Aspar's – "

"But you and the Aspar believe in different gods!" I said.

"No. We know the same gods. We just are favored by different particular gods. My people follow the instruction of the Mother Goddess, as told to us by the Oracles."

"And the Aspar?" I asked.

"They obey Raxes, the heir to the Old Father."

"But they don't have Oracles," I said.

"Certainly they do! Why should Raxes not have Oracles? He'd be foolish."

"But..." I sat up, bothered by what I was realizing. "Do you mean to tell me that... you believe in Raxes?"

"How can I not?" she asked. "He is real. He is son to the Great Mother."

"Her son? And... he instructs his followers... to make war with you?"

"Yes. Because we follow his rival, the Mother."

"Are you telling me... " I stumbled over my tongue. "... that the gods are at war with each other? Mother against child?"

"Of course! That is why we fight the Aspar!"

"Why... why would the gods want you to fight?"

"Because, eventually, one side will win. And that side's god will rule."

"Unbelievable."

"As unbelievable as good people going to eternal torment."

"That's different! If – "

"Shep," she said with amusement. "Do you know what time it is?"

"I... no."

"It's quite late. I'm afraid we've talked the night away. And I must lead a contingent into Aspar tomorrow, and you must go with me."

"Me?"

She nodded. "The Oracle has declared it. It is the will of the gods."

"Which gods?"

She bit her lip to keep from laughing. "It's time for bed," she said firmly.

She was right. I rose to go. I have to admit I had a little trouble getting to my feet. Wine was not something I'd had a lot of experience with. I turned to thank Xhylanna –

And found her standing, naked, before me.

"Where are you going?" she asked.

"To bed," I said. And then I felt foolish. I didn't actually know where I was to sleep.

"But bed is right – " she broke off and put her hand to her mouth. "I'm sorry," she said. "That was stupid of me. I keep assuming you know our customs. When a man dines with me, he stays all night."

"I... Oh," I looked around the lavishly appointed room. I should have realized that it doubled as a bed chamber. "That's fine. I'll stretch out on the floor – "

"Shep, it's an insult for a guest of the High Priestess not to have sex with her."

"I... Oh, God! Xhylanna, it's a sin if I do... have..."

"Sex."

"Yes!"

"You don't want to?"

"I...well no, I... it's not a matter of what I want! It's – "

She stepped forward. "Part of you disagrees."

"I – please don't do that!"

"Can't you just ask Jehovah to forgive you tomorrow morning?"

"It's not supposed to work that way!"

She was naked, and fully pressed against me. I was naked. My head swam from the wine.

"God forgive me," I muttered into her lips.

SEVEN

"Was that a sin?" she asked when we lay, sweating and spent, in each others' arms. Her head was cradled against my shoulder.

"The Bible says it is," I replied sadly.

"Perhaps your Bible is mistaken."

I was far less offended by this statement than I should have been, I suppose. "The Bible is the inerrant word of God."

"Jehovah? He wrote it?"

"It was written by those he... inspired."

"Oracles?"

"Prophets."

"They sound about the same. And Oracles are sometimes wrong. The gods are much smarter than we are. It's hard for us to understand their message, at times."

"I had thought of that," I admitted. I stroked her hair. Candles which her servants had lit and placed all around the room prior to dinner threw pools of light over it, making her look as though her tresses themselves were flame.

"Would you like to sin with me again tonight?" she asked playfully. "I'm sleepy, but I think I could manage it. And I can tell that you're prepared for more."

"You... seem to have that effect on me."

"It's quite a novelty. Men of Jentana – when I bother with them at all – do not have the stamina to engage twice in one evening. Are you always able to do so?"

"I... I can't honestly say I've ever had opportunity."

"Why not?"she asked, puzzled.

"Until I came to your world, I'd never... experienced... this."

"You'd never had sex?" she asked in surprise. "But surely you've been an adult for years!"

"But unmarried," I reminded her.

"Unbelievable."

"The Lord has proclaimed that His people are to be chaste and virtuous."

"The gods behave mysteriously, I suppose."

"On that we agree."

After a moment's silence, I asked, "Did you enjoy... that?" It seemed only good manners to ask.

She giggled. "Couldn't you tell?"

"I... that is, you did seem... moved... by the experience."

"You do not have the training our men would have received," she said without making it sound judgmental, "but you have a natural aptitude. It's very different to have sex with a man who is one's equal, physically and intellectually. I think I could grow to appreciate it."

"You, er, intend for us to... continue... that is...?"

"I've already asked to go again, haven't I?" She traced the lines of my chest with her fingertips. "But you seem reticent."

"I... it is only..."

She gave a sharp intake of breath, as one does when one has suddenly remembered something. "I'm sorry! Where are my manners? I should send for Hylas."

The sudden change in subject surprised me, but I was attempting to learn to adapt quickly on this world. "I would like to talk to him," I admitted. "Although it's late. He's surely sleeping."

"Perhaps, but he expects you to send for him, doesn't he?"

"He does?"

"Of course. The catamite is usually invited into the bed, after hostess and guest have observed the formalities. Especially among the Aspar, I'm sorry to say that there are men who cannot perform if only a female is present. You don't seem to have that problem, but I certainly understand if you want – "

"C – catamite?" I managed. I knew of the word. It brought to mind the excesses of English poets like Lord Byron, or the sins of the pagan Roman Empire. "Hylas is not – " I began.

"Surely you're not going to tell me you can't even have sex with your protégé," she wondered, astounded.

"Sodomy is also forbidden in scripture," I replied.

"How disappointing! He's such a pretty boy. I was looking forward to seeing you take him."

I did not know what to say to such a statement. Xhylanna did not seem to be a degenerate in any way. She believed in pre-marital sex, but so did many men of my acquaintance on earth. I knew Christians, even a few Quakers, who did not believe that it was particularly sinful for a man to have sex with a prostitute, since it kept good women virtuous. A man, they thought, had stronger drives, and could not help such indulgences. God understood, because He knew that women were more sinful, and tempted men. I was not sure I agreed.

Yet here was a woman who was not a street whore, but a head of state. She was intelligent, well-spoken, considered herself a child of God, in her own system... and she openly confessed that she would enjoy seeing me bugger a boy in her bed.

"Shep?" she prodded me. "I've upset you."

"I... yes, I'm upset."

"I suppose your ways are just different."

"Different?" I demanded. "They're not merely different, they're – my God, don't you see how evil and depraved...? Did you honestly believe I was capable of committing such an atrocity?"

She smiled a sad smile. "What atrocity?"

"Men... do not lie down with other men!" I blurted.

"On your world?"

"On my world! And I wish I was there now!"

"No man ever...?"

"Oh, I suppose... yes, there are some who... but it's a sin! They are jailed!"

"Jailed?"

"Imprisoned. Punished under the law."

"I see. It is a strong taboo, then."

"I should say so!"

"How do boys learn then, the ways of men?"

"From their fathers," I said. "From serving apprenticeships, with tradesmen or scholars. And there are universities."

"Who teaches a boy to have sex?"

"He... well... no one, really."

"How sad."

"I fail to see how anyone could be sad about it!"

"I could," she said thoughtfully. "I think it benefits young men to be taught the ways of pleasure by someone they trust. It removes their fear

and awkwardness with women. It promotes a closeness that softens the
harshness of male bravado."

"It feminizes men," I said.

"Yes, exactly!"

"I don't believe that's a desirable goal. Men should be encouraged to
manly qualities."

"Such as?"

"Integrity. Moral courage. Hard work. Leadership. The inclination to
provide for a family."

"The men of Aspar believe as you do. That men are morally superior."

"I didn't say – "

"You said men should not behave as women."

"I only meant – "

"What did you mean, Shep? Do you think I am not courageous? That
I possess no talent for leadership? That I am immoral?"

She had shamed me. I responded quietly, "I cannot say you are not
courageous. Your people follow you, and you are gracious to your
enemies. I suppose the only flaw I can see is this tolerance for perversity – "
She began to respond. I held up my hand and finished gently, "but I am too
tired to discuss that further tonight. You are the equal of any man I have
ever known."

"Thank you. I hope you will remember, at least while you're here, that
men do not have exclusive possession of virtue. That is Aspar thinking, to
say that all good is bound to the male spirit and body. That is why they
believe their semen carries the power to pass on virtue from one man to
another."

"Hylas tried to explain that to me, yes."

"He did?"

"When he asked to... receive my... semen."

"And you reacted as you did just now?"

"I did," I said. And why did I feel shame at admitting it? It was as if I, not this entire backward world, were immoral.

She shook her head. "That poor child! How devastating for him."

"Devastating?"

"Shep, boys of Aspar choose their mentors very carefully, with more care than they use choosing a wife. Indeed, wives are often chosen for them; but each boy chooses his own mentor."

"Well," I said, giving the matter careful consideration, "I suppose, in a warrior culture, the relationship to one's elder males is of more import than is any bond to a female."

"And, considering they use their females only for breeding and pleasure, and then usually kill them, I'd say the only real feelings of love they have are for other males, wouldn't you?"

"I... " I hesitated. I knew where she was going, and it was so... foreign! "I... suppose so."

"Shep," she said evenly, "you've told me that your people believe that sexuality should occur between one man and one woman, and that that sexuality is a sacred, godly thing."

"It is," I agreed.

"And, how would you feel if the woman you had selected, the woman who had agreed to become your wife, told you when you asked for sex that you were a pervert and that your needs were an abomination?"

Actually, I'd talked to men who had been through that very experience. It bred resentment, and led them to spend much time dining and drinking together at exclusive clubs. I thought it unfortunate. When I married, I hoped to have a happy and fulfilling partnership on all levels.

"Well?" she pressed.

"It would seem very unfair."

"And, if you were still a teen-aged boy, and desperately in love with the one who thus turned on you?"

"I – "

"You'd be heartbroken."

"Are you comparing me," I asked indignantly, "to a frigid bride who refuses her husband on their wedding night?"

"If such things are possible in your world – "

"They are!"

"The husbands don't simply rape the unwilling wives?"

I realized I was clenching my teeth. "Not if they are gentlemen."

"Then be glad Hylas is a gentleman, as you say. That, or his poor, child's ego was so bruised by your effrontery that he suddenly considered himself unworthy of your love. Either way, he would have been well within his rights – among my people or his – to have put a knife to your throat and forced himself on you."

"That's barbaric!" I cried.

"That is the law, Shep. You entered into a contract with Hylas. You agreed to be his mentor. And then you deprived him of one of the benefits he most wanted from you. No one would be on your side, were it known. And I suggest, for your own sake, that you see to it that it not become known."

"I will certainly not speak of it, I assure you!"

"That's good, but I'd also advise you to get over your parochial bigotries and fulfill your obligations."

"Meaning what?"

"Meaning, if you know what's good for you, you'll summon that beautiful boy in here right now, and give me the pleasure of seeing you take his pesky virginity from him, at the same time shedding the rest of your own."

"I won't! I can't!"

She shook her head sadly. "Then you're a fool. Noble..." She crinkled her nose in a smile, "and not a bad lover, for an amateur. But a fool." She sighed. "I suppose we'd better get some sleep. Tomorrow will be a very busy day."

She rolled over and was soon gently snoring by my side. In the silence, I reached inward to the Lord. Heavenly Father, what is it that You sent me here to accomplish? For I'm afraid I may have already failed You.

———

I walked toward the simple farmhouse. It wasn't near any village. These humble people lived on their own, providing for all their own needs. Well, providing whatever the gods didn't provide.

Gods? God. There was only one God.

Wasn't there?

Then what was I? Why was I uncertain about the nature of things? I spotted my quarry. He perched on a fence, throwing slop to hogs. The Firechild.

Here, among mortals, his natural radiance was suppressed. His mother and I had made that happen when we had brought him here to live with surrogate parents. We did not want God the Father to identify him as the product of the union He had brought about. His wrath would be devastating to the boy.

Even without the aura of his divine heritage, he was beautiful, wild and untamed. Despite the years of separation, my love for the child remained, as strong as my love for his mother. Never mind that I was not his father. He was mine.

The parents, an old couple now, smiled and bowed to me. They offered me their best wine and their best seat. They knew why I was here. "You've come for the child," they said. "You've chosen him." They did not know that it was I who had sent him to them. They had heard that emissaries of Heaven sometimes claimed exceptional children as their own. They were honored that I had picked their son. They made over me as if I were king of the land.

Well, I had created them, hadn't I?

What? No! I didn't create humans! Only the Almighty could – what was I thinking?

I was not God.

And yet...

We left the rude farmhouse, the Firechild and I. He was ecstatic, burbling with smiles and laughter and energy. He couldn't wait for the adventures we'd have, the things that I would teach him. He was so fortunate to be the favored one of a god...

No! No, I cried out.

———

"No!" I sat up in bed. Where?

Xhylanna slept beside me, turned away, her head pillowed on her arm. Had my cry been made aloud? If it had, it had not disturbed her sleep.

I was drenched in sweat, as though the room were bathed in sweltering heat; and yet it was not.   Had I been hot in my dream? I remembered the Firechild. Why did I name him that? Of course, dreams often made no sense; but why did I keep dreaming of him, and of his gray-eyed mother? Who were these people that I professed to love?

This Firechild. He felt... wrong. Once again I reflected on the connection between the devil and fire. Yet, in my dream, I loved him. What man professes to love a boy not his son? Was this merely my mind reacting to the disturbing conversation I'd had with Xhylanna before going to sleep? Was my mind saying something to me about the love Hylas claimed to feel?

Most troubling of all, why, in my dreams, did I have this ever-increasing sense of confusion over the supremacy of God? I dreamt of other gods. I dreamt – Heaven help me! – that I myself might be a god.

Surely, surely the dreams came from Satan. Yes. I had left myself vulnerable, sinning with Xhylanna. Beautiful Xhylanna. How could loving her be a sin? But it was; I knew it was. The Holy Scripture said it was.

And again, I reached out to the Lord, to the Light, as does one lost. Surely, I was lost. Would He find me, I wondered? Even here?

———

The next morning, the encampment was broken down. The Jentana mounted their fliers and horses and began a slow pace toward the City of Aspar, with some of the servants simply walking alongside. Hylas and I rode in Xhylanna's craft, standing beneath the transparent dome, which allowed an incredible view of the landscape below, and the towering spires of Hylas's home. I imagined that the view from a balloon was like this. I had never had the opportunity to ride in one. I wondered what the carnival impresarios would make of a conveyance like this one.

We were met near the City limits by a contingent of fliers from Scorpius. Weapons were aimed, and defensive preparations taken, but no shots were fired. Xhylanna informed the leader of the Asparian guard that she was on a diplomatic mission only, and that she was returning the Prince and a companion. No doubt it was this last bit of intelligence which staved off an attack. I didn't imagine the Aspar cared much for diplomacy.

I did not know my intended part in this drama, but I had spent my morning prayer time asking the Lord to make me a vessel of His peace among these savages. I hoped that my obedience would, in some measure, atone for my sins of the previous evening. I know that God does not make trades in forgiveness, but I had to admit that I felt the need to do good works, if only to soothe my own conscience. In the morning light, I castigated myself for succumbing to Xhylanna's charms, and to the numbing effects of the wine. The evil, haunting dreams were the result of my sin, I knew. I knew I must resist further encounters, and yet her sweet face hovered ever just behind my mind's eye, and my flesh tingled always, as if it were still pressed, warm and firm, against hers.

Xhylanna came to terms with the guard, and it was agreed that a force of twelve should be permitted to enter the gates. Xhylanna led, of course, with the Oracle by her side. Hylas's presence, and mine, were de rigeur, and the party was rounded out by Escara and seven of Xhylanna's amazon warriors, for so I had come to think of them. None of the Jentana males were brought. Their presence would have probably been an insult to the Aspar.

As we marched through the gates by twos, flanked on each side by a double number of Scorpius's guards, I whispered to Hylas, "To think we were here only yesterday."

He did not meet my eye. Dear God, I had not wanted to hurt the child. How could I turn him from his sinful ways?

We were met in the plaza before Scorpius's tower by the Warlord himself. A crowd gathered at a respectful distance to watch our return, and to gape, no doubt, at Xhylanna and her beautiful entourage.

As his father approached, Hylas set his face in a mask.

The old warrior met his eyes, imperious disdain written on his face. "Prince Hylas," he said, as if this were some foreign prisoner of war, and not his own flesh and blood. "It seems your attempts were for naught."

"I was honor bound, my lord," he said, "to save my mentor." He kept his voice cold, not intimating to his countrymen what a disappointment I'd been to him.

Scorpius looked at me briefly, calculatingly. Then he turned back to his son. "It would have been wiser to let the City elders weigh matters of honor for you," he said. "But what is done is done. I trust your mentor's essence will serve you well in what is to come next."

At this, Hylas's resolve failed him. He could remain impassive no longer. His cheeks flamed red with shame, and he cast his eyes, which I could see were beginning to leak tears, to the ground.

There was a murmur of surprise, and I believe even disgust, from the assembled Aspar. They knew, from this simple gesture, all that had passed – or not passed – between the boy and myself. Scorpius, his face as red with anger as his son's was with shame, stalked over to me. I knew his intent, and did not flinch. I stood and allowed his fist to drive into my jaw. The impact drove me backwards, and Escara, beside me, was obliged to catch me and steady me on my feet. Even as she laid hands on me, however, her eyes bespoke deep contempt. She was shocked, I saw, by what I had done. This whole world was mad, condemning a Christian for refusing to sin!

"You filth!" Scorpius cried, and then literally spat in my face. "You have ruined my only son, and you deny him what is his by right?" He swallowed and clenched his jaw. "I will enjoy killing you."

Xhylanna interposed herself between us. "My lord Scorpius," she said, with such dignity and calm that one might imagine she had witnessed none of what had passed. "I have come under a flag of truce. I have returned your missing child – "

"He is a subject," said Scorpius quickly. "He is no longer any child of mine."

From the corner of my eye, I saw Hylas's chin quiver.

"Just so," said Xhylanna. "I have returned two who fled your city. Despite your grievances against them, I had believed that you would want your countrymen restored to you."

Scorpius raised an eyebrow. "To stand trial, yes."

"Then they shall stand trial," said Xhylanna calmly. "But I cannot, in good faith, return them to you, if you plan to kill them outright. Killing, off the battlefield, and with no trial by combat, is an abomination to the gods."

He cast his eyes upon Hylas again. Finally he said, "What would you have of me, Priestess?"

"You prepare an attack on our lands on the Island of Wisdom. Your advance scouts have been sighted this day."

He nodded. "In retaliation for your kidnapping of our... of a citizen of Aspar. We cannot allow such an affront to go unanswered. You understand."

"I do. That is why I came to speak to you in person. I'd brought gifts along, but having happened upon the two fugitives, I thought I would offer them first."

"Do you believe I will allow you to attack us, and then buy us off with gifts?"

"I did not attack you."

"But – "

"One of my generals led the attack," she pressed on. "She did not ask my consent, and was aware she would not have received it."

"And where is this general? If you were sincere, I would expect to be presented with her at once, so that my lords and I could perform the ritual violation of her body, and then execute her, as is our right."

"It is your right," Xhylanna agreed. "Sadly, the General was killed in her assault on you, when the Amal lost control of themselves. We are still picking through the dead. If I can find enough of her for you to violate, I will bring those parts to you, for your amusement."

I thought surely that this insulting jest (a lie, for Escara lived!) would inflame Scorpius, and he would dismiss this diplomatic contingent once and for all. Instead, he smiled and nodded his head deferentially. "That would be appreciated," he said.

"Then you will accept our tribute, and call off the attack?"

"Do you fear it that much?"

Xhylanna smiled. I would not believe, as she presented herself here, that she could fear anything. "I simply do not wish to lose the women or the resources. It is my job as High Priestess to keep our borders safe. My people would not think highly of me if I allowed the misguided actions of one maverick general to get them killed."

Again, he nodded. They did not seem to be conversing, as much as performing to a prescribed script, doing a dance, as it were.

"I must consult my lord advisers," he said.

"Of course," said Xhylanna. "I will withdraw, until you send for me."

As she turned to instruct her troops, Scorpius held up a hand. "And you will leave these two with me," he said. "As hostages, against our final agreement."

For the first time, Xhylanna looked uncertain. I had thought this the plan all along, of course. What would be the point in bringing us, if not to ransom us to Scorpius? I had no illusions that our pleasant conversations and our night of intimacy meant more to her than protecting her nation. For all the effort she had put into convincing me to embrace the shared ways of the Jentana and the Aspar, I was still but a pawn in a warrior's game.

So why did she falter? Was it because she was being asked to surrender us without securing the peace she desired? Once we were out of her hands, did she have any leverage?

The Oracle made her decision for her. "It is the will of the gods," she said. "They are to remain, until the peace is brokered."

Xhylanna muttered, "So be it." She made a polite farewell to Scorpius, and asked if his men could escort her outside the City. He as graciously agreed, and she and her retinue turned and left us. As four of the Asparian guard closed about Hylas and myself, seizing our arms and binding them behind us, Xhylanna looked back, only once. Was I merely imagining the sadness in her lovely gray eyes?

Scorpius also watched her retreating form in silence. When she had rounded a corner, and was out of sight of the plaza, he lifted his wrist and addressed his Speaker. "When the Jentana have cleared the gates, secure the city perimeter." When he had received acknowledgment, he nodded to the guards holding us.

"Take them to the great hall," he commanded. "They will die this very hour."

EIGHT

Hylas and I were led separately to the field of the Great Hall, and placed at opposite sides of its expanse. As a crowd filed in to witness our deaths, I was confronted with the last face I ever expected to see again.

"Philip!" I blurted as my old friend, clad now in the scant trappings of an Aspar warrior, approached me.

He surveyed me and shook his head in disgust. "You do have a talent for getting yourself into trouble, Shep."

"And you for staying out of it," I said bitterly, "no matter the cost."

"I wouldn't be so holier than thou, old friend," he replied. "They intend to kill you."

"I'm well aware of the fact," I said. "There's precious little I can do about it."

"There's a great deal you can do about it," said Philip. "You simply refuse to see the obvious. You can fight for your life."

"I will not kill another to save myself."

"Shep," he said impatiently, "kill or be killed is the way of the natural order. You must either be predator or prey."

"God did not intend any species to prey upon itself," I maintained. "And Jesus clearly said not to resist an evil person. He – "

"Jesus!" Philip spat. "Shep, Jesus is no more real than Raxes or the Mother Goddess, or any other mythical deity. When will you get that through your head? Mythology is not worth dying for!"

"You're wrong," I said quietly.

He pointed across to where Hylas was being unbound and handed a sword and knife by his guards. "Scorpius has decreed that the two of you are to fight. To the death. If you want to live – "

"I don't," I said. "Not at that price. I have harmed that boy enough. I will not raise my hand to him."

"And I suppose," Philip asked smugly, "that you expect the same consideration from him?"

"Not really," I replied.

"I should say not! He's a warrior born. He'll kill you where you stand, if – "

"Then so be it," I said.

He looked at me long and hard. "You're a damned fool."

"I hope I'm neither, but I won't argue. Now please step aside, and let's have an end to this ugly business. Tell them I'm ready." I said. Then, for the moment seemed to beg closure, "Goodbye, Philip. I pray God will find a way to spare your soul, despite your stubbornness. If you are able, please tell Hylas that I bear him no ill will, and I die happily at his hands, that he may live."

I must say that the expression of stupid disbelief on my old friend's face was almost worth dying for. I was convinced that now I must die. I had escaped death so often in the past few days, but surely, there was no escape from this. I wondered how soon Xhylanna would learn of my death, and of her betrayal by the Aspar.

Seeing that there was no convincing me to play Scorpius's obscene game, Philip walked away from me, across the field to where the Warlord's seat of honor overlooked the center field. Scorpius and his retinue had now taken their places there.

I watched some conversation occur between Philip and the Aspar leader. There were shrugs, and exasperated hand gestures. Scorpius's face became red as they spoke. Then, waving Philip away, he stood and tapped the speaker on his wrist. His voice, amplified by the device, echoed throughout the hall.

"The stranger says he will not fight," he announced.

The crowd jeered and booed, loudly. Debris began to fly from the stands, as they lobbed rocks and trash at me.

Scorpius held up his hands for quiet. When the crowd had calmed itself, he went on. "This fool believes that fighting and war are against the will of the gods. Did you ever hear anything so ridiculous?"

There was an uproar of harsh laughter, and again, objects began to fly. Most of the detritus came from too far away to even reach the field, and landed amidst the audience itself. More than one brawl erupted, as a rock here, a rotten piece of fruit there, missed its goal and struck an unwitting Aspar.

"It is my understanding that the stranger plans to allow himself to be killed by he who was once Prince of this city." He looked at me disdainfully. I nodded at him in agreement. "Where, I ask you, is the sport in that? What kind of creature is this?"

The crowd roared its approval of his words, and, from one of the closer seats, a small rock flew out and struck me on the shoulder. I ignored it, but wondered absently if, like St. Stephen, I was to be stoned to death by this barbarian horde.

"Well," said Scorpius, fixing his eye on mine, "I will tell you, my strange friend. Even in your death, you shall not be allowed to insult the gods, nor their chosen favorites here on New Earth. If you will not fight, then you will suffer. The one who accompanied you here," he gestured to Philip, "tells me that you would rather die than raise your hand against another. That you cannot abide violence against your fellow man. I believe we might test that resolve of yours."

He nodded at the other side of the field, and Hylas's guard, following instructions no doubt conveyed privately via the speakers, reclaimed the weapons the boy had been given. His wrists were bound once again behind him, and he was led to the center of the green by two guards.

Scorpius looked my way. "Arm him," he called to my guards, "and bring him forward."

My bonds were cut away. A sword and knife were placed in each of my hands. I resisted even to the point that they were forced to close my fingers about their grips for me. Then, awkwardly bearing the instruments of death I wished no truck with, I was led forward to stand mere feet from Hylas. My guards looked to Scorpius for instruction. To my surprise, the Warlord waved them away, and I was left to stand, armed and unhindered, facing Hylas and his guards.

"Guardsman, raise your sword," Scorpius instructed. The man to Hylas's left did so. "On my signal, you will run it through the boy's chest. Be sure to pierce his heart cleanly. He need not suffer to make my point."

The guard poised to strike, the point of his blade positioned so that the arc of his descending arm would carry it to Hylas's exposed chest. The boy met my eye, and I could not quite discern what I saw there. Fear, surely, for even the bravest warrior trained cannot help but fear impending death. Anger? Perhaps. In his eyes, he had reason to be angry with me. I believe I also saw regret. Regret that I could not live up to his expectations? That he had brought me – or I him – to this final, ignoble end?

"Stranger," said Scorpius to me, "you have taken my son. It hurts me little to cast off this, the shell of what he once was. I wonder... does it hurt you as little? Are you as willing to stand and let him die as you are to accept your own death? You have blades with which to fight. No other shall intervene. Raise your hand to save Hylas, and you shall be permitted the death you seem to crave. Allow him to die... and I shall choose another to take his place. You shall watch that one die as well. And I swear to you, full a hundred men shall fall before you, ere I tire of the game and finally slit your miserable throat. Would you go to your weakling god with all those deaths on your conscience?"

I did not answer.

"I shall give you a few moments' time to consider," said Scorpius. "And I, meanwhile, shall ready your next victim. Your erstwhile companion, I think..."

He nodded, and the guards by his side seized Philip. From this distance, I could not hear his words, but the high notes of the punctuating shrieks were carried to me on the air. Philip struggled in his captors' grasp, but all in vain. Restrained, he shot at me a look of pure and utter hatred.

I used the moments left to pray to God for instruction. I knew only one thing for sure: I could not simply stand and let Hylas die, after all the harm I had led him to. How was I to save him, though? I called out to the Lord for wisdom. Surely, there had to be a way...

And then I remembered – of course! Upon my arrival here, God had gifted me with the power to stop a man in his tracks, and to summon a wind to cloud the vision of an army. He had blessed me with the power to peacefully end a violent attack. Surely that was the power He intended me now to use, to escape this crisis, to show these animals the power of a man of God. I shut my eyes and concentrated, focusing on Hylas, and how I wished to save him. The other times I'd worked this holy magic, he had been in danger. Surely now –

"Your time is up," shouted Scorpius. "What will you do, Shepherd Autrey?"

I continued to pray, not even acknowledging him. If I could but paralyze the arm of the guard, then Hylas and I might find a way out.

Infuriated by my silence, the Warlord called out, "Guardsman, kill the boy."

This, this was where God would intervene. I had faith that He would save Hylas. I opened my eyes, to be ready to find an escape, but I saw only the guard's arm, the sword firmly in its grasp, begin its descent to strike the fatal blow. I saw the look on Hylas's face as death stared him down. It was a look of cold acceptance.

And then I was in motion, little realizing what I was doing. I drove the long blade in my right hand through the chest of the guard. His blade fell to the ground, and he followed it, my sword still protruding from his breast, blood beginning to ooze to the point of entry. Fallen, he did not move. His eyes, still open, saw nothing.

God forgive me, I had murdered a man.

Why had I done it? After a lifetime of commitment to the principles of Christian brotherhood, why had it been but the space of seconds for me to decide to end another man's life? Not even to decide, but simply to unthinkingly plunge a sword into his breast? I did not even know how to use a sword. At least I didn't think I knew. Obviously, I was mistaken.

And why, in two similar circumstances, had mere concentration been enough to defeat our foes, and, in this instance, it had yielded nothing? Was this a test, I wondered? Was the Lord seeing how I would perform if my supernatural advantages did not deliver me from worldly evil? Was it, perhaps, even a test of my resolve, my faith in the Lord, that He would deliver my soul, no matter what happened to my body? The Shepherd Autrey I had been until his moment would have told anyone who asked that, when threatened with death, a Christian should stand his ground and trust in the Lord. If he died in so doing, then the Lord had purpose for his death, and would ease the mortal's earthly suffering in the by and by.

I was no longer that Shepherd Autrey. And this man I had become simply had no answers.

The dead guard's opposite number turned to his Warlord for guidance. Scorpius was momentarily too astounded, and, I fear, too pleased with the sudden bloodshed to immediately instruct him. Before he could speak, there was a thunderous explosion, louder then the worst I had heard upon the battlefield back home, and one of the spires which overlooked the meeting complex crumpled, the better part of it bursting into flames and tearing free to fall out of sight, presumably to the street below.

There were screams and shouts of indignation. "It's the damned Jentana!" someone cried above the throng of voices.

And then all was chaos. Whether or not Xhylanna's people were the cause of the disruption I did not know, but I knew that this might be my only chance to act. My soul was surely damned for my crime, but I could still spirit Hylas to safety. I leaped behind him and quickly used my remaining weapon – the knife – to sever his bonds. I think the boy was in shock. I had to seize him by the shoulder and jerk him into motion. Fortunately, in the confusion, even the surviving guard was paying us no mind.

As in all structures of its kind, there were, in the great hall, tunnels beneath the stands, allowing ingress to and egress from the field of exhibition. I made for the nearest one, pulling Hylas by the arm and elbowing my way through the crowds. No one attempted to stop us, their attentions were too focused on the skies above the city, where now I saw that Xhylanna's huge flying craft cast its shadow in the late morning sun as it hovered among the towers of Aspar. About it, like bees buzzing around a hive, a dozen or more of the small fliers circled. Quickly these were joined by fliers of the Aspar, and aerial combat ensued.

So she had not abandoned us. Did she know what had happened to me, I wondered? And then I reprimanded myself for such selfish indulgence. Xhylanna was too smart to allow herself to form an attachment to me. She came back and attacked because the Aspar had closed off their City, and she knew that treachery was afoot.

As Hylas and I had nearly cleared the outer walls of the coliseum, a voice cried out to us to stop. This was it, I thought. We'd been noticed. I wondered if, in my new incarnation as a bloodthirsty savage, I should have remembered to fetch the weapons from the dead guard. To my surprise, however, it was Philip who called out to us. It was Philip running so hard that he looked as if he would collapse at a moment's notice. I slowed and allowed him to come near.

"Take me with you," he begged me, "please!"

"And why should I?" I demanded.

"Because Scorpius was going to have me killed!"

I looked over his shoulder to where I knew a dead body – killed by my hand – lay oozing blood into the sod. "And you think I am of a kinder nature?"

"I - I was wrong, Shep! I didn't realize – I – Oh please! Get me out of here!"

"Keep up with us," I sighed. "I'll make no attempt to wait for you."

"Oh, thank you, Shep! I – !"

"Shut up and run, you fool!"

We made it perhaps ten city blocks, ducking falling debris as whatever destructive shells the Jentana employed hit the towers above us and showered stone and metal supports onto the streets. Then, turning a corner, we were again apprehended. This time, it was by a force of Jentana warriors, led, I was disappointed to see, by Escara.

"The Priestess sent us to retrieve you," she said brusquely. "Against my advice, I feel moved to tell you."

"Xhylanna? But... how?" I wondered. "How did she know – ?"

The woman smirked at me, and seized my arm. "We are not as foolish as you take us to be, nor as you yourself are." She jabbed a finger at the weapons belt Xhylanna had insisted I wear. Part of what I thought was merely a decorative clasp I now realized was a tiny speaker, a miniature of the ones the Aspar Guard wore on their wrists.

Xhylanna had known – where I was, and doubtless all that was happening to me – all along.

———

Nestled in Xhylanna's craft, Hylas, Philip and I were born swiftly away from Aspar. Once we were in place, the Jentana seemed to have little interest in remaining to toy with their foes. I was surprised, but grateful, to be of this level of import to them.

Hylas and I were escorted to Xhylanna's cabin to await her. She was commanding the attack force from the fore of her ship. One of our guards asked if Philip should be brought along to be de-briefed by the Priestess. "I don't really care what you do with him," I told her. "He means nothing to me. I brought him along out of simple Christian charity." I still burned with anger at Philip for his attempts to sway me to violence, no less with anger at myself, for I had been swayed, even if not by him.

When we were alone, I asked Hylas if he were injured at all. He had been so silent during our flight from the arena, and I feared he was in shock. To my surprise, he responded by bursting into tears and flinging himself into my arms. I could do nothing but hold him while his body was wracked with uncontrollable sobs.

When he had managed to calm himself a little, I said, "I'm sorry, Hylas, for the way your father treated you. I don't believe, deep down, that it's what he wanted – "

"Th – that isn't it, Shep."

"Eh?" I asked. "Then what's shaken you so?"

"I thought you hated me," he admitted.

"Hated you? Good lord, you saved my life!"

"No more than you saved mine. And now you've done so twice. You... I know how you hate killing, and yet you..."

"I'm not proud of what I did back there, Hylas. I have sinned – broken one of the Ten Commandments, as well as Christ's admonition to love others as myself. I can never atone for what I've done."

"Would you rather I had died?" he asked, pain evident in his tone.

That was the question, wasn't it? There had been only two possible outcomes in that moment when the guardsman raised his sword: that Hylas would die, or that I would somehow strike the guardsman down. Since my new-found powers to prevent violent action had inexplicably failed me, Hylas's life had depended on my taking violent action, or on a miracle.

And why had I not held out for a miracle? Or accepted that God might, with regret, allow Hylas's death as part of a greater good? Why? I had to admit that it was because this innocent boy, who looked upon me with such frank and unashamed admiration, was someone I was not willing – not able – to sacrifice to my faith.

"Never," I told him firmly. "Never would I have allowed you to be harmed, my friend. I don't know why you admire me so, but I do believe that God has placed you in my care. If I must sin in the cause of sparing your life, then so be it. The Lord will tell me, in time, what must be the fate of my soul."

He laid his head on my shoulder and again wrapped his arms tight about me. "I thought you had deemed me unworthy," he said.

"No. I don't believe I have ever had a more devoted friend. I could not call you unworthy in any way."

"You mean it?" he asked with painful innocence.

"I do. I am sorry that misunderstandings have come between us. We have saved each others lives, and are bound by that in brotherhood. More, I have cost you your family and your home by my intrusion in your life. I will do everything I can to make that up to you."

I'd never seen anyone look so pleased. What, I wondered, had I done to command this child's affections so?

The door to the cabin opened, and Xhylanna entered. The battle over Aspar had apparently dimmed neither her beauty nor her energies. She looked fit and completely collected. She smiled when she saw us seated on one of her lavish couches.

"Welcome back," she said.

"Thank you for rescuing us," I replied.

"I never intended anything else. I must apologize for not briefing you on my plan, but I felt it more effective this way. The Oracle had predicted that the Aspar would not deal honestly with us."

"Then why did you even attempt to meet with them?" I asked.

She looked sad. "I am a warrior, Shep; but, like you, I believe that peace is preferable to war. I must give diplomacy every chance to work. That is why I delivered both of you unto the Aspar. I had thought, despite his anger with Hylas, that Scorpius's affections for him remained."

"I'm sure they do," I said, trying to spare Hylas's feelings.

"You don't know the ways of our people, Shep," said Hylas. He was sad, but matter-of-fact. "From the moment I defied him, Scorpius no longer had a son." I noted he used the Warlord's name, not calling him, "my father." He went on, "To him, you and I are but killers, who deprived him of an heir. His son died in the moment of my betrayal."

"That seems to be true, Prince Hylas," Xhylanna agreed.

"I am no longer a prince, my Lady," he said. "I belong to no state. I suppose I am now your slave."

She shook her head. "No, Hylas, not my slave. I have granted Shep the status of Ambassador to the Jentana from the people of earth."

"Earth?" wondered Hylas.

"Doesn't he know?" she asked me.

"I did attempt to tell him," I said.

"You mean that silly story is true?" Hylas laughed. "I thought Shep had hit his head in battle, and was hallucinating."

"That silly story," Xhylanna chuckled, "was confirmed by my Oracle. As unbelievable as it sounds, Hylas, your mentor is an earth man. As such, he is an honored guest in my home land. And so are you."

"Xhylanna," I asked. "What of the Aspar? Didn't you endanger the peace by attacking them to rescue us?"

"There was no peace to endanger, Shep. I placed you and Hylas with Scorpius as a test of his openness to reason, and his honesty. If any gift would sway him, it would have been the return of his son. It was Hylas's kidnapping which began this latest round of hostilities, after all. As soon as I heard that he had ordered you killed – " she gestured to the speaker on my belt.

"You might have alerted me that you were eavesdropping," I said.

"It would have been less effective, had you known. At any rate, Scorpius's attempt to execute diplomatic hostages, as well as his attempt to lock down the City as soon as we cleared the gates, let me know that all diplomatic options are now closed. The gods directed me to test him in this way, and now they have shown me that the answer is war." Again, she looked extremely sad. "There can be no peace between Jentana and Aspar. Now there must be war, until one of us is defeated completely."

"Xhylanna, that must not be!" I protested. "Surely – "

"We cannot speak of it now, Shep," she interrupted. "I must direct out return home. I thought you might wish to come forward and watch our approach to Jentana."

I was eager to see Xhylanna's home. I nodded my agreement that I would like to observe, but resolved that she and I would speak further on the question of war with the Aspar. God had delivered me to these people, and given me the ear of one of their leaders. Surely, I was intended to work for peace among them, and spread the message of Christ.

Our craft dropped out of the clouds, giving my stomach a jolt, and revealing a glittering seascape beneath us. Like the skies of what Xhylanna's people called New Earth, the seas were purple, deep and rich purple, sparkling like an amethyst. Rising from the waters, warmed by the sun, and lush with red and gold foliage, was a large island. From our vantage point, I could see impressive buildings, but only sparsely scattered over the land mass.

"It's beautiful," I said to Xhylanna, "but where is your city?"

She smiled. "Just wait, Shep. There's more here than you would probably guess."

Our descent continued toward the island, but, where I thought we might level off and prepare to alight gently on its surface, as the ship had done outside the walls of Aspar, the pilot continued nearly straight down, arcing over the edge of the island, but not preparing to right us and touch down on it.

"What – ?" I wondered, seeing through the clear canopy that we were headed straight for the water. I admit I was alarmed.

Xhylanna squeezed me hand. "Just relax, Shep. I promise you, we're not committing mass suicide."

But what other purpose she intended I could not imagine, for the ship continued its descent and plunged into the water, breaking the surface, and still not righting itself. The violet waters closed in over us, and the ship momentarily darkened before electric lights flashed to life to compensate.

"A submersible!" I said in amazement. "Of glass!"

"Don't you have such things on earth?" asked Xhylanna.

"We have submarines," I replied. "They've been used in the war my people are – were – fighting. But they're tanks of iron, and easily scuttled. Dangerous." I looked about and above me, where I could see water covering every inch of the transparency over us, and the light from the surface beginning to dwindle and fade. "Can this beautiful craft really survive the pressure of the water?"

"Oh, yes," observed Xhylanna. "And we're going to go far deeper."

And indeed, we did. I have no idea how deep the craft plunged, for, in the darkness, it was impossible to gauge our speed. We traveled a considerable distance, however, eventually seeing only by the exterior lights of the craft, which cast ahead of us, revealing the wonders of the undersea world. I had never seen its like.

And then Xhylanna pointed, and I saw a spot of light amidst the purple darkness. It grew as we sped toward it, and I eventually realized that I was looking upon a cluster of buildings, lit up like – in fact, it was! – a city. A city beneath the sea! The whole was encompassed by a transparent dome, not unlike the domed ceiling of this vehicle.

"In the name of Heaven," I muttered.

"The island above is merely used for farming crops and raising livestock," explained Xhylanna. "We have never allowed the Aspar to know the truth – that our true residence is here. Welcome, Shep, to your new home. That is the city of Jentana."

NINE

The city was the most beautiful I have ever seen, even if completely unearthly. There was no natural light, it was so far beneath the waves. Light sprang from every window, however, and from lamps all over the city. Even the walls of buildings had their own special luminescence. I gathered that most of the lighting was electric, but the Jentana seemed also to adorn surfaces with a chemical substance that absorbed light that was cast and radiated it back when the source was not present. Even more than Paris, then, Jentana was a City of Lights. To walk its streets made one feel he was ever attending a nighttime carnival.

Xhylanna's palace was no less lavish than that of Scorpius, though it lacked as many of the martial trappings, and was more prone to display phenomenal works of art, sculptures, tapestries and paintings. That the Priestess's people were talented artisans was everywhere evident. And here I saw no slaves, only the poor, male servants, who at least, Xhylanna said, were paid and cared for, not executed once they had served some barbarian's pleasure.

I could have lived here happily forever, were it not for the specter of war that overhung these people. Indeed, Xhylanna told me I was welcome to do just that. I asked how one went about securing lodgings here.

"There are rooms to rent, I believe," she said. "Once you find some way to earn money. I imagine that the state budget could afford to give you a stipend, for a time. But you needn't bother. You are welcome in my home for as long as you wish to stay."

"Thank you," I said. We were gathered in a parlor of sorts in her palace. A comfortable room, larger than the whole of her flying submarine. And in that, she'd had a considerable private stateroom. Servants had brought us wine, cheese of some sort, which I could not refuse, and various local fruits. I assumed these products came from the island above. There was also, naturally, a generous selection of seafood. I was afraid to try nothing, for were these people not as human as I? Hylas, being a desert-dweller, had been raised to distrust seafood. We had tried to coax him to sample something that looked like crab, to no avail. He found enough to keep him from starving, but the principal meats of these people were from the sea. Sooner or later, he would have to give in, if he were to stay here.

"You are welcome in my bed, as well," added Xhylanna, smiling.

I started at this frankness, especially in front of Hylas.

She noticed, and came to sit next to me, leaning heavily against my side. The warmth of her, the fresh scent, her sweet breath, all confounded my senses.

"I didn't mean to make you uncomfortable," she said.

"I... well... such conversations are usually... private." I nodded to Hylas, who looked mildly surprised.

So was Xhylanna. "That's a strange custom. Is Hylas not your blood-brother by virtue of shared battle?"

"I... suppose," I said.

"Then you have no secrets from him. And I wish to have none from you, Shep. I... I have not had a lover in some time," she said slowly. "My fellow females can be quite satisfying, but I keep my distance because of my position of authority."

"You... sleep with women," I said, trying to keep the shock from my voice.

"I suppose the women of your world do not enjoy love play together," she said, a little impatiently. It seemed my mores were becoming as tedious to her as hers were distressing to me.

"Women of my world... do not enjoy such pleasures at all," I replied. "It is a physiological difference."

"What? That's ridiculous. Your women are – Shep, I'm just as human as you are! We're descended from the same earthly ancestors!"

"So it appears, anyway," I agreed.

"Then how could there be a physiological – Holy Mother, did you not hear me the other night?"

"Everyone on the ship heard you, my Lady," muttered Hylas, grinning over the rim of his goblet.

I blushed furiously to think that my degeneracy had been so obvious. My partner in sin was phased not at all. She turned to the boy and asked, "And did it not sound to you as though I was enjoying Shep's attentions?"

"It surely did," Hylas giggled. Then he looked at my shamed face, and began to laugh so convulsively that he could not speak.

"I'm glad you both think this is funny," I said petulantly.

Xhylanna shrugged. "Sex is preposterous in so many ways, it cannot help but be funny." She stopped and kissed me firmly. "But about this I am in earnest, Shep. I have wished for years for a lover, someone I would not have to worry over because I was also her priestess – someone who could be my equal in every way. I've never felt very passionate about sex with women, though it's fun. I've never met a man who could even remotely be called my equal." She took my face gently in her hands. "Until now. I would very much like to have you as my lover, Shep."

"Are you asking me to... marry you?" I asked hesitantly.

"I've told you already that my people consider marriage a primitive and exploitative institution. I'm asking you to just... be with me. I'm asking you to love me."

"I... am very... taken with you, Xhylanna. You are beautiful and intelligent, and I believe you are good to your core, even though you engage in warfare and promiscuous sex."

"Even though," she said wryly.

"But... To take a lover, outside of the Holy bonds of matrimony, I... I do not know. My time here has changed me. I don't know if it has changed me that much."

I thought perhaps she would be angry at my hesitance. She was not. "Your time here has changed me, as well, Shep. You have no idea how hard it was, after just one night with you, to send you into danger in Aspar. Even with the assurances of the Oracle that the gods commanded it, I did not wish to leave you. I suspected that Scorpius might try to kill you – "

"Xhylanna, I knew that you did. I do not fault you. You had your people to protect, and I was but a stranger. I bear no grudge – "

"But I do not want you to simply not resent me, Shep!" she cried, "I want you to love me! And sending you in as a pawn in my game was perhaps the most painful thing I've ever done. And that tells me the depth of my feelings for you! I believe the gods intended us to be together." She sighed. "But I won't push you. I want your love, given freely. And I do not want you to believe that loving me is a sin. Please think about it. I must meet with my generals. Ask for anything you need. The servants already know that you are my most honored guest." She stood, and left us.

When she was gone, Hylas said, "You are very lucky, to be loved by such a woman."

"Yes," I agreed.

He looked at me intently. "And you are in love with her."

"I... " I thought about that. Was I? All my life I had avoided women, for the very reason that their beauty and charms tempted a man to sin. I had always intended to marry, but my own aloofness kept me from women, and women of earth, of course, waited for a gentleman to approach them. Now here I was, beloved of a woman who did not believe in marriage, a woman I had already known in the Biblical sense. Of course, my morality told me I should marry her immediately, and deliver her from sin. Her morality told her to do no such thing. But I wanted...

Yes. I wanted to marry her. It was not guilt, or obligation which brought about this feeling. Xhylanna and I disagreed on many things, but on this point, I would not argue: whatever gods there were in all the universe did intend us to be together, else our impossible meeting would never have happened.

"Yes," I told Hylas. "I do love her. I... I don't know what to do, though. It's a difficult situation. My beliefs say I must marry her."

"What does it mean," he asked, "to marry someone?"

"Er, ah... it means that she has my exclusive love. That I will put no other before her. That I will not allow another to come between us. That I will make caring for her the priority of my life."

"If you love her, then are not all those things already true?" he asked.

"I... suppose they are," I admitted. "But marriage is more than intent. It means that God has blessed a union."

"Xhylanna says the gods have blessed your union, and she's a priestess. What does your god say to you?"

"I... I have not had the time to pray about it. I certainly don't believe that God would allow me to love a woman who was wrong for me."

"Then there you have it. You love her, you'd do anything for her, and the gods approve. You're married already."

His simple logic made me laugh. He was such a pure creature, so desirous that the world could be a happy, fair and loving place.

"I wish it were that simple," I said.

"Well," he fell back against the couch and helped himself to grapes, popping them from the stem and dropping them into his mouth two or three at a time. "In the meantime, this is a very nice place to think about the question."

"It is that." I reclined myself, and attempted to shed the nervous energy of the last few days. I needed to be calm and still, and hear the voice of the Lord.

Hylas wriggled over next to me, placing a hand on my thigh. I thought nothing of it, until he said, "Xhylanna's meeting will take hours. Now that we're alone, would you like to take me?"

I sat up. "What?" I demanded. "Surely you don't mean – " I broke off. His face fell, and he went white. Yes, he had meant...

"Oh, Hylas," I said mournfully, "I thought we'd settled this."

His eyes teared up. "So did I," he said hoarsely. "You killed the guard to save me! You told me I was worthy!"

"You are worthy," I assured him. "You are worthy as my... as my blood brother, as Xhylanna called you. You are my dear friend, my comrade in arms!"

"What do I have to do?" he demanded. "What is it that you want from me?"

"I want only your friendship," I said weakly.

"No! I mean – ! When will you claim me as yours? As your protégé?"

"I..." I blinked my eyes because they burned. God help me, I was nearly in tears myself. "I can't do that, Hylas. It's not a matter of you being worthy it's – "

"Shep," he pleaded. "Don't you understand that I'm not ready for a woman? Someday, I'd love to have someone as beautiful and noble as Xhylanna in my bed, but... I can't! I can't do that, until I am loved and taught by a man!"

"What?" I demanded.

He swallowed and tried to keep his voice even. "Just as you say you can't have a woman who hasn't... married you, I can't have a woman until I've been loved by a man, a greater warrior. My mentor!"

"I... I didn't know – "

"But that's the way it is," he pressed on.

"Why?" I demanded. "Men of Aspar do not value women."

"No," he admitted. "We do not. That's part of it. We must always remember that our first loyalty is to our fellow males. And so, even though we mate with women to produce children, new warriors, we must first be taken by a man. It is the law our gods have bound us under. As the god Raxes was taken in his youth by the Pretender, so must each youth of Aspar give himself in this way."

"I am sorry, Hylas. I did not know that you believed this. I... "

"And it is not only because of the custom, Shep. I have waited all my life for the man who would claim me. All my friends have long ago found their mentors. I waited, and I found you... Shep, I want this. I want you to have me."

"Hylas," I said gently, "you must understand that, to me, it would simply be compounding sin upon sin. I have already fornicated with Xhylanna, and with that poor girl your father's guards killed. I have committed murder. On top of all that, I simply can't – "

"Then," he said with resolve, "I will live without the touch of another."

"No," I protested, feeling sorry for him, despite the absurdity of his religious code, and the preposterous nature of what he was asking from me. "Surely, there is some other man who can... fulfill your needs."

"You are the only man," he said firmly. Then, his voice breaking, he added, "I want no other." He leaned back into the pillows of the couch and covered his face with the crook of his arm.

I moved to him and took him by the shoulder, trying to think of what on earth – New Earth – I could say to bring him comfort.

"Please," he whispered. "Just go. Just leave me alone."

Helpless, I left him.

I had intended to go for a walk, clear my head, and explore this strange city. One of the disadvantages I immediately recognized about an undersea community is the absolute boundaries it imposes upon its denizens. Like living on an island, or even in a prison, there were limits to how far one could go before encountering a wall, and those limits were easily reached by a man in the course of a short walk. This would have the effect of reducing privacy, since the odds were high that you would always meet someone wherever you went. I was one who enjoyed my solitary walks. Like Thoreau, I found being alone in the wilderness allowed me to feel in proximity with God. Never had I had a greater need to be in the presence of the Lord, and never had I felt more isolated from Him.

I had hoped to roam Xhylanna's palace gardens, that they might offer some substitute for a rambling forest. Unfortunately, Philip accosted me before I had found an exit from the building. He had a look of urgent purpose about him.

"And what deviltry are you about?" I asked him.

He grimaced, wishing, I'm sure, that I would forgive him his amoral nature and resume our friendship. I had no such intent.

"I've just been questioned by the Generals," he said with some satisfaction. "It seems I can be of some aid to them in their efforts."

"Which efforts are those?" I asked, not really caring.

"Why, the effort to make a decisive strike against the Aspar," he said. "No Jentana has had the access to their city that I have. I can provide them with valuable intelligence for making a strategic strike on – "

"You'll do no such thing!" I barked.

He straightened himself and gave me a defiant look. "I'll do what I like, thank you very much, Dr. Autrey."

"Oh, Philip, come now! I know you've never been... particularly committed to morality or spiritual matters, but... we can't allow ourselves to be caught up in war! The Lord has declared – "

"The Jentana and the Aspar worship different gods," he said sternly. Then, with a little smile, he added, "Who knows? It's possible that this planet is outside Christ's jurisdiction."

The jibe made me angrier than it should have. "Nothing in the universe is outside Christ's jurisdiction," I said, "least of all, you. Philip, I beg you, for the sake of your soul – "

"Shep, have you considered how pleasant life might be here? If only we don't allow the Aspar to destroy it?" He waved his hand at the surrounding grandeur. "Look at the life these people have built for themselves! And they've made us welcome among them!"

"It's very nice, yes, but – "

"But," he interrupted, "they are not proponents of your Christian charity. They do not take kindly to freeloaders, and paupers are conscripted into the ranks of the servants. A person must have means, to live well here."

I said impatiently, "I don't understand what you're – "

He leaned in close, and said in a conspiratorial whisper, "They're going to pay me – handsomely – for the intelligence I have to offer."

"But," I stammered, "it's blood money!"

He shrugged. "They're going to go to war anyway. I'm not causing the violence."

"But you'll happily profit by it!"

"Is it any different from selling whiskey to men who might become dipsomaniacs? You know," he went on, looking pleased with himself, "your young friend Hylas knows Aspar better than any of us. He could supply – "

"You expect the boy to betray his countrymen?" I demanded.

"Why not? They tried to kill him. And you. You know, Shep, you really do need to learn to recognize opportunity. I suppose I understand your revulsion at being asked to commit buggery, though I must admit I wish I could have been there to see the look on your face."

"I wonder how you would have reacted," I muttered. I had no shame left over, after all my experiences, to waste on Philip Meigs.

"To a chance to sod the son of a king, and win his eternal gratitude for my services?" He snorted a laugh. "I'd have pounced on the silly little bugger."

For the first time in many years, I had to actively suppress a desire to punch a man. "I'll thank you to stay away from Hylas," I snapped.

He laughed. "My dear boy, you're beginning to sound like a jealous lover. Is he... getting to you?"

I grasped him by his forearms – a disadvantage of scant clothing was that he had no coat lapels for me to seize – and backed him into the wall. "Let me remind you, Philip, that I killed a man today. You might not want to antagonize me, now that my control has shown prone to slipping."

I couldn't believe I had said it, and was immediately seized with guilt. Was I making sport of the grievous sin I had committed? What effect was this place having upon me? No. I knew I could not blame place or person for my own shortcomings. The Lord had sent me here to test my commitment to peace. I was failing that test... miserably.

Philip looked at me with his darkest smile. "Observe the gentle friend of man," he sneered. "How the mighty have fallen, eh Shep? I always knew that, someday, your armor would crack, and all that smug talk of loving your fellow man would be seen for so much folderol."

I released him, and backed away slowly.

"How soon is this planned attack to occur?"

"Why immediately! They can't wait. The Aspar will be expecting – "

"Is Xhylanna aware of this?"

"Yes," he said brightly. "In fact, it was she who asked me. I believe she's considering an appointment for me to her council of – "

I broke and made my way down the corridor, toward the chamber where I knew Xhylanna and her Generals would be meeting. It had been pointed out to me in the brief tour before lunch.

Behind me, Philip laughed, and called out, "Don't be in such a hurry, old man! I'm sure they'll delay the attack to hear from such a renowned killer as yourself!"

There was a guard now, at the chamber door, since a meeting was in session. She held out her arm as I approached, but listened politely as I stated my need to see the Priestess. I was asked to wait, but did so only briefly before Xhylanna herself came to the corridor.

"Is something wrong?" she asked.

I felt suddenly foolish. Of course, something was wrong. The Jentana and the Aspar were bound and determined to kill each other. But what did I intend to do about it? Ask them to sit down and have tea? Would I have demanded to meet with Lincoln and Davis with such audacity? What made me think I was qualified?

I reminded myself that I was the only Christian, the only man of peace on this entire world. The Lord had placed me here for a purpose. There was no doubt in my mind that, as always, my admonition from Him was to witness to the fallen.

"Philip tells me you're planning an immediate attack. I – I must talk to you about it!"

"Of course," she said. "I was planning to send for you anyway. We need as much information as can be gathered from those who have been inside Aspar."

"So I heard," I said bitterly. "Philip seems to think you're going to make him rich."

She laughed a tired laugh. "It is nothing to me. Your friend will be a harmless court pet – "

"He is not my friend!" I hissed.

"I'm actually glad to hear that. He's a coward and a fool."

"Xhylanna, I didn't come here to help you in your war efforts. I cannot. I came to try to convince you – "

She took my arm. "I've called a recess. Let's walk for a few minutes." She led me away from the chamber door.

"I did not think the guards needed to hear you, before the Council did. Of what did you want to convince me?"

"Of the sinfulness of war!" At her dubious expression, I said, "Xhylanna, have your people ever been at peace, truly at peace?"

She shook her head. "Not for long. Have yours?"

"Some of us. Some of us live at peace with our fellow men, despite the wars around us."

"Then you live in a land of luxury, Shep. War has not consumed your resources sufficiently for you to see that war must touch us all. Eventually, it forces us all to take sides. I'm afraid you won't be able to maintain any kind of neutrality here."

"But I must," I said. "God commands it. And He commands that I spread the word of peace to others."

"It will not be well received," she warned me. "There is great anger on both sides, for the recent indignities suffered. That is why I led you away, for a time. The lower ranks would not understand your commitment to peace. All they know is hatred for the enemy."

"Why are you fighting the Aspar, anyway?"

"You know that, Shep. Because they are angry that our general kidnapped Hylas – "

"You mean Escara."

She raised an eyebrow. "I do, although I was forced to cloak that truth from Scorpius. Temporarily. It will not matter soon."

"But before the kidnapping, what was the root of the hostility? Why would your general even do such a thing?"

"We are... enemies."

"Why? Do they claim land that is yours?"

"No."

"Is there some natural resource of theirs that you need?"

"We have all that we need."

"Do you believe that they oppress their people and must be stopped?"

"You've seen yourself what they do to captives of the Jentana," she said soberly.

"But... why do they do that?"

"Because we are enemies. Really, Shep – "

"But why must you be enemies?"

"Because the gods have decreed it. I don't know about Jehovah, but our gods – particularly Raxes – have a great interest in human warfare. That is what it comes down to. We do the wills of our gods. Are we so different from you in that?"

"Only in that my God would never ask us to go to war," I replied.

"What would you have us do, Shep? Leave ourselves defenseless?"

"Break the cycle," I said. "Risk making peace with the Aspar. Go to them and negotiate – "

"They will kill us!"

"That's fear talking."

"I am afraid for my people," she admitted. "It is only the secrecy of our location that has protected us thus far. If the Aspar could find this city, they would eventually develop the technology to attack us under water."

"All the more reason to end this nonsense as soon as possible!" I insisted.

"I wish there were some way, I really do. I have tried, however, and - "

"Send me," I said.

"What?"

"Let me go to the Aspar, as a negotiator. I'm a third party, I'm neutral."

"You're not neutral! They hate you! You tarnished the honor of their prince!"

"Oh, that," I said. "It keeps coming back to that."

"It's important to the Aspar," she said.

"That has been made abundantly clear to me. Still, I believe I might be able to broker an agreement between your peoples, a treaty. Won't you allow me to try?"

"I'll allow you anything," she said carefully, "provided that my people agree to it. If you want to address my Generals, you may. I warn you though, they will not listen."

"I am obliged to try."

═══════════

Within the hour, I stood before the Council of Generals. The Jentana, it seemed, had some semblance of representative government. Xhylanna, as Priestess, served as a sort of chief executive and moderator, but the Generals, military leaders, spoke for factions of the people. In a small way, I suppose it was like addressing Congress. The thought daunted me, but I was resolved that the Lord wanted me to do this.

I told them of Jesus, His divine birth, his ministry, the many people He had healed, the Sermon on the Mount, and His sufferings on the cross. I told them of the Golden Rule, and the Ten Commandments. I recited as much as I could remember of the Quaker Testimony on war.

I proposed my plan to go into Aspar and hold peace talks with Scorpius.

They listened politely. It was their way, to listen to a reasoned argument. Much like a Friends Meeting, any of their company was welcome to stand and speak. They let me go until I was finished. Then Xhylanna thanked me, and asked if anyone else would speak.

Immediately, Escara stood. She had been eying me the entire time. Indeed, from the moment I had come into the chamber, her black eyes had burned with hatred as they had looked my way. Now, carefully keeping those eyes from meeting mine, she asked bluntly, "After the earth man is killed, will we invade the city immediately? Or will we wait, to maximize the element of surprise?"

I buried my face in my hands, and ignored the rest of the proceedings.

When I left, however, walking alone because Xhylanna had additional matters of state to attend to, I was approached by a woman, one of the Generals who had sat in silence in the back of the chamber. I had noticed her particularly because she was petite, as Jentana go, with light blonde hair that was almost white, and clear blue eyes so pale they seemed to fluoresce in the darkness beneath the sea. I had seen her looking at me with a strikingly blank expression. I'd wondered if I was boring her.

She introduced herself as Colys, leader of a large family in the City, and General by virtue of her family's wealth.

"It's been a long time since anyone spoke of peace with any real passion," she observed.

"I thought your people believed in peace," I said bitterly.

"We do. But our belief has been sorely tested over generations. I'm afraid we do little more than pay it lip service." She looked me up and down. "You have great courage, to be willing to go into Aspar. It's likely they'd kill you on sight."

"Very likely," I agreed.

"Then why go?" she asked.

"Because I must obey the word of God," I said.

She nodded. "You know this war cannot be stopped."

"I fear that is true."

"But your courage speaks well for you. If a man can show such courage, I wonder if there might not be some hope for civilizing the Aspar. I'm going to tell my family of what you've said today. Perhaps... perhaps we will come to support a proposal to send another diplomatic envoy."

"Why did you say nothing in the Council?" I asked.

She looked at me guardedly.

"The opinions of the other Generals are closely aligned. They are hungry for war, for victory. It is... not safe to speak in opposition to them. Anyone who disagrees with Escara, especially, risks losing her position. Even her life."

I sighed. "It is rarely safe to speak of peace."

"I am impressed by you, earth man; but watch your back. Even Xhylanna's patronage has its limits."

―――――――――

Somewhat heartened – if perplexed – by my conversation with Colys, I returned to the parlor where I had left Hylas. I was anxious to tell him that I'd made at least some progress towards peace. The room was empty, however. Finding a servant in the corridor, I asked if he knew my young compatriot's whereabouts. He replied that rooms had been prepared for us, and Hylas had retired to them.

Well, that wasn't surprising. The boy was upset and wanted to be alone. As I walked, I rehearsed what I might say to him. I needed to assure him that I held him in the highest regard – no, the deepest affection. I had to explain to him how my people viewed sodomy, and why I could not engage in it. But I could be, in every other way, his mentor. If only he would be reasonable...

I came to the apartment indicated and entered, calling his name, quietly. He didn't answer. If he was here, perhaps he was asleep. We had certainly earned sleep, after all. Sure enough, I found him in a bed chamber off the main room, draped across a well-appointed bed, face down. I thought to let him rest, and speak to him when sleep had made him more agreeable.

Then I saw it – a patch of red on the gold, woven cover of the bed. It was a stain that had spread from where Hylas's arm touched the fabric.

I dashed to him and seized him, hauling him roughly face up. Thank God, I thought, for he was still warm and breathing. As I turned him, however, a knife dropped from his opposite hand, the hand which had been obscured by his body. The metal clattered to the floor, and I saw that the blade was liberally stained with blood.

And then I saw the horrific wounds on the pale wrists, and I cried out despite myself. I didn't need to be a doctor to know that they were self inflicted.

I had driven the poor child to suicide.

TEN

I waited in Xhylanna's chambers for some word. My own skills had allowed me to stop the bleeding and stabilize Hylas, but he had lost a great deal of blood. Without a transfusion, he would surely die. I offered my own blood, but Xhylanna's physician assured me that it was not necessary, as blood was kept on hand at all times. I was amazed. To be able to store blood? It was beyond the medicine I knew. The only transfusions I'd ever heard of were performed from one live donor to another.

Even so, with blood ready at hand, I feared for Hylas's life. How long he had been there, quietly dying in misery, I did not know. I only knew that I had caused both his misery and, very likely, his death.

Xhylanna tired of me pacing the floor, and seized my hand, to pull me down on the couch with her. She embraced me tightly, and then brushed the hair from my face. I realized only then that I had gone into a cold sweat as I'd worked to save Hylas.

"He'll be all right, Shep," she said soothingly.

"You can't know that," I said.

"I've lost more blood than he in battle, and I'm still here. My physician is superb at her job. She will keep him alive, and make him well."

I sat back. "And if she does? What if he tries again?"

"If someone really wants to take his own life, we cannot stop him."

"It's my fault," I said.

"No – " she began.

"Yes. I accepted an obligation to care for someone from a culture I didn't understand. And when I couldn't provide what he needed from me, he felt he had no other way out."

"He does love you."

"How clear he has made that fact!"

"And I think you are not indifferent to him."

"No," I admitted. "I am fond of him. I don't understand how so sane and healthy a boy could have so diseased a desire of the flesh – "

"Have you thought that, just maybe, it's because his desire for you is just as sane and as normal as yours for me?" she asked.

"Don't be ridiculous!"

"I'm not," she said sharply. "Shep, you're in a different place than the one you came from. We have different customs. Does that make us wrong?"

"If the customs violate God's laws!"

"And does it violate your god's laws? Did he ever say, 'Hylas shall not love Shep, and Shep shall not do Hylas the kindness of a little sexual gratification?'"

"No, but He said 'Know ye not that the unrighteous shall not inherit the kingdom of God?' And he included in the unrighteous fornicators, adulterers, the effeminate, and abusers of themselves with mankind.'"

Her eyes widened. "He said that?"

"Well, the Apostle Paul said it."

"An Oracle?"

"More a priest, like yourself."

"I see," she said skeptically. "And... how does it apply?"

"A man who is effeminate behaves like a woman – "

"What's wrong with that?"

"Well, it means he... accepts a subservient position, as a woman – "

"As a woman should?"

"No. I suppose... that Paul was a product of his time. The key words were 'abusers of themselves with mankind.' Those who engage in sexual congress with their own sex."

"And could that not also be this Paul just being a product of his time?"

I hung my head. "I... I just don't know. It could be. I'm so unclear on right and wrong just now. I once thought I knew exactly what the Lord expected of me, and it was so easy not to stray, because – "

"Because you didn't care."

"What?" I demanded. "Of course I cared! I became a doctor because I wanted to ease the suffering of my fellow man."

"And woman?"

"Yes, of course. That's what I meant."

"I know. And I know you care about people in the abstract, Shep, but... what person have you ever cared about?"

I shrugged. "My parents, I suppose. They're both gone now. I thought Philip was my close friend, but..."

"Have you ever been in love?"

"I haven't really had time."

"And now you feel a brotherly bond to Hylas. You might be in love with me – " she said leadingly.

I gave her a weak smile. "I might."

" – so, for the first time in your life, you have something to lose. Your moral convictions are being challenged. Right and wrong become less important, don't they, when you have something to love?"

I shook my head. "How easily I drove my sword into that poor man..."

"Because the alternative was Hylas's death."

"I should have trusted in the Lord!"

"Why? Is your god not busy enough with his own agenda, that he should have time to swoop down and intervene in every human endeavor?"

"It was a test of my faith," I said. "God tested my principles against my affection for a stray I had picked up... and I failed. I am lost."

"Lost?"

"Condemned. The Kingdom of Heaven is not for me."

"What about Jesus? I thought he had paid the price for your sins."

"Of course."

"Then he paid the price for this one."

"I – "

"Shep, it only makes sense! You say you have faith. Faith in what?"

"That Jesus will deliver me, someday, to Heaven."

"Well do you believe it or don't you?"

"Of course I do!" I found I was shouting.

"Then, damn it, Shep, believe it! If you have faith that Jesus will save you and forgive you, only until you commit your first real sin, what kind of faith do you have? What kind of savior is he? If I were he, I would be insulted that you had stopped trusting me now." She reached forward and took my hand in both of hers. "Don't you see, Shep? You didn't lose faith when you killed to save Hylas. You merely acted on impulse! You lost faith when you believed that your crime – if you call it one, for I don't – would prevent Jesus from saving you. If he is that powerful – "

"He is all-powerful," I said.

" – Then he can do anything he wants to. And, oh, Shep, if I were your god, I would want to save you!"

She pulled me to her and kissed me over and over again, all about my face, my neck, the back of my head. I sank into her arms and wept, not knowing what else to do anymore. I had been torn from my home, had no idea how far I'd been transported to get here, and now this pagan priestess with whom I was desperately in love had just given Christian witness more powerful than any I had ever heard in a meeting house. I wept not only for my guilt and shame, for my fears for Hylas's life, but for my confusion. I was in a world I didn't understand at all. I wept like a frustrated child, denied a dangerous plaything.

There was a quiet knock at the door, and Xhylanna's physician entered. I sat up, attempting in vain to erase the evidence of my unmanly tears from my face. She did not even seem to notice.

"The boy is resting, Priestess," she said. "I have repaired the wounds in his wrists. They will not scar."

"Then..." I said dumbly, "He's all right? He's going to live?"

The physician cocked an eyebrow in amusement. "Obviously. He was in little danger, except from his own stupidity. I must say it was quick thinking of you use his bedclothes to apply pressure and stop his bleeding."

"I have... some medical training," I said, knowing that, here, that was the best I could claim. Compared to this woman, I was surely no doctor. "May I see him?"

She shook her head. "He will sleep for a day or so. I will tell you when he wakes."

Xhylanna nodded her thanks, and the doctor left us. My priestess placed her arms about me.

"You saved his life again. I told you he would be fine."

"So you did," I agreed. "But... I wonder..."

"What?"

"Would it be against your religion... to pray with me? I feel a great need to say thank you to the One who really saved him."

━━━━━━

Three days passed, and I was not surprised to be visited again by dreams. This time, I dreamt of a snake. Not unusual, I suppose. Many people dream of snakes. It's a common fear. This was the snake, however. The Serpent of the Garden. I recognized him easily.

The Firechild was afraid of nothing. So he did not flinch when the snake slithered upon his shoulder as he lay in the garden, drying in the sunlight after a swim. He merely regarded the animal with curiosity, peering into its slitted eyes.

"Hello, Serpent," he said easily.

"Godling," the creature hissed. The voice came not from its throat, which was not designed to produce sound, but from everywhere about.

"You are mistaken," said the Firechild. "I am favored of the gods, but I am mortal."

"Godling," the creature maintained. "Child of the Gray Lady."

"The Gray Lady is beloved of my teacher," said the child. "His wife. And he is not my father."

"Who is your father?" asked the serpent.

"A humble farmer."

"No. You were given to the farmer as a babe, that you might be raised among mortals. Your mother wished to be ever a virgin. You were forced upon her. She wished to hide you among mortals, never to look upon her shame again."

The child's eyes grew wide. His mouth was slack. Astonishment settled upon him. As it registered, the fire came up in his eyes. His face glowed red with rage.

"The Gray Lady loves no man or god," the serpent pressed.

"It... it isn't true," the boy muttered, but his fiery eyes said that he knew the truth. "My teacher loves the Gray Lady. He loves me! He would have told me – !"

"Nor did he tell you who your father was," said the serpent. It fixed its evil eyes on the boy. "Who is your father, child?"

The boy grasped the snake by its neck and squeezed, attempting to squeeze the life from it. The serpent, unflustered merely continued to hiss silently, and then it vanished altogether. Even as it was gone, its voice echoed, "Who is your father?"

I came upon him now. I had not watched as the serpent taunted him. I did not need to. I had seen this happen ages ago, before the Firechild was born. I could not bear to watch it actually happen.

"Is it true?" he asked me, tears in his eyes. "Is she my mother?"

"She is," I admitted.

"And who is my father?"

"Does it matter?" I asked. "He never claimed you."

"No," he said, his voice cold. "You claimed me. You claimed me and you lied to me. You did not tell me I was a god. You did not tell me my mother never loved me!"

"That is not true!" The Gray Lady's voice, plaintive, rang throughout the garden, and she appeared before us. "I did not hide you because you were unwanted. I hid you to protect you."

"And did you want me?" demanded the Firechild.

She hesitated. "You had a destiny. You will claim the throne of Heaven! God would have destroyed you to keep you from fulfilling it. I had to keep you from His sight."

"Did you want me?" he repeated. "Did you love me?"

She did not answer.

"It is true," cried the boy. "What the serpent said. You love no man or god!"

She looked at me, her eyes belying his words. She loved me, and he knew it.

"And you," he looked upon me. "You claimed me to train me for this... destiny?"

"I did."

"Then you loved me no more than she!"

"That's not true," I said. "I could not love you more were you my own child!"

"But I am not your child," he replied. He regarded my beloved, the Gray Lady. "I am no one's child."

He vanished.

From that dream I awoke feeling the worst desolation I've ever felt. I felt as a man must who has lost a son. Yet I had no son, and the dreams were constructs of Satan. The presence of the Serpent confirmed that.

Please Lord, I prayed, *take these dreams from me!*

During those three days, Xhlyanna spent much time in preparation for the attack on the Aspar. I spent most of my time with Hylas. He was weak, and still not bubbling with enthusiasm, but he agreed that it was not time yet for his life to end. We spoke no more of that which he wanted from me. He seemed pleased to simply have my company.

I confess I spent those nights in Xhylanna's bed, although only two of them with her, for she was kept up planning well into every night. When we learned that Hylas was going to live, I was both too weak and too happy to resist her advances. After that... sin became easier. It is a slippery slope. To my credit, I did ask again if she would marry me. The suggestion seemed to offend her less, but that was all.

On the afternoon of the third day, Colys came to see me. She invited me to come and meet her family. I was loathe to leave Hylas for any length of time, but this was an opportunity to witness to many who had not heard the Gospel.

"Go," urged Hylas, waving me away from his bedside. "I'm tired of looking at you anyway."

It was a weak joke, but it was a sign that he was recovering emotionally, as well as physically. I was thankful. I followed Colys to her home.

Being a domed city, Jentana is naturally circular in layout. At the city's center is Xhylanna's residence, which also contains the assembly rooms of the Generals. Radiating out like spokes on a wheel from this point are several roads which stretch toward the dome's circumference. These divide the city into segments like pie slices, creating neighborhoods roughly triangular in shape, and buildings quite different from what I was accustomed to seeing at home. Imagine a building with a footprint not square, but triangular!

Such was Colys's home. It was a beautiful edifice, bespeaking the wealth of its occupants. No home in Jentana appeared to be poor, but certainly those of the Generals who ruled the city were more opulent. This house dominated a city block – diamond shaped – and was backed by a triangular garden. An undersea garden has a very different atmosphere than the city gardens you would be familiar with on earth, something like a conservatory, but without the need to enclose the structure in glass, there being no sun whose rays the plants within would collect. I was reminded of tales of the Elysian Fields in classical mythology – beautiful meadows filled with light and life deep within underground caverns below the surface.

Colys led me to a flagstone patio on which lounge chairs were arranged in a circle. On a table were heaped refreshments of all kinds. Gracious living, I thought, like something one would expect in London, or on a rich Southern Plantation in the not-too-distant past. In one chair reclined an old woman. Colys introduced her as her mother. Aside from the Oracle, who is old but timeless, I had my first glimpse of age among the Jentana.

The retired General, Colys's mother, was one of the oldest people I've ever met. Still she was neither frail nor failing. She appeared healthy, handsome with a noble bearing. A strong voice greeted me as she said, "My daughter is much impressed with you, man of earth. She told me of your speech before the Council."

I told the lady it was hardly a speech, merely my own impassioned attempt to forestall what seemed inevitable violence. If there was eloquence to my words, if my ideas were creditable, it was because they were the Lord's, not mine.

The old lady nodded. "Like you, I was always taught to credit the Mother Goddess as the font of all wisdom." She smiled and gave a little shrug. "In my old age, however, I have come to see that some receive the waters from the fountain more quickly than others, and drink more deeply from them." She looked up and gestured toward the house. "My daughters are coming. They, too are eager to meet you."

Colys's four sisters, like the General herself, were pale and delicate, like living moonbeams. They were not cold as moonlight might be expected to be, however. They were quiet, reserved, but gracious. Each arrived accompanied by a male servant. This was my first up-close encounter with the men of Jentana. Contrary to my expectations, they were not effeminate. They were not rugged he-men, either. They sat quietly by the women's sides. They pulled out chairs for them, as well-mannered earthmen would. They fetched refreshments, as many a considerate husband might for his wife where I came from. Like children of my time and place, though, they also did not speak unless spoken to.

"We thought it appropriate," said Colys, seeing me watch my fellow males closely, "that our men attend. I hope this doesn't make you uncomfortable."

"Certainly not," I replied. "On my world, there are many places where women are not welcome." I saw looks of disapproval on several faces as I said this. "Some religions even keep women out of their services. I am proud to say that those of my faith welcome women, however, even in the ministry."

"Even in the ministry?" asked the mother. "You imply that most priestesses in your world are male?"

"They are," I said.

"Like the Aspar?" asked the old woman. "Male priests for a male god."

"Unlike the Aspar," I stressed, "the one true God does not hold women in contempt. Jesus, his son, preached love and brotherhood – sisterhood too – for all. Indeed, He urged us to reconcile with our brother first, before we make offerings to God. In Jesus's eyes, you cannot love God without loving His children."

"And who are his children?" asked one of the sisters. "Which of your people were sired by your god?"

"All of them," I said, a little taken aback.

There was some giggling, but the mother glared disapproval and it silenced. "Your god must be very busy," she said, "bedding so many mortal women."

I suppressed my inclination to cry blasphemy. One of the men offered me a cold drink, something like iced tea. I was grateful and took a long sip before saying, "you misunderstand. God does not come to us in the flesh. We are His children because he created Adam and Eve, from whom we are all descended. He creates our souls and the world our bodies occupy."

"He literally asks you to love every person in the world?" wondered Colys's mother.

"It is as I told you, Mother," said Colys. "The earthmen truly believe in peace. Real peace."

"So there is no war on your planet?" asked her mother.

I shook my head. "How I wish that were true. You see, many, most, I am ashamed to say, who claim to believe Jesus's words somehow have convinced themselves that war and killing are still justified."

"How could anyone reconcile a doctrine which says to love everyone, indeed to place love for man and woman above love for the gods, with a belief in war?"

I chuckled. "How does one reconcile a belief in wisdom and in the productive arts," I gestured to the grandeur about me, "the creation of cities like this, with the arts of killing and war? Jentana should not be embroiled in petty violence. With your art, your architecture, your medicine – " I thought of Hylas, and how inept I'd felt as a physician when I saw how easy it had been for the Jentana doctor to save his life – "you should be setting an example for all the people on this planet! As the Lord said, a city on a hill cannot be hidden, nor does one hide one's light under a bushel. The light of this city should shine on all the world! With compassion and patience, you could teach the Aspar to repent from their barbaric ways! Together, without the distractions of war to hold you back, think of the heights of civilization and technology you might scale!"

The Mother nodded. "So the Mother Goddess would have it."

I scoffed, "Is not the Mother Goddess at war with her own son?"

"She is," acknowledged the old woman. "But not of her own doing. The circumstances of his birth were... difficult. Her father... arranged his conception. She had wanted – "

" – to remain forever a virgin," I finished. "But an arrogant warrior of Heaven forced himself upon her, and then she had the child in secret – "

"You know the history of the Mother Goddess?" she asked, surprised.

"I know my dreams," I said, suddenly self-conscious. I had not meant to blurt out what I did. I was just so surprised to hear recited back to me those images I thought had come to my mind from Satan.

The old lady became more animated than I would have thought possible. She bolted up in her chair and leaned in close to me. "You dreamt of this?" she asked in wonder.

"I did. I dreamt I was her lover... "

"The Pretender," she said helpfully.

"Is he the one who was cast out of Heaven?" I asked. I had heard Scorpius speak of the Pretender. I thought him analogous to Satan.

"He was the first. And after him, the Mother Goddess. Both plotted against her father – "

"And I knew – the Pretender knew – that her child would be the one, the one who overthrew the King of Heaven. I dreamt of a Gray Lady... a Firechild... and I... I was the one who cared for them both. I took the boy from humble parents and raised him... "

She nodded emphatically. "The Pretender raised Raxes, was his teacher. The Gray Lady – an apt name for the Mother Goddess! – dared not know her child until the time was right for him to overthrow her father."

"He rejected us. Them. The Pretender and the Gray Lady. The Firechild ran from them, because the serpent revealed the truth – "

"The serpent!" she spat. "The serpent was Raxes's father, the Warrior. He never reveals the truth, except it is twisted to serve his own purpose. He corrupted Raxes, the Firechild as you call him. He does burn with divine fire and rage to this day. It is his father's doing. His father knew it would foment war among the gods."

I shook my head. "A blasphemous dream! To dream I was Lucifer and plotting the overthrow of God!"

"I do not know that name, but the dream is hardly blasphemous. Don't you see?" she grasped my hand. I looked in her eyes and saw that she was overwhelmed. Near tears. "Their mission was to spare humanity the meddling of the old gods. The old father god, he used us for sport, as the warrior did. As so many others did. The Mother Goddess and the Pretender wanted to change all that."

"You speak of many gods," I said. "I know only one. He would never sport with us. And none could ever overthrow Him. If the Pretender is the Lucifer I know, he is doomed to failure. God is all-powerful."

"If any god is all-powerful," asked Colys pointedly, "why would he need to exile his enemies?"

"To prevent the corruption of Heaven," I answered.

"And how could Heaven be corrupted, if its ruler is all-powerful?" she asked.

I did not have an answer. It troubled me. "All this talk of other gods... and these dreams... I thought they came from Satan. From Lucifer. The evil one. Now you say they come from gods you worship – "

"You are the prophesied one," said Colys's mother. "Only he would received these dreams."

Colys added. "You see why Escara despises him so."

The old woman nodded. A wave of excitement seemed to wash over her, indeed, over everyone present. "It is time," she said gravely.

"Time?" I demanded. "Time for what?"

"You are not the first among us to say these things," said the old lady. "Many of us feel that the battles with the Aspar long ago turned away from being an effort to protect our city and our sisters. Instead, they are fought to the glory of a few like General Escara."

"Why do you allow this?" I asked.

She leaned back, enfolding her hands before her, as though in prayer. "Because Escara is influential... and dangerous. Those among the Jentana who disagree with her tend to die in battle, or to be revealed as having committed some crime against the City."

"A powerful leader then," I agreed.

"But your presence here, in fulfillment of prophecy, will excite many," said Colys.

"What is this prophecy?" I asked.

Her mother explained, "Long ago, our oracles predicted that a man would come from old earth. He would carry with him the favor of the gods. He would break the centuries-old cycle of war, and bring a new golden age to our world."

"There can be no doubt that you are that man," said Colys. "And that means it is time for us to prepare. The time for people like Escara is passed. The time comes when we can control our own destiny."

This began to sound dangerously like a revolutionary council. I was accustomed to being among people who wanted to take drastic action to change society for the better, but I was concerned by the tone this meeting was taking. I had no love for Escara, but she was a powerful General in Xhylanna's city. If I was implicated in standing against her, where did I stand with Xhylanna?

"I... I didn't come to encourage any kind of violence," I said carefully. "I don't know very much about your politics."

"You know enough," the old woman assured me. "You will know what to do when the time comes." She looked to her daughter. "We must meet with the other Generals, Colys. They must know that the time is upon us. We must act quickly, lest Escara silence all of us." She turned her gaze on me. "Be careful, Shepherd Autrey. Escara already suspects who you are. She will stop you, if she can... any way she can."

When I returned from Colys's home, Escara was in Xhylanna's chambers. She looked disdainfully at me when I entered.

"Where have you been, earth man?"

"Why do you ask?"

She drew herself up and her face reddened. "A man does not speak to me in such a manner."

"Escara – " Xhylanna began.

"Really, Priestess, could we not teach him respect for his betters?"

"He is from another land, Escara," said Xhylanna. Before the General could argue, she interrupted firmly, "and he is my guest. Like you, he will be treated with respect."

Escara nodded unhappily.

"I don't actually see that it's a secret where I've been. I do have the freedom of the city, do I not?"

"Of course you do," said Xhylanna testily.

"Then I have been to the home of General Colys. She invited me to meet her family."

Escara nodded. "It is as I said. He meets with the malcontents, and encourages divisiveness in our city."

"I encourage peace in your city."

"In a time of war," said Escara, "to encourage peace is treason. Were I Priestess, you and your two barbarian companions would have been executed as soon as we had learned all you knew."

"You are not Priestess, Escara," Xhylanna snapped at her. "Remember that well."

Again, the General nodded. "Very well, Priestess." She looked at me, hatred flashing behind her eyes. "But already there are murmurings in the streets. Women of influence, of good families, repeat his words of conciliation with the Aspar."

"Perhaps because they see the sense of them," I said pleasantly.

"I am tempted," Escara shot back, "to lead a push to allow you to go to Aspar, earth man. Scorpius, at least, would not be so careless as to leave you alive to betray him."

She stalked out.

"Pleasant woman," I said.

"Shep..." Xhylanna began.

"What? Don't tell me you agree with her!"

"No. She's an opportunist and a fool, like your friend Meigs. But, she does have a following in this city. She's only half-joking about being priestess herself. If I were to die, she would be, I've no doubt."

I put my arms around her. "You're not going to die, are you?"

She did not smile. "Only the Fates can know. And, if I become unpopular, it could happen without the Aspar lifting a finger. Those in power in Jentana... never leave it peacefully."

"What could make you unpopular?" I asked.

"Entertaining an outsider whose views might be considered a threat. Especially a male outsider, for whom I display an unwomanly level of affection."

"I... I do not mean to make your job difficult, Xhylanna, but... I must be what I am."

She nodded. "I know. And I am not afraid of Escara. Just be careful, Shep. These are dangerous times."

It was that very night that the Aspar attacked.

———

The attack was made by air, using the fliers. It was not directed against the undersea city, of course, for the Aspar did not know that it was there, and had no way of attacking it even if they did. The Island of Wisdom was their target, and that would be devastating enough to the Jentana. They would lose their livestock and all of their surface crops.

Xhylanna assembled her forces and sufficient vehicles, not only to make the surface, but to engage the Aspar fliers once they arrived. I asked what

I could do. "Nothing," Xhylanna said. "This isn't your fight, Shep. And I'd rather have you here, and safe."

I protested that I could treat anyone who was wounded, and, if Scorpius were among the battle forces, I might yet make overtures of peace to him. I made the mistake of saying some of this in front of Escara.

"Are we to allow you anywhere near the line of battle? You would betray us to them in the name of peace!"

"I would betray no one, General," I said. "There can be no betrayal when all men – that is all people – are brothers and sisters."

"I am not sister to those animals," Escara spat.

Xhlyanna silenced her, and clasped my hands. "Shep, you must trust me. I can defend the city best if you are here, and safe."

"And I am to wait here, not knowing if you are safe?"

"I will signal via speaker with status reports. You can listen." She pointed to the speaker unit on the wall of her bedroom. There was one in every room in every building in the city. "Someone will show you how to tune in to my ship's signal." She embraced me, kissed me once, and said, "I must go."

They left for the surface, and I stayed, feeling useless, and fearing that I would not see Xhylanna again. This anxiety was a curse of war that I knew of, but had never experienced, for never before had one I loved gone off to war. I could not help but hope, in some piece of my heart, that her forces would be victorious, for that would increase her chances of coming home safe. Was this how so many became embroiled in the causes of war, because they felt taking sides might help protect their loved ones? It was a devil's bargain.

Then again, would I not bargain with the devil for Xhylanna?

"You look simply miserable, old boy."

I was not happy to see Philip. I would have preferred to be left alone, pacing the parlor in Xhylanna's apartment, listening to the drone of communications from the ships above on the speaker. At least I could hear my beloved's voice, calm and competent, in command of everything. Still, I was sure I did look miserable, but I was also sure that Philip did not care.

"What do you want?" I demanded impatiently.

"Merely checking on your welfare, Shep, the City being under siege and all. We earthers should stick together, don't you think?"

"Like you stuck with me in Aspar?" I asked.

He rolled his eyes. "Oh, come now, Shep, it wouldn't have done any good for me to be executed with you. I was positioning myself to be of maximum advantage, of course. Strategically, being close to Scorpius – "

"You'd be farther away from the bloodshed," I observed cynically. "Don't waste energy inventing lies, Philip. I know what you are. I can even find it in myself to forgive you for being so utterly spineless, as you can't help what you are. But please go away. I just want to be alone right now."

He should have been angry. Any man of character would have been furious to have been thus described. Even a man of no character but colossal vanity like Philip should have been incensed, but he was not. "I'm a better friend than you give me credit for, old man, and I've come to prove it to you." He leaned in and whispered conspiratorially. "I know where there is a ship. We can leave this city."

"Why?" I asked warily. "Why would you want to leave?"

"Don't you want to be assured that your priestess is safe? To render aid to the wounded?" He pressed, saying pointedly, "You might even have an opportunity to see Scorpius – to press for peace when he is weak from battle."

He said all this too easily, like he had rehearsed. It was as though it was a sales pitch, and he a merchant, standing to gain a great profit. He was nervous, I realized.

"What's in this for you?" I asked.

"I only want to help you," he replied. "I told you – I'm a better friend than you think."

"No," I said firmly. "You're up to something. I realize now that you've been up to something as long as I've known you. Why should this be any different?"

"Because," he said urgently, "because it is different." His eyes were imploring, his tone very nearly pleading. "Just accept that I want to help you, Shep. You know you want to go to the surface, and I know a way for you to get there. Must you always question my motives so?"

"Always," I said. "Because there is always so much to question with you. Now go... please."

———

Fifteen minutes later, the speaker in Xhylanna's bedroom went quiet. I rushed to the outer chamber and found that speaker quiet as well. Frantically, I ran through the palace, searching for any device which would allow me to keep hearing Xhylanna's voice, which would assure me she lived on.

All were silent as the grave.

Hylas encountered me in my travels and informed me what had happened: the battle had destroyed a relay antenna on the Island of Wisdom, and so the city could receive no communications from above. Whatever was to come, we would wait in silence.

I considered this information for a matter of moments. I then took Hylas by the arm and dragged him to Philip's rooms. He met us at the door, pleasantly surprised, and opened his mouth to ask questions. I cut him off.

"The ship you offered. Where is it?"

I did not want to take Hylas. He needed more rest, though the Jentana doctor had worked miracles on him; but neither Philip nor I had knowledge of piloting the Jentana craft. Hylas, at least, had flown the similar ships of the Aspar. I also needed his knowledge of his world. We were heading into danger, and we needed every advantage we could enlist.

Our appropriated ship broke the surface some distance from the island, and it looked as though we had ascended into hell. Beside me, in the pilot's seat, I heard Hylas exclaim quietly, crying out to some god or other.

The sky was on fire, or it appeared to be. In fact, the surface of the Island of Wisdom was literally aflame, and the cause was obvious: even as we watched, what looked like balls of fire arced through the air from the Aspar fliers like shooting stars, striking the ground and detonating. Around the points of impact, conflagrations erupted.

Scorched earth, I thought, like the strategy of Sheridan in Virginia. The Aspar were rendering the Jentana farmland barren.

Hylas shook his head. "I'd seen the fire bombs tested. I didn't know that we – they – had amassed such quantities. They came prepared."

"Attempting to starve the Jentana out," I observed.

"Possibly," Hylas agreed. "But they do not know where the Jentana homeland is. They knew of the Island of Wisdom, and always considered it an unimportant target, a staging platform at best. Aspar reconnaissance had often tried to observe operations here, to gain more clues to the Jentana's actual base of operations, but they had always been driven off. A direct attack on the island was ruled out, because it could render it unusable, and eliminate the only known link back to the real Jentana city."

"I wonder what changed their minds," I said absently. I was busily scanning the skies, looking for Xhylanna's flagship.

"Whatever it was," said Philip, "I suggest we keep our distance, and find a safe haven. Our Jentana friends don't appear to be faring well."

I ignored him. I had spotted Xhylanna's ship. It was floating on the surface of the water, an ugly gash in its side, framed in burned and torn metal. One of the Aspar incendiaries must have struck it. I keyed the ship's speaker and called to Xhylanna – one of the few things I had learned to do. Our ship's speaker had flared to life as we had neared the surface. Communications between ships and city were gone, but, apparently, ships could speak to each other.

Escara answered from the flagship, demanding to know what we were doing here.

"We came to help," I said.

"You have violated orders," she barked. "I will see you executed – "

"See me executed then, woman, and be damned!" I snapped back. "But where is Xhylanna?"

There was a pause. Then, with a trace of noticeable satisfaction in her voice, the General replied, "Xhylanna was wounded when we were hit. A head wound. She is dying."

I didn't stop to think. "Get me over there!" I shouted to Hylas.

He did immediately as he was asked. Our craft lurched into the air, keeping low, and angled in toward the wounded flagship. At the time, it did not occur to me that my own medical knowledge was far behind that of the Jentana. It did not register on me that, if they could not save her, I could certainly do nothing. I only knew that I was a doctor, and the woman I loved was badly wounded.

"Are you crazy?" exclaimed Philip, intruding on my purposeful state. "Shep, they've lost! We've got to get out of here!"

"I've got to get to her!" I shouted back at him, shoving him back into a seat from where he'd hovered over me. "If you want to leave, then jump and swim for it!"

Hylas brought our small flier down to rest only a handful of feet from the side of Xhylanna's ship. Before he'd even righted us in the water, I was on my feet and making for the hatch. I must have cast a line and steadied our ship to theirs. I must have made a great leap from one hull to the other. I remember nothing. I only know that, presently, I was at Xhylanna's side, cradling her in my arms and weeping.

She was conscious, though not truly awake. Blood smeared her lovely face, and still oozed from a horrid split in her scalp. It darkened the fiery red of her hair, and matted it against her face.

"Shep?" she said, barely able to form the words. "Told you... to stay..."

"Never!" I exclaimed. "You cannot order me to be anywhere but by your side, my love."

She tried to mutter a response, but she was too weak. Her eyes closed, and she coughed – a wet, sickening sound.

"She's dying!" I cried out. "We've got to get her home!"

"I told you she was dying," Escara snapped, "but we've no time for the wounded. The Aspar struck us a near fatal blow on their first volley. They're forming to attack again. Is your ship flight-worthy?"

"What?" I demanded. "I suppose..." My thoughts were all for Xhylanna. Yes! My craft could take her home! Was it safe to move her?

Escara was giving instructions to a junior officer. I disregarded her, examining Xhylanna to determine if she could be moved. Then I heard something about scuttling this ship, if capture were imminent.

"What?" I demanded, leaping to my feet. "What are you planning?"

Her face was a mask of contempt. "The less you know, earth man, the better – for all of us!" She turned to leave.

"Where do you think you're going?" I asked.

"I am taking your ship, you fool! Someone has got to lead this battle!"

"But you can't – Xhylanna – "

"Xhylanna is of no use to us now." She cast a disparaging glance at her leader on the deck. "And soon, I think, will be none to anyone." She turned to her pilot. "My orders stand. And if he tries to transmit to his allies, kill him!"

"Allies?" I spluttered. "What allies?"

Escara narrowed her gaze scornfully. "Someone shared our ships' specifications with the Aspar. They'd never have made such a precision attack, otherwise. Who else could it have been?"

"But I didn't – "

"We can debate this if you survive, earth man," she said, and she stepped through the hatch and was gone.

Hylas and Philip had joined me, I don't know when.

"We must find a way to get Xhylanna back to the city," I said.

"We can't go back to the city!" Philip ejaculated. There was alarm in his tone.

"Why?" I wondered, searching his eyes. "Do you know something the rest of us don't?"

"It's... dangerous!"

"My people have no way to attack the Jentana city," said Hylas. "They don't even know where it is."

"Correction," I said. "They didn't know where it was, when we left." I continued to lock my eyes on Philip. "They have since learned – from someone – specifications on the Jentana battlecraft. That same source might have supplied them the location of the city as well!"

"H - how would I know," stammered Philip, dropping his eyes to avoid my gaze. "W - what are you implying, Shep?"

"That you might have betrayed our location to Scorpius," I said evenly.

"I would never – "

"For the right price, Philip, there's nothing you would never. Now go find a place to sit down, before you get shot." I turned to the pilot. "Is there any way to get Xhylanna to safety?"

She looked uncertainly at me. Surely she shared some of Escara's distrust of me, as an alien, but she also must have some loyalty to Xhylanna. Her gaze strayed to her priestess's prone form.

"I have my orders," she said. "And the ship is not diveworthy."

Xhylanna moaned in her sleep. "Can't you help her, Shep?" Hylas asked. "You know... the way you stopped the guards in Aspar?"

"I don't think – " I began. Then I considered it. Who knew what my mind could accomplish, here? True, my newfound abilities had failed me in the arena, but... what could it hurt? I knelt and took my beloved's hand in mine. Hers was distressingly cold.

"Xhylanna," I whispered, over and over. I closed my eyes and concentrated, searching for the light within, willing that light to bathe the woman I loved, I now realized, more than my own life. Peripherally, I was aware that the pilot asked what I was doing. I ignored her. Let Hylas respond. I must help Xhylanna. I must summon the will power.

I shook my head. "It's not working!" I muttered. She was dying under my hands. There was nothing I could do.

I felt a warm, light touch on my shoulder, and realized it was Hylas's hand. When I did not flinch, it grew firmer, his fingers squeezing the muscle. I was grateful for his brotherly comfort, but Xhylanna – ! I felt a heat, and a sparking, like static. I'd felt this before...

From where Hylas's hand touched me, there was a charge, a dynamic surge of warmth which filled me with a sensation of potential, of being ready to spring from a starting position, and knowing I could run faster than the wind. That was it, I realized. Each time, before, when my mind had summoned the power to influence events around me, Hylas had been there. Hylas had been in contact, touching me. The power was not mine – it was his! He fed it to me!

Eyes still closed, my mind still open to the presence of the Light, I took Xhylanna's face in my hands and prayed as I'd never prayed before. Heat surged through me, and I heard the pilot gasp in surprise. Hylas's hands – both of them now, tightened their grip on me. I opened my eyes.

Xhylanna, Hylas and I were bathed in light. It came from no apparent source, but I knew, from the heat where our bodies touched, that it came from, and flowed through, all of us. It was as if the spark of the divine had fanned into a flame that did not burn or blind, merely warmed and, I hoped, healed.

My prayers were answered. Xhylanna stirred. Her eyes opened. Already, her color was returning. "Shep?" she muttered.

"Rest, my love," I choked out through tears of gratitude. I knew – I knew! – that she would recover. That she was healed. Silently I thanked God for this miracle, and for letting me be a part of it.

Xhylanna smiled, and closed her eyes. Her breath was even, her pulse strong and regular. The light from about us faded. I turned to Hylas and drew him into a bear hug. "Thank you," I said.

"I did nothing," he protested.

"You did everything."

The pilot had leaped from her seat, and was gaping at us. I expected, at any moment, that she would draw a weapon and kill me. Instead, as I faced her, she dropped to her knees.

"My lord!" she exploded, burying her face in her hands. "Forgive me, my Lord! I did not know you were a god! I – "

"I am no god!" I said in horror.

"Please forgive me, lord! I meant no offense! I am your servant!"

I shook my head in amazement. Was there no end to the

misconceptions of these people? I took the poor girl by the hand and lifted her to her feet – no easy task. She weighed nearly as much as I did.

"You have seen a miracle," I said firmly, "but I am not a god. I am merely God's servant, a tool for use by His healing hand." I gestured to Xhylanna. "It is the Almighty, who sent Christ to dwell among us, who has saved your priestess."

She shook her head. "You cannot fool me, my lord. It was your love. If you are not a god, then you are surely touched by the gods. I will be proud to stand beside you as we die."

"Die?" I asked. "Who said anything about dying?"

Philip leaped forward and grabbed my shoulders. "The Aspar, you fool! While you were engaging in parlor tricks, they've come 'round for a second attack! They're going to blow us out of the water!"

He pointed frantically to the front, where, through the dome, I could see three Aspar fliers, bearing down on us.

"They'll be in range in seconds," said Hylas. "Their guns will destroy us."

"Are there no lifeboats?" I demanded of the pilot. "Some way to get back to the City?"

She shook her head.

"The City!" screamed Philip. "We can't go to the damned City! They've already sent their bombs! It's probably already destroyed! We have to – "

I advanced on Philip, backing him up against the supporting struts arching beneath the bulkhead of the ship. "What do you know? Tell me!" I shoved him hard, and his head cracked against metal.

"I... I gave them the location of the city. Scorpius sent me with you to – "

"A spy," murmured the pilot, drawing her sword.

I held up a hand to stay her. "And what have they done?" I demanded.

Philip licked his lips. I'd nearly knocked him unconscious. "L - loaded explosives – on the first Jentana ship they could capture. Sent it back with an Aspar crew on a suicide run... to destroy the city."

"No," the pilot moaned. Then she screamed and raised her blade to strike. I stepped between her and Philip.

"No!" I shouted. "No more killing!"

"Shep, let her do it," said Hylas, with a sneer that looked completely out of place on his angelic face. "He deserves to die."

I looked forward to where the Aspar fliers closed in on us. "He's going to," I said coldly. "With the rest of us. Let him die in the battle he has made."

The pilot stepped back, apparently liking my argument. Philip slumped to the deck.

I moved to crouch beside Xhylanna, to say my goodbyes. Christians believed that those who did not confess their sins to Christ were damned to hell. Oh God, I begged, Heavenly Father, give me more time with her. I'm happy to die, if I can but carry her to Heaven with me.

Hylas knelt beside me, and took my hand, squeezing it between both of his. "My brother," he said, tears in his eyes. "I know our ways seem wrong to you, but... but I have never loved as I love you. I... I'm proud to die by your side."

And again, I felt the heat from our touching, the power.

And I knew... this was not over.

ELEVEN

"Shep," said Xhylanna, her throat raw, "I can't go on any longer."

I rolled over onto my back, pulling her on top of me. I was hot and bathed in sweat. I shoved the damp blankets away, wanting to let the air cool my body; but I wanted even more to keep her close.

"And I thought you Jentana had so much more stamina than any man," I grinned.

She chuckled. "You're not just any man. And despite your miracle cure, I did spend three days in the hospital."

"So you did, Mrs. Autrey."

"Mrs. Autrey? What – ?"

"We're married. You take my name."

"Oh," she asked, amused, "and what do I do with mine? Give it to you?"

"Well, you don't have a second name."

"No." She considered it. "If I did, would you take it?"

"I'll take anything you wish to give me, my love."

It had been a small ceremony. The Jentana did not really understand it, and those who did still suspected that either Xhylanna or I had become the other's slave. But Hylas stood with me, and Colys and some of her family attended out of curiosity. The Oracle watched politely. In Quaker style, we spoke our own vows, and there was no need for priest or shaman.

From Xhylanna's perspective, it was only fair that she marry me. Certainly, it violated her people's code that marriage was slavery. But I had – albeit grudgingly – violated my people's code which said that sex out of wedlock was sin. Her near-death experience, she told me, had made her realize that the happiness she found with me meant more than the approval of small-minded people. We knew that there was no hint of slavery in our relationship.

I suppose, in her way, she was humoring this silly savage that she had fallen in love with. And she had fallen in love with me. There was no doubting the fact. Her first thought, when she'd finally awoken, had not been for the city, or the state of the battle, but for me. I knew this, for she cried out my name even as her eyes opened in the hospital. I had not left her side, despite the nagging of Hylas and the doctor.

She could not believe all that had happened while she recovered from her wounds. Hylas and I had stopped the incoming Aspar fighters with our minds, causing their guns to fail to fire. I don't know how we did it, for I didn't know how their weapons worked. Left with the choice of ramming us, or simply flying around and trying again, the fliers chose the course which would allow them to survive. By the time they came around again, they found their engines failing, and their craft, aerodynamic in design, left to glide gently to the sea below. Other craft in their fleet soon followed. Most of the soldiers manning them were too unnerved to fight on, but Hylas and the Jentana easily resisted the few who wanted to make trouble.

Using a confiscated speaker, I contacted the submersible which carried a death cargo to Jentana City, and, thus in contact with the pilot, was able to summon the force of will to end his mission as well. The hatch of the cargo bay in which the bombs rested malfunctioned, and they sprung into open water. The bombs, detonated by some complex system, and not by shock, fell harmless to the ocean floor. The pilot of the craft, knowing he surely would be killed by Jentana forces if he continued on course to the City, re-surfaced.

To my knowledge, not a life was lost in the entire operation.

Scorpius was brought to the flagship under guard. He would not look at Hylas or me, and his son wanted no part of him. Hylas left the deck when his father was brought on board. Escara accompanied Scorpius, planning, I believe, to execute him aboard the flag vessel for all to see. At the same time, no doubt, she intended to step up as the new High Priestess. She was disappointed to discover that that office was not vacant. Still, she intended to kill Scorpius.

I stepped forward to challenge her. "Why?" I demanded. "What will it accomplish to kill their leader? We have stopped their attack. What else do you want?"

"Revenge!" she spat at me. "For all the dead on the Island of Wisdom! For generations of atrocities!"

"Will it bring back the dead?" I asked, looking in her eyes for some flicker of reason or compassion, but finding only a blind need to carry out her campaign to its end.

"Not all of us can bring back the dead," she said scathingly. "Some have to settle for what mere humanity allows us to accomplish."

"I do not believe you should execute a head of state – or any prisoner of war – without Xhylanna's approval. She will recover fully in a few days. Why not wait? Or... would you rather put it before the Council?" I asked pointedly. "You'd have to, you know."

I had no idea of any such thing, but I assumed, in a pseudo-republic like this, that only a majority vote would carry the day in the absence of their leader's wishes being known. Apparently, my assumption was correct, for Escara lowered her sword.

"I could cite my authority as commanding General," she said. "But it seems I'd be a fool to ignore the wishes of him who saved our priestess."

"I think you'll find it's the right decision, General."

She scowled, raising an elegant finger to point at me. "Make no mistake, earth man. This is not over. I will show you for what you are."

Scorpius had no kind word for me either. "Bastard!" he spat at me. "Why plead for my life? I would rather die than breathe air on a world where you walk about! You insult me by pleading for my life."

I gave him my most placid smile. "Then I fulfill my principles and enjoy myself, my Lord," I said.

He colored and struggled against his bonds, swearing that, as long as he lived, he would seek nothing with more determination than my death. It seemed I had made two fast enemies that day.

But this was not that day. This was this night. My wedding night. I'd never been so happy in all my life. Still, between encounters this evening, I asked, "What will happen to Philip?"

Xhylanna shrugged. "He'll be tried as a spy, and probably executed."

I sighed. "I would like to say that he should not be killed. That decision should be reserved for the Almighty."

"He'll have a fair trial, my love. But you heard his confession with your own ears. He nearly got the City destroyed."

"So he did."

"And it would have been destroyed, if not for you, my alien prize." She snuggled her face close to mine, and added in my ear, "My husband."

We found... little else to talk about before we slept that night.

———

I was awakened again in the night by touches at once soothing and exciting, by caresses which inflamed me, by kisses which promised and invited. "Don't you ever get tired?" I muttered sleepily, but lips engulfed me, and I sank back, joyously resigned to my fate.

Short of what I considered to be the goal of the exercise in question, my lover broke from me and nestled against me in spoon fashion. A series of pulls and tugs and applications of pressure left little doubt in my mind what request was being made. This was a new addition to our repertoire, but nothing conceivable was unwelcome.

I entered and gave my whole being over to seeking this release. Thrusting madly, producing gasps and even yelps from the lips which strained to brush my own, I sought to quench this fire that had been sparked within me. I tried to enfold her in my arms, but each attempt was met by two hands which returned my own hands behind me. The frustration of this dance only added to my building tension. Like some mad animal, I growled and bit. Sweat dripped from my hair and ran down my chest, spilling everywhere. Our sweat mixed as our passions heated our bodies to what must have surely approached a combustion point. I was amazed at the heat we generated, so like that produced... when...

I froze. Everything went cold, except the body pressed against me. I reached around, and this time was not resisted. My lover knew the evidence I sought, and knew that there was no reason to resist any longer. I reached. I felt. The skin was smooth and soft, the hair silken, the lips full and warm... but these were not the curves of my beloved, taut and sinewed though they are. This was not the taste of her flesh nor her delightful scent. Had I not been so tired and... distracted... I might have noticed earlier.

"Hylas," I said at last.

"Yes, my brother," came the answering, terrified whisper.

I lay still for a long while, I do not know how long. He lay equally still, trembling, whether from fear or unspent passion I do not know.

I said nothing. What could I say? What could I do?

After a while, he grew impatient with me, and began to move again. He was tentative at first, but gained confidence when I did not resist.

I shall probably burn in hell for a very long time, but no one can say I do not finish that which I have started.

━━━━━━

When I awoke, Hylas was still there, watching me. I wished him a good morning, but he said nothing. He simply looked and chewed his lip. Still I did not know what to say. There was no etiquette. My training as a gentleman and a Quaker had covered many things, but never this.

"Are you mad at me?" he finally managed.

Was I? I sighed. "I suppose not. Mind you," I pointed a finger at him, "on earth, an apprentice who played such a trick would find a strap taken to his backside!"

"I could find you a strap," he offered.

"No," I said.

"It's your right. Most of my friends were beaten by their mentors. I'd call it small price to pay for finally becoming a man."

Finally, I laughed and tousled his hair. "You have a very poetic way of describing a mortal sin, my blood brother."

The door opened and Xhylanna came in, bearing a tray of juices and breads, and a steaming beverage that the Jentana drank as Americans did coffee. "I thought you two would sleep all day," she said.

"Since we didn't sleep during the night," I added.

She stationed the tray by the bed and fell into my arms. "Are you mad at me?"

I nodded at Hylas. "That was his question, and I've already answered it."

"Oh, it's my question too," she said soberly. "You mustn't blame Hylas. This was my idea." To my raised eyebrow, she continued, "I thought it was just silly for two people to love each other as much as you both do, and never... you know. Besides," she clapped Hylas on the shoulder, "our young prince is a man now. It needed to be done."

"Strangest wedding gift I've ever heard of," I answered, reaching for the breakfast tray. I was too happy to dwell on a sin that was beginning to seem – God help me – less evil in the light of the new day.

The door flew open with a crash, kicked by an armored boot. Escara and four of the Jentana guard marched in, weapons drawn and pointed at me.

"What is the meaning – ?" Xhylanna began.

Escara ignored her. "Shepherd Autrey, the Council has ruled that you should be placed under arrest and brought to trial. The charge is espionage."

"That's ridiculous!" I said.

"We have a witness," said Escara. She nodded at one of the guards, who went into the hallway and returned... with Philip.

He smirked at me. "'Fraid I had to tell them the whole story, Shep old boy. Please don't be too angry with me. You really didn't think that no one would find out that... you planned the entire attack?"

———

A trial among the Jentana is a somewhat less formal affair than it is in the United States or England. There are no courtrooms specifically set aside for the purpose, no professional judges, and juries seem to be composed entirely of volunteers. Each juror must still be acceptable to both parties, of course, but there seemed to be no end to the supply of willing volunteers. This followed, since no audience was allowed at the trial.

Xhylanna had no choice but to allow the trial, as it was called by the Council. I am sure that Escara and Philip had conspired and arranged the whole thing while we enjoyed our wedding night. The General's hatred of me must have been strong indeed, that she would ally herself with the true betrayer of her people, or perhaps she was just that gullible.

I was hard pressed to find Escara gullible.

My wife preceded over all as judge, ironically. She was leader of the Jentana, and there seemed to be no provision for conflict of interest. How could there be? These people did not recognize the institution of marriage, and felt filial bonds all for all. The Priestess's affection for one, in the eyes of the law, could be no greater than that she felt for another, and her devotion to her office was assumed to supersede all bonds. Quite an assumption, in this case, considering that I would be summarily executed if found guilty. The pain of being forced to oversee the trial which might condemn me was just another knife Escara could twist in her rival's back.

I asked why Hylas was allowed to stand with me at the trial, if no audience was permitted and no family bond recognized.

"He is an interested party," Xhylanna had explained to me, in the few, brief moments we had to talk before the trial began. "Our laws do recognize the bond of servant and master, and it is established that he is so bonded to you. Whatever your fate, he will share it."

"Without a trial?" I asked.

"The master speaks for all under his power," she replied. "That is the way of my people."

Apparently, guilt by association was not prohibited here.

Escara was the first witness called to testify for the prosecution. There were no attorneys. Witnesses simply lined up for or against, and were heard by Xhylanna and the jury. Xhylanna decided when they had said enough, though she asked the jury, in each case, if there were additional questions. Had she dismissed a witness too quickly, I assume the jury could have objected.

"I watched the alien closely, because his loyalty to Jentana was always in doubt. He is linked to the son of Scorpius, for one. He is also an outworlder, for another, with no loyalty to any city-state of this world. When he fled the city during the attack, taking with him only his male companions, it became clear to me that he had foreknowledge that the city itself was in danger."

"And what did he do, upon fleeing the city?" Xhylanna asked. I could see that she was working hard to maintain an appearance of objectivity in the face of these infuriating lies. "Where did he go?"

"Why, he came to the flagship, Priestess. Where better to observe his plans coming to fruition? Where better to divert suspicion from himself?"

"You do not believe there could be any other reason for his arrival at the flagship that day?"

"I am well aware," said Escara with exaggerated patience, "that my lady Priestess would like to believe that her savage plaything wanted only to be at her side. The jury will find the evidence overwhelming, however, that his motives were far less noble."

"And how did this evidence come to light, General?"

"I questioned his companion – the other earth man, Philip Meigs. Autrey had claimed that Meigs was the sole agent for the Aspar, and had him arrested on this false pretense. Autrey banked on his own... association with you to protect him from further suspicion. He was supreme in his arrogance, even as he brokered pardon for Scorpius and his men. What could be more disloyal to Jentana? Meigs told me all, however, in exchange for a promise of leniency from the Council in his own trial."

When Escara stepped down, it was Philip's turn. His testimony, as I expected, was a masterpiece of lies.

"The entire plan was engineered by Scorpius, of course. Brilliant tactician, that man. He paid Autrey to take his son into the wilds, knowing that your forces were coming, and that you would apprehend them and return them to him. He knew also that Autrey's... powers of... persuasion... would cause my lady Priestess to become... attached to him. So he contrived a staged execution, and lured you to rescue this man whom you believed to be in love with you."

I locked my eyes on Xhylanna's. I knew it would be bad form to stand and proclaim my love for her then and there, but I had to assure her that my love was true. I also needed her reassurance that she believed it. Her eyes answered mine, and the faintest smile played across her lips. Whatever else happened, there would be no doubts between us.

"Confident that you would bring us back to your city, Scorpius had but to wait for our signal to invade."

"And why were you sent along?" Xhylanna asked him.

He affected an embarrassed smile, "Well, Shep was going to be... very busy with you, my lady. It was assumed that he would never long be out of your... sight. And so I came along to send the signal. Once the attack was underway, it was my job to arrange our escape, knowing that Scorpius planned to destroy the undersea domes with one of your own ships."

"If all you say is true, Meigs," asked Xhylanna, "then why did Shep save me on the flagship? My wounds were fatal, if left untreated."

Philip made a grand gesture of not meeting her eyes, as if to spare her additional pain. "It was, ah, felt, my lady, that... you were more... malleable than General Escara. As long as you lived, and felt gratitude to Shep for saving your life, he could control the City through you. In time, he would have gained a godlike status, preaching to your people and performing these 'miracles,' which are but tricks of Aspar science."

It was a clever pack of lies, I had to admit. It was nothing to what was to come. The final witness was a young warrior I had never seen. She identified herself as the sole survivor of the crew of the ship Scorpius had seized to destroy Jentana City.

"How did it come about that the Aspar seized your craft?" Xhylanna asked her.

"We were forced out of the air by a squad of their fliers. Before we could submerge, they had gotten lines attached to the hull, and then they boarded. The Warlord himself, the one called Scorpius, led the party. He... killed everyone... but me."

"Why did he leave you alive?" Xhylanna asked gently.

"He said I was... too young. It... was my first mission, my lady. He said I'd make a nice plaything for his son, when they returned home."

Next to me, Hylas colored and looked away from the girl. Whether it was the pain of the lie that Scorpius might still consider him his son, or shame at the practices of his people, raping and killing innocent girls, I did not know.

"What else did he say?" asked Xhylanna.

"He instructed one of his soldiers to go to the flagship and fetch his son and Shepherd Autrey. He said that Autrey was a hero... that he'd delivered the Jentana to Aspar once and for all."

"That's a lie!" I cried out. I could not help myself. Philip's lies, I'd been prepared for, but what this child was saying... had Scorpius really said those things? Was his hand in this as well, seeing to it that I was executed, so he could have his revenge on me? I had thought I had two opposing enemies in Scorpius and Escara. Were they working together?

Xhylanna shut her eyes in pain and said quietly, "The prisoner will be silent during testimony."

After that, it was my turn. I didn't make a particularly good showing. Escara had built a convincing case, and it included just enough of the facts that it meshed with my own story closely. Yes, I had been blessed by Scorpius to mentor his son, yes I had fled the city willingly when the Aspar attacked. No, I could not deny that Philip had supplied intelligence to the enemy, nor that he was my oldest friend. My attempts to disavow his actions were met with mute, hard stares by the jury.

When I had nothing else to say, Xhylanna asked if I wished to call any additional witnesses. Hylas was ineligible, for the same reason that he was allowed to be here. He was bonded to me. Colys, who had attempted to volunteer, was dismissed for having no direct knowledge of the attack on the city. Her testimony was inadmissible.

"Well, then," I said, "I'll call the pilot of your flagship, my lady. She witnessed all of my actions. She knows that it was Hylas and I who intervened to prevent the attack – "

Xhylanna looked uncomfortably to Escara, who had stood. The General could barely contain her satisfaction as she said, "Regrettably, my lady, the pilot suffered extensive internal injuries during the attack. She died, only last night."

"What?" I demanded. "She was not injured!"

"Her injuries were not evident," maintained Escara.

The truth spilled over me like ice water. "You...killed her," I said quietly. Then, more forcefully, I cried out, "you murderer! That girl did nothing wrong!"

Escara rolled her eyes, "Really, Priestess, must we tolerate these outbursts? Bad enough that he claims to have stopped the invasion – "

"I did!" I insisted, and then I realized how pathetic that sounded, when there were no witnesses. The pilot was dead. Xhylanna had been unconscious. The end of the battle had been fantastic, true, but how much more fantastic for one man – or two – to claim to be the author of it all?

One last line of attack occurred to me, and I took it. "How," I asked Escara, "do you explain the sudden end of the battle? The failure of the Aspar guns to fire? The dropping of their fliers from the sky?"

"I do not have to answer your questions," she spat back.

"But the question remains, Escara," said Xhylanna. "If Shepherd Autrey was not responsible for the defeat of the Aspar, how did this inexplicable thing occur?"

"The way that all inexplicable things occur, Priestess," said the General. "It was the will of the gods that we win, and their direct intervention which turned the day." She looked at me with a forced expression of pity and shook her head. "The creature is not mentally stable. I think it would be merciful to call for the vote."

The jury was gone for minutes, only. During their absence, Xhylanna gave me a single, mournful glance, and then looked away and closed her eyes. I could not imagine the pain this must be causing her, to have her countrywomen turn against me, and, by extension, against her.

When they filed back in, the forewoman, or whatever they called the position here, wasted no time. "The earth man is guilty," she announced. "The entire party of refugees from Aspar conspired to destroy our city. They are sentenced to die."

I was growing numb, I must admit, to death sentences. In a week, I'd collected more than I imagine most murderers do.

Xhylanna's breath caught. Escara stood immediately, her sword drawn. "The sentence of the earth man Meigs," she gestured to Philip, seated next to her, "has already been commuted, by vote of Council. As to the rest," she stepped toward me. To two of the guards she snapped, "Remove the whelp. He dies last," even as Hylas reached to seize my hand.

They were too fast for us. We could not touch and activate our paranormal abilities before he was dragged bodily across the room. Escara faced me. "Your choice, earth man. Pick the weapon with which I will kill you. I will use the same on the boy."

"Your face should be sufficient," I said. My patience was exhausted. I would not play her games.

Enraged, Escara raised her blade to strike.

"Wait!" cried Xhylanna. She rushed forward to stand between Escara and me.

"Have a care, Priestess," said the General. "Your office demands that you carry out the jury's sentence, no matter your personal feelings. If you cannot perform as our laws require, then you will be found unfit to hold that office. The next trial will be yours."

"There will be no trial," said Xhylanna calmly. I wondered if she would stand against Escara and the Council, if she commanded enough loyalty. She did not believe she did, if her next words were any indicator. "I do not contest the charge." She looked at me and smiled sadly, reaching out to stroke my cheek. "I have taken this man as my husband. My destiny is bound to his. I cannot stand by and allow him to be killed. The law be damned."

She reached to her side and removed from her belt the only weapon she carried. It was a jeweled dagger. Hardly practical, I assumed it was a badge of office. Nevertheless, Escara stiffened and assumed a defensive stance.

With cool determination, Xhylanna snapped open her fingers. The dagger dropped to the floor. "I resign the office of Priestess."

The Oracle stepped forward, saying quietly, "Child, the only resignation is through death."

Xhylanna nodded. "So it is. So this is the day I die." She stepped back and wrapped one arm around my back, clutching my hand with the other. "The method of execution, Escara, will be flame pistol. I would die with the same shot that kills my beloved."

I tried to push her away from me. "Xhylanna, no! I won't let you – "

Her eyes met mine. "You have no choice, Shep. We are equals, remember? We do not make decisions, one for the other."

"I..." I did not know what to say. I should urge her, I knew, to go on without me. To bring peace and justice to her world. Yet I knew that, were it she who were condemned, and I who had the choice, my choice would be no different. I would rather die than go on without her.

"Are you ready, Shep?" she asked quietly.

"What if," I asked desperately, "we are not together in the hereafter? You have not accepted Jesus Christ. If your gods are real, they surely cannot be pleased with me."

She kissed me gently. "The gods brought us together, my love. Who can say, then, that they are not pleased?"

"I love you, Xhylanna."

"And I will love you, no matter what comes next." She straightened her shoulders and faced the General. "We are ready, Escara. Make it a clean shot. And take care of our people."

Escara raised her pistol. "My people," she whispered with venom and squeezed the trigger.

Nothing happened.

Escara looked in astonishment at the gun, clicking the trigger repeatedly. It did not discharge. In a fury, she seized the pistol from the belt of a nearby guard and leveled it. It, too, failed to give satisfaction.

"You can test every weapon in the place," said Hylas behind me. He came forward, smirking and arrogant, his arms crossed defiantly over his chest. "They will not work."

Behind him, his guards stood rigid, clearly trying to move, clearly unable.

"Hylas?" I wondered.

He grinned at me. "I thought I felt different after... " – a small blush crossed his face – "last night."

"Truly," observed Xhylanna, "it seems you have passed him a gift of manhood, Shep. He has the power, alone, to frustrate the weapons of war."

"I bet Shep has it too," he said. "Something in our... joining... freed the power."

Escara bit back a curse. "You openly flout the law of our people!"

"No," said Xhylanna. "You openly flout the law, Escara! You murdered my pilot, and plotted with this creature," she pointed at Philip, "to convict my husband of a crime that was not his. I wonder," she said with revulsion, "if you even plotted with Scorpius."

"Lies!" barked Escara. She pointed to the members of the jury who stood, astonished, to the side. "They have spoken! You are all condemned!"

"So we are," agreed Xhylanna. "But, in so finding, my city betrays my husband. It betrays me. We will go." She took my hand and beckoned to Hylas to follow us.

"A moment, Xhylanna," said the Oracle. "This proceeding has had its foundations too firmly rooted in the affairs of mortal women. The stake of the gods has not even been discussed."

"Do you suggest that the gods want this... refuse... to dwell among us?" demanded Escara.

"No, Priestess," said the Oracle, for it was now Escara's title, by default. "They must go, there is no question. Yet no consideration was given, during the trial, to the prophecy."

Escara rolled her eyes.

The Oracle, ignoring her, continued. "Prophecy spoken by Oracles generations before me has told us of a man from another world. This was a man who would work the will of the gods among the people."

"Among the Jentana?" I asked.

"The prophecy says only, 'the people,'" replied the Oracle. "It could mean Jentana and Aspar alike, as well as other tribes in city-states all over this world."

"Do you believe Shep is the promised one?" asked Xhylanna.

"This is madness!" spat Escara, but I think even she was coming to realize that events were unfolding in spite of her objections and fell silent.

"Only the gods may determine who is the promised one," said the Oracle.

"And how will they do that?" I asked.

"You must meet the gods," said the old woman, as if the answer were obvious.

"Meet the gods?" I demanded. "One does not meet God on this side of the grave!"

"Certainly one does," said the Oracle, "if one is willing to attempt the journey."

"But God lives on a spiritual plane!" I retorted. "If you people believe in gods, then surely you must understand that they are not just... here somewhere with us. Not in the physical sense!"

Xhylanna looked at me strangely. "Shep, your beliefs in your god are very... different. Do you mean to say that you have truly never seen Him?"

"No one living actually sees God," I replied.

"Amazing," said the Oracle, with the only honest expression of emotion I had yet heard in her voice. "How can you be expected to believe in a god you never see? Ridiculous! I assure you, Shepherd Autrey, that our gods are not abstract concepts. We know precisely where they are."

"You do?" I was amazed.

"Of course," said Xhylanna. "We simply do not go to them. To do so, unbidden would be death."

I spread my hands in disbelief. "I suppose you're going to tell me that it's as simple as jumping aboard one of your fliers and setting sail?"

"It is," said the Oracle, "exactly that simple. The gods have spoken. You will leave by the first morning light."

TWELVE

Now, before I go on, let me explain exactly why Philip accompanied us on our journey. I did not want him there, by any stretch of the imagination. He had taken an active hand in engineering my false conviction, and thus in removing Xhylanna from her office as High Priestess. My reputation aside, he had caused the Jentana to be saddled with a conniving glory-hound for their leader. He had very nearly caused Xhylanna's death, not to mention Hylas's and mine. I can think of no better fate for him than to dwell under the regime he had helped to put in power.

So why did I ultimately take him along? For one thing, I felt that his presence here on New Earth was my responsibility. I still did not understand the mechanism of transport which brought us here, and I was now fairly certain it was not the admittedly phenomenal mental power which Hylas and I had awakened in each other. It had to have been some form of divine intervention, yet it had been I who had reached out to the infinite for rescue, and, immediately after, Philip and I had appeared on the field of battle on the plains of Aspar. I was convinced that, had I not begged the Lord for rescue, Philip would not be here to trouble these people.

I also suspected, despite Escara's promises to the contrary, that Philip's life was not worth a Confederate dollar. Even if the devious new Priestess did not simply reverse her decision and kill him, some faction or other, knowing that he was a willing participant in the plot to bomb the city, would eventually assassinate him. Even if they didn't believe him the prime mover, his involvement was motive enough for a revenge killing. This my Christian nature could not tolerate. The only way to keep this scoundrel safe to truly suffer the consequences of his many sins was to keep him with me. I supposed it might offer him the additional chance at redemption that Christ offers to even the most depraved, but I must admit I wondered how even Christ could find any redeeming quality in Philip Meigs.

Nevertheless, we took him – secured in his seat with manacles – when our submersible flier departed the City that morning.

Morning light is a surprising term to be used by denizens of the deep. They cannot see the sun under any circumstances from their vantage point, and yet the idiomatic expressions of surface living die hard. In fact, monitoring equipment on the Island of Wisdom had, until recently, allowed them to view the goings-on and conditions above, but all that was now ruin. We departed at the predicted hour of sunrise over the island.

We had spent one final night in Xhylanna's apartments, collapsing, exhausted, into bed after packing what belongings of hers we thought we would need. Once our preposterous mission was over, we would be starting a new home. Nor did we know where that new home might be. And all this assumed that we survived this alleged encounter with these alleged gods, and that was hardly a certainty, to hear Xhylanna talk.

When I say "we" collapsed into bed, I do mean all three of us. This night, I was quite happy to have both my wife and Hylas beside me. There was no sex. I still was ambivalent about the encounter I had been tricked into with my young protégé. It having happened, though, I was not as revolted by the memory as the conventional morality of earth would have me be. Tonight, however, sex wasn't even a question in any of our minds. We three were the only friends we had, wanted to be together for purposes of emotional security, and needed to be together to offer each other what protection we could. I did not yet know if my powers, like Hylas's, had taken to functioning on their own. I was not willing to test the possibility with Xhylanna's safety on the line. It was better that Hylas and I be within arms' reach of each other.

The night, thankfully, passed without incident.

There was no ceremony made of our departure. Enough of Escara's guards (only hours before they had been Xhylanna's) accompanied us to our ship to ensure that we actually left. Escara herself was nowhere to be seen, nor the Oracle, but Colys met us in the grotto where the amphibious fliers were housed.

"I thought you'd be jailed," I said, "for trying to aid the exile."

"No," she observed. "Escara is ambitious and treacherous, but she's not a fool. She knows that my family commands a great deal of influence in the City. She needs me as an ally. She'd love to put me on trial for treason as well, and she isn't shy about admitting it. But there are already discontented rumblings about her ascension to the priesthood."

Xhylanna smiled with irony. "I suppose that's something to be grateful for. Some of my sisters will miss me."

"More than you might imagine, Priestess," said Colys.

"Priestess no longer," my beloved reminded her.

"Still more sacred to the gods than Escara, I think," Colys replied. Impulsively, she rushed forward and embraced her former leader. When she pulled back after a time, I saw tears forming in her eyes. "Luck to you, my old friend."

And then the General turned to me. She clasped my arms in the manner of a warrior comrade and said, "You are worthy of her. I did not think a man existed of whom I could say that. You have changed everything for the Jentana."

"I have caused your leader to lose her power," I countered, and suddenly felt the shame that had hidden in a corner of my heart.

Colys shook her head. "You have fulfilled prophecy. You could do no less. It would not be my first choice to see Xhylanna deposed, but if that is what must happen for us to change and meet our destiny... to break the cycle of war... " She looked again at her former Priestess with open admiration. "I cannot believe otherwise than that a greater destiny still lies ahead for you."

We embarked refreshed, if troubled for what the future held. Now we were an hour into a flight which Xhylanna had informed me would take until past lunchtime. As she piloted us toward our unlikely destination, she seemed the calmest, the most relaxed and happy, that she had in the short time I had known her.

I reached out and took her hand. She smiled at me.

"Regrets my love?" I asked.

She shook her head and stretched luxuriously in her seat. "I have been leader of my people since my seventeenth summer."

"A gentleman does not ask how many summers ago that was."

"More than enough, I assure you. I had planned to spend – looked forward to spending! – the rest of my life leading the Jentana. And, now that those plans are all washed out with the tide... Shep, it's as if the weight of the world were suddenly lifted from my chest. I can breathe! I'm alive!"

"We have no idea what happens next," I reminded her.

"I think that's what feels so good, my love. Maybe life shouldn't be all planned out for us."

If surprises were the stuff of happiness, I reckoned we must be the happiest people alive. Nothing expected had happened to me since Philip and I had left Baltimore, less than two weeks ago.

I looked through the transparency at the sea below us. We had long ago lost sight of the blackened husk that was the Island of Wisdom. All that was visible now was the even violet of the ocean. For a while, I had glimpsed the occasional bird which recalled the albatross or seagull, but now even they had receded.

"Are we still ascending?" I asked, some time later.

"Of course," she replied. "You don't expect the gods to dwell near the earth, do you?"

"I don't expect them to dwell anywhere."

"So you've said. A perverse creature, your God, to dwell in obscurity as He does. Our gods have never hidden themselves from us, though it is admittedly rare that they actually walk among us. To my knowledge, no god has visited New Earth in my lifetime, although they don't always make their presence known."

"So they... don't live on New Earth? Are we... actually leaving the planet?"

"Not quite. You'll see, soon enough."

"But surely you don't claim that the gods often visit your people?"

"Our religion is obviously more concrete in its foundations than yours, Shep. For instance, how many generations has it been since any of your people actually saw a god?"

"Well... counting the resurrection as the last worldly appearance... over seventy. Of course the Catholics will claim that they have seen the face of Jesus in everything from the clouds to patterns of mildew on their walls – "

"The Mother Goddess attended the festivities when my predecessor became high priestess, about fifty years ago."

"Surely not – "

"The goblet from which she drank wine was on a shelf in my bedchamber. Didn't you see it?"

"Your goddess drinks?"

"Doesn't yours?"

"We have no goddess – "

"Barbarians! No wonder your culture is so backward."

"But I suppose it's true that Jesus drank wine, during his mortal lifetime."

"There you have it."

"But this notion of gods and goddesses coming down from the heavens to dwell among you as often as a cousin visits from England, well – "

"Can the gods not come down from the sky as easily as we go up to it?"

"Well, surely – "

"And is their home really so far away from us? If you'll look just to your left, it's coming into view now."

I looked, and, to my astonishment, I saw it. Floating among the clouds, with no visible means of support, was a city the size of Washington. I had seen much that challenged belief in my time on this world, but this had to be the capstone of my experience.

The City of the Gods. I marveled at its beauty for exactly ten seconds. Then our flier was struck by lightning, and began to spiral downward toward the sea below.

———

"I can't get him stabilized!" Xhylanna cried. My brain took a split-second to process that "him" referred to the ship itself, in a reversal of earth tradition. Then it took another to process the fact that the four of us were about to die. My stomach, meanwhile, was putting hellacious effort into returning all the components of my breakfast whence they came. I had never been drunk, much less so drunk that the room felt as though it were spinning, but I had had the sensation described to me by others less fortunate. I now knew the utter hopelessness of wanting discomfort to stop so badly that death seemed a pleasant alternative.

Philip screamed hysterically from his seat. I considered telling Hylas to kill him and get it over with a few seconds early. I also considered that Hylas or I might stop this horrible plummet, if we could but concentrate. I certainly could not concentrate.

The ship was only feet above the water when it suddenly righted itself, ever so gently, flew straight for a few moments, and then, just as gently, began to ascend again. "What the devil?" I demanded.

"I don't know," said Xhylanna.

I looked to Hylas, thinking perhaps he had saved us with his newfound power. He sensed my question and shook his head. Philip blubbered in terror.

Xhylanna fought with the ship's instruments. "I still don't have control. The ship is...acting on its own..."

She finished the sentence mechanically, as if the end no longer mattered. She was now staring straight ahead of us through the dome. My head still reeling, I stumbled forward, seizing onto the back of her seat to steady myself. When I looked, I saw the cause of Xhylanna's astonishment, and gaped. Before us, hanging in the sky as easily as did the city we had just seen, was a man. He looked so comfortable, so graceful as he floated there, that one might think walking a quaint, outdated practice. Surely, the human body was designed to simply defy gravity in this way, he made it look so easy.

Like all the denizens of New Earth he was nude, but cloaked, unlikely as it sounds, in flame. It seemed to come from his pores, and it bathed his body, which glowed red and hot within the halo of the flames.

The Firechild.

Yes, it had to be he. The boy from my dreams, now grown to manhood. I felt a pang of.. what? Affection? Regret? The sensation from my dream, of cradling his tiny, fiery body to me... and then of his fiery anger, directed at the Gray Lady and myself... The pain of seeing anger in the eyes of one I loved so... Why was he so consumed by bitterness, when I wanted only the best for him?

Foolish thoughts. Sinful. I dismissed them. This was not a creature I knew. This was a threat, a dire one. In keeping with his fiery appearance, he seemed supremely angry. There was no doubt his anger was directed at us, and that he was the source of the bolt which had struck our ship from the air. Our presence had distressed him, and he had attacked. Why then, I wondered, had he spared us and brought us back here?

Xhylanna closed her eyes, bowed her head and, unbelievably, began to pray out loud to the Mother Goddess. She begged for intervention, and for mercy. I did not wish to disturb a holy interlude, even one devoted to a false god, so I turned to Hylas. "Who is he?" I wondered.

He had turned even paler than usual. He swallowed and whispered, "Raxes. He is the god of the Aspar."

Philip found his voice. "Talk to him, Shep! You know how to speak to gods!"

"That is not a god!" I blurted.

"Shep, be quiet, he'll hear you!" Hylas hissed.

"I have heard him," said a voice which reverberated through the very walls of our craft. It was a harsh, angry voice, which belonged to one ever primed for battle. It was brash, and arrogant, and challenging.

"So you doubt my divinity, mortal?" Raxes asked me. "Then I shall at least let you live long enough to confess it, before I kill you in searing torment."

I summoned my courage and tried to equal his glare. "God does *not* kill."

"Aside from being thoroughly ungrammatical, that statement is untrue. Gods do kill."

"There is only one God, and he so loved the world that he sent his only begotten son, that whosoever believeth in him should not perish – "

"You sound like my mother's husband!" Raxes interrupted petulantly. "Please do not tell me that men have taken to worshiping the Pretender again! If so, I shall make a point to engineer a war and cull the herd."

Again someone referred to the Pretender, whom I took to be Satan, when I quoted the Lord. These people were confused!

Hylas came to stand next to me. "M – my Lord Raxes," he said, "my blood brother is from old earth. The people there worship different gods. They do not know about you."

"Which is why we left that dreadful world," observed Raxes. He studied us for a moment. Then, with a flicker like a candle dying, he disappeared, only to re-appear... right next to me.

He looked as human as I, save for the flame which still ensconced his body. It gave off a good deal of heat, but not near as much as would a healthy bonfire. Of course his body was perfect. He was tall. Very much the classical description of a pagan god.

"Who are you?" he asked Hylas.

"Hylas, of Aspar, my Lord."

"Son of Scorpius."

"No longer," Hylas said without sentiment. A clarification, nothing more.

"Really? I'm sure there's an interesting tale therein. But I always thought you showed promise, young warrior. What are you doing here with a female, and this womanly man who worships peaceful gods? And what," he stabbed a burning finger at Philip, "is that obscenity?"

"That is another earth man," I said.

"No wonder we left," he snorted. "You're a sorry lot."

Hylas bowed his head. "We do not mean to displease you, my Lord."

"Hylas," I demanded, "why are you kowtowing to this... ill-tempered hooligan?"

"Shep," said Hylas urgently, "he's a god!"

"I could reduce you to cinders where you stand, mortal!" said Raxes.

"And I could kill that mewling sac in the corner," I snapped. "I've been tempted to a few times recently. I've killed one man. I've seen hundreds of others killed. What does it prove? So you can kill me, does that make you a god?"

"Have a care, mortal," muttered Raxes.

"Shep, don't be a fool!" cried Xhylanna.

Raxes looked to her. "Dare you to speak in my presence, Jentana? Do not think that my Mother's patronage can prevent me from burning the tongue from your head!" He raised his hand, which began to glow from red to yellow as its heat increased. "In fact, I believe I will do just that. Females should be seen and not heard."

He took a step toward Xhylanna. Instantly, I reached for Hylas's hand. Together, surely we could resist this false deity. Hylas, however, backed away from me, uncertainty, even fear in his eye. He believed in this creature. To ask him to stand against Raxes was too much.

At least I had distracted our attacker. He turned from Xhylanna to me. "You thought to attack me, did you? With those puny powers my mother granted you, you thought to stand equal to a god? You are mad!"

His mother? His mother had granted me the power? Of course. In my mind, I saw a flash of sharp, gray eyes, and a smile, wise and knowing... The vision strengthened me, and reminded me who it was this creature threatened.

I stepped forward and locked my eyes with his. "I would stand against anyone who threatens my wife."

For a moment, his radiance grew brighter still. I braced myself for the attack that would surely follow, but then he rolled his eyes and spat out a hard breath in frustration.

"You carry the protection of my mother and her consort," he said through his teeth. "I cannot harm you... yet. But your time will come, mortal." He stepped back from me, but did not look away. "We will meet again." Then, as quickly as he had appeared, he was gone, carried away in a brilliant flash. Nor had he gone alone.

"Xhylanna!" I cried in desperation, as my beloved also vanished. Philip was gone as well, but I cared not at all. I turned to Hylas, thankfully still beside me. "We must – " I began.

There was not time to formulate a plan, however; for, bereft of Raxes control, our craft resumed its downward dive. We were both thrown off our feet and toward the rear of the cabin as the ship plummeted, nose first.

Using the seats and each other for leverage, Hylas and I clambered forward, to the controls. I still did not know how to fly the craft, but I held the boy steady in the pilot's seat as he attempted to slow our descent and bring up the nose. I tried not to look at the clouds as they flashed by the transparency of the dome. I set my jaw firmly, trying to stave off a wave of vertigo-induced nausea.

My stomach felt as though it had turned completely within me as Hylas leveled us, hard and fast. I feared permanent internal damage; but when his white knuckles relaxed on the lever which controlled ascent, and he nodded to me that all was well again, I had time to take stock of my condition. I was alive and whole and all parts in their proper places.

And Xhylanna was gone. Despair gnashed at me. For the first time in my life, I felt utterly hopeless. What could I do against such a being as Raxes? He had my beloved, and was bent on revenge.

Hylas, sensing my desperation, met my eye with calm resolve.

"We must return," he said quietly. "We must go back and enter the city of the gods, as we'd planned. Only the Mother Goddess can help us now."

THIRTEEN

What astonished me about the City of the Gods was not, in fact, its grandeur. It was the sheer... reality of the place that struck me. Certainly it was an amazing feat of architecture, and far and above the cities of earth in its achievements. But so were the cities of Aspar and Jentana. Yes, it floated in the clouds, using technology I could not fathom. (Or was it magic? How was I to know?)

But the City of the Gods had a sewer system. It had trash cans. Oh, yes, they were trash cans which actually made the trash vanish once it was placed inside, but they were still trash cans. Their presence informed me that the residents of this allegedly divine capitol had to contend with the same silly problems that any other being did.

As Hylas arced high over the city and then brought our craft down, I had to accustom myself to the sight of people – gods, it was still claimed – flitting through the air under their own power and dashing at impossible speeds down the street. But I did not feel that I had left the land of the living. I spotted a library, an opera house, even a bank! The gods used currency? Well, I reasoned, why shouldn't they? But the architecture... what was it about the buildings which so troubled me? Of course...

Despite the emotional state brought on by Xhylanna's abduction, my curiosity was aroused. Perhaps my mind was attempting to compensate for the emotional blow by keeping itself busy.

"The buildings are all classical in design," I said. "Like Greek Revival style. Nowhere else on your planet have I seen such an earth influence."

Hylas shrugged, seeming distracted. "It is the style of the gods. You would not see it among mortals."

That was the trouble. I had seen it among mortals – often – on earth. Why should this city, of all places on this alien world, have earth architecture?

Hylas landed our craft in an area designed for the purpose of receiving airships. There were two or three others there when we arrived, not unlike the ships of the Jentana or Aspar. Were these ships belonging to other "mortals," I wondered, or did the "gods" also transport themselves in ships?

A boy was waiting for us when we stepped out of the ship, onto the perfectly ordinary green of the landing field. Yes, it was green! In another astonishing parallel, this city displayed everywhere the green grass of my native world. The sunlight seemed not so crimson here, and the sky a paler violet. One might almost believe one was on earth.

Our host looked to be a teenager, short for his age, but tightly muscled. Although naked, he wore sandals adorned with small, silver wings. He also wore a silver cap on his head, as if it were a badge of office.

"I am Vintinus. You're all expected. The Queen has prepared some – "

"I'm sorry," I interrupted, "but we're in rather desperate circumstances. There's no time – "

The boy smiled pleasantly, if a little smugly. He had one of those faces that told you he was up to no good. When he smiled, you just wanted to slap the smile right off his face.

"The Mother Goddess is fully aware of the situation," he said. "You can relax. Raxes will not harm his captives until he has presented demands. Mother is not accepting demands until she has met with you."

"How can you be sure – " I started to demand.

"It's how we do things," said Vintinus.   "Formalities are always observed. Your encounter with Raxes was merely one more step in an ongoing conflict between gods. We do not take steps out of order. If your wife is fated to die, she will do so only after protocol has been followed."

"She will not die at all!" I blurted out.

"Shep!" cried Hylas. "This is the messenger of the gods! You need to be respectful!"

I had had enough of this comedy of manners. "I think I need to cast a few people over the edge of this city!"

"Shep..." Hylas breathed. Clearly, he was afraid of this ridiculous boy. I suppose he thought that this slim youth would somehow magically kill me. What an idiotic thought! Looking back, I also know it was a very realistic fear. I should have listened to Hylas. I didn't know how much danger I was actually in. The whole situation was just so unreal.

But Vintinus only laughed at my threat. "I'm afraid the Queen Mother would never allow it. She has invisible guardians to prevent anything from falling out of the city."

"Invisible guardians?" I said dubiously.

"It's how she does things. No one gets hurt... unless she wants them to." He smiled, less offensively this time. "My friend, I understand that you're anxious; but you've come to the right place. If anyone can save your wife and friend, it's the Mother Goddess. Take a deep breath and – " he produced, Heaven help me, a golden lyre from out of nowhere. It was the first really heavenly object I had seen here. Much more evocative of divinity than a trash can, I must say. He began to strum on it, and finished, " – let me play you a song."

"No I – " I began, but my head suddenly... lightened. At the sound of the few notes he plucked, tension drained from the muscles of my neck and back. My breath came more easily, and my pulse slowed. Despite my fear for my beloved, I was suddenly... calm.

Vintinus nodded approval. "Much better. We wouldn't want you to endanger your health by being unduly upset. The Queen Mother is so looking forward to meeting you, and would be unhappy with me if you had some silly stroke before she did." He jerked his head toward the center of the city.

"Come, I'll take you to her."

"Do we tip you?" I asked as we walked.

"Tip?" wondered Vintinus.

"Money, for services rendered?"

"Shep!" squeaked Hylas. He looked as if he were about to whack me on the head, as one would a misbehaving puppy.

But the godling was not offended. "You have nothing of value," he said. "If you had, I'd have stolen it already."

"The gods steal, as well?" I asked.

"I do. It's the messenger's job, to go through all the possessions of a visitor. Make sure he has nothing dangerous. But if you come across some interesting trinket in your travels, I'd be happy to receive a tip when next we meet. What fun!" He gestured toward a carefully landscaped path which led off the landing green. "Shall we?"

He led us down city streets, pointing out this item of interest and that, chattering all the way. Hylas acted as I suppose I would have were I to visit Jerusalem, or Bethlehem.

We arrived at an imposing building, near what I thought must be the center of this amazing city. I was impressed by it as an example of classical architecture, but I could see that Hylas was impressed in an entirely different way. As we mounted the steps, following Vintinus, Hylas hesitated. His expression said that he was nervous or anxious, and that he was hoping for me to change our course.

"Is something wrong?" I asked.

"I – " he began. He pointed up the steps and whispered, "That is the Palace of the Gods!"

I nodded, somewhat baffled. "Yes."

There was a pause, while I wondered why he was stating the obvious. I think he wondered why I didn't understand the full impact of his statement. I think we each thought the other was experiencing an intellectual low point.

Finally, he said, "I do not wish to be in the presence of the gods."

Vintinus chewed his lip and, I think, suppressed a laugh. "Bad news, friend..."

"I do not wish to enter the Hall of the Gods," Hylas amended.

I asked carefully, "That was the goal of our trip, was it not? To meet with your Mother Goddess?"

"Not his Mother Goddess," corrected Vintinus.

"Still," I maintained, "we had instructions from the Oracle. Don't even men of Aspar accept the validity of the Jentana Oracle?"

"Of course," said Hylas. "But... "

"What, then?" I demanded. "We came to meet the gods, and now you hesitate!"

"You and Xhylanna came to meet the gods!" he replied. "Xhylanna is a priestess and you're... well, you're you. You two are the kinds of people who meet and speak to gods. I am just... me. I expected I would... wait outside."

I clapped him on the shoulder. "You are my blood brother," I said. "You are worthy to go anywhere I do. In fact, I insist – "

"Shep, they're going to bring us into the Presence of the Queen Mother. They're going to offer us nectar and ambrosia. They're going to expect us to sit and chat like visitors in the home of a friend. Would you sit and chat in the presence of your God?"

I considered it. Hylas had a point. It might be overwhelming, but...

"My God loves me," I assured him. "and would never do anything to me that was not for my ultimate good. I fear His wrath against the unjust and His judgment of my sins, but I could not fear Him. I would give anything to be in the presence of the Almighty."

Hylas thought for a moment, and then nodded quietly. "All right," he muttered. "I'll go."

As we began to walk again, Vintinus asked me "The Almighty who?"

Hylas shook his head. "Don't get him started."

———

Gold. Gold everywhere. The doors were gold. The walls were crusted in gold. The furniture was gold-leafed. I'm well versed in descriptions of the City of Gold and the Pearly Gates, but I could not help thinking of Jesus and the money changers in the Temple. I didn't think He would have approved of this opulence. It seemed to me that it was the sort of dream a laborer might have of what a rich man's house should look like. It was showy and impractical. I kept my thoughts private, however. Hylas was nervous enough.

I thought my friend might faint when we entered the Great Hall, as Vintinus called it. It was a circular room. Room? The word "room" hardly does it justice. "Rooms" are in mortal homes and built to mortal proportions. This was... a chamber? An expanse? Ever been to the Capitol

Building in the City of Washington? It's like walking into that rotunda, only where the Capitol is dark this was bright. The light of the sun seemed to stream in, from where it was not apparent. Where the Capitol's dome causes the voices of visitors to echo in an often hideous cacophony, this enormous enclosure seemed to encourage a gentility of sound. Soft music lilted in the air, which was sweet and gently moving. It was like being outside on a calm, late Summer day when the rain had not fallen that week, and did not threaten to fall soon.

In a circle stood golden thrones, some occupied by beautiful, golden-skinned young men and women. Other such perfect specimens stood about, some clothed in pristine robes, some artfully nude. They did not pause in their activities as we entered. Some drank wine, some played games or just chatted with each other. One throne, opposite the grand entry doors, stood high about the rest.

On that throne, She sat. She, the Gray Lady.

Is it possible for reality to be more beautiful than a dream? If it is, then so she was. Her gown was many layers of flowing white and green silk, embroidered on the edges in threads of many colors. Her hair, as I remembered from my dreams, was a deep auburn which shone so that it might be heated like the wick of a candle. And her eyes... those piercing, flashing, gray eyes.

She alone looked up as we entered. She smiled at me and all was right with the world. I was far from home. My best friend was a traitor. I had fought and killed and been tricked into immoral sexual congress. The woman I loved had been kidnapped, but I suddenly knew, for that instant, that everything would be all right. I had no doubt the feeling would pass when I looked away, but what a precious sense of well-being the Gray Lady's smile delivered.

Hylas knelt. "Praise to you, Mother of Heaven and New Earth," he recited, his head bowed. "Thank you for allowing us in your presence."

"You are very welcome, child," she said graciously. Her voice! Oh, God, her voice! "But I would not dream of allowing Shepherd Autrey to be harmed. I've been quite looking forward to meeting him. And I imagine he has many questions for me."

"I have many questions... ma'am," I agreed.

"Rise, Hylas of Aspar," she said. "Do not worry yourself with formalities. Like my father before me, I am comfortable walking among mortals, and I want you to be comfortable." She winked at me.

"If I may," I asked, "who was your father?"

"Your people have forgotten so much since we left, Shep, that I don't know if his name will mean anything to you. But my father was called Zeus, and I am his firstborn, Athena."

"Ridiculous!"

"Ridiculous?" wondered Hylas. "What's ridiculous?"

I gestured at the terrace around me, the beautifully landscaped area on the roof of the palace where we were being fed on (literally, if you believed the claims) heavenly delicacies. Hylas had finally relaxed in his surroundings, thanks in large part to the high alcohol content of the delicious drink Vintinus called nectar. My young companion now looked sleepy, and his speech was not as clear as it usually was.

"All of this!" I answered him.

"You call the palace of the gods ridiculous?"

"Completely. Athena? And this boy Vintinus – Mercury's great, grand nephew? I'm to believe that the gods of antiquity simply moved to a new location two thousand years ago and started their own shop?"

"So you have heard of our gods?"

"Certainly! I don't know that horrid Raxes who tried to burn us from the sky, nor this young imitator who escorted us here; but I've heard of Zeus and Athena in books of fable and myth. They're not real."

"Not real? You just spoke to Ath – " he broke off and corrected himself with reverence. "To the holy Mother Goddess. How can you say she's not real?"

"Easy. We died when the ship crashed an hour ago. I'm in Heaven's foyer, having an hallucination. Besides, this isn't even accurate to the Greek Myths! Athena was not the mother of the gods. She wasn't anyone's mother. She was an eternal virgin."

Hylas threw up an unsteady hand. "Virgin? She's the mother of Raxes!"

"The Athena I learned about would not be at war with her own son," I objected. "And the gods didn't live in the sky, they lived on Mount Olympus."

"Mount Olympus! Have you been there?" Vintinus had returned with a fresh, golden pitcher of nectar. He smiled happily as he overheard me.

"Uh... no," I admitted.

His face took on a dreamy aspect. "I always wanted to see it. They tell me that this city looks very like the one we lived in on earth, atop the mountain, but I always wished I could have seen the original. I was born after we came here."

Athena returned to us, seating herself opposite me on a couch. She reclined so casually, folding her feet up under her like a little girl would, it was hard to believe she was a goddess.

What was I thinking? Of course she wasn't a goddess! These creatures weren't gods, they were... I didn't know what they were; but there is only one God.

She ruffled Vintinus's hair affectionately, disturbing the winged silver cap of which he seemed so proud. "Many things have changed since we came here. If you do know our history, Shep, I imagine we're very different from what you'd expect."

"I expected nothing," I said, trying not to be rude, but wanting to stand firm in my faith. "I do not believe in any gods but my God. I never thought I'd meet someone who claimed to be Athena."

She laughed softly. "Still you doubt us. I suppose I don't blame you. In the last few days your life has changed so drastically, a lesser man might have gone mad."

"The Lord has blessed me with a strong faith," I said.

"That is good. You're going to need it, if you're going to win Xhylanna away from Raxes."

The mention of my beloved's name caught me off guard. I felt suddenly guilty for sitting here eating, when she was heaven knew where, exposed to unknown dangers. I set down my goblet harder than I'd meant to. Athena seemed to guess my thoughts.

"Do not castigate yourself for tending your own needs, Shep," she said. "Xhylanna is safe, I promise you. Raxes will not harm her. He needs her."

"Why?" I asked.

"Because she is his instrument of revenge against you. You stole Hylas from him."

"I stole – ?" I began.

"You certainly did. Until you came, Hylas was a model citizen of Aspar, consecrated to Raxes's path of battle, rage and violence. Before him lay a carefully planned life: he was going to select a mentor, be schooled in the arts of war and one-sided physical pleasure, go into battle, and either die a hero or become King of his people.

"Instead, he has bound himself to a man of peace, gained power to end violence, and he's beginning to question the rightness of killing his fellow man in battle, and of killing women after raping them."

Hylas hung his head, embarrassed to be talked about this way.

"You have angered my son more than he has ever been angered," Athena finished gravely. "He has never lost so promising a follower. You must carefully prepare for what is to come."

"And what is that?" I asked.

"A challenge.   My son is battling me, through you."

"Why doesn't he just battle you himself?"

A new voice answered me: "Because gods do not battle gods."

It was a strong voice, deep and resonant. I followed it until my gaze turned on the arched doorways which led to the terrace. There he stood, tall and impressive. Not a big man, for all his height. He was lithe, with an athlete's body.   His commanding presence had its roots in the questing, black eyes that looked on me, in the compassionate, intelligent countenance, in the air of ageless wisdom which surrounded him. He looked like the model for Michelangelo's David with the face of DaVinci's Christ, neither of whom, I knew, looked anything like the Semitic originals.

It was his abdomen which drew my attention, however. Etched in pale, white lines on his flesh were scars terribly recognizable to me. I had borne them in my dreams.

"It's you," I whispered. "You're the one I dreamed of being."

He smiled at me. It wasn't the sweet smile of Athena, so pleasant that a mortal might become addicted to seeing it. It was at once comradely and fatherly. It bolstered one's confidence and made one feel strong.

"I needed to impart information. Dreams seemed the best way. How many students have wished they could learn in their sleep? You have. You have lived my history, Shep."

Athena reached out, took the newcomer's hand and guided him to sit beside her. "This is my husband," she announced with marked pride. "I believe you know his name."

"The Pretender?" I asked.

"That, too," said her husband. "But on Earth I was called Prometheus."

I felt foolish for not having realized his identity, especially after Athena revealed hers. Do not think for a minute that I was lulled into believing this madness they spouted. I knew there were, in truth, no gods of antiquity. Still, within the fabric of their insane tapestry, I should have been able to trace the threads. I had read Homer, after all, and Sophocles and Ovid. I was educated. Prometheus was the one who gave gifts to mankind, and was exiled from Olympus for doing so. Chained to a rock, his liver ripped out each morning by an eagle, only to grow back by nightfall... That explained the scars.

"You look well, considering your ordeal," I said.

He smiled and reflexively traced the scars with his fingertips. "It was a long time ago. I could heal them completely, but I choose to carry a reminder of the past."

"An odd choice, for the patron of foresight," I said.

"Lately, I seem to be doing a lot of looking back. My brother Epimetheus would laugh, could he see me now. I used to mock his single-minded obsession with the past, but our current situation is rooted in past events. It is important that you understand why."

"I, important? I am only a mortal." I paused and added, "who doesn't believe in you." I saw Hylas flinch.

"Gods, mortals," sighed Prometheus, "I never cared much which was which. I can see folly bringing them all to their eventual downfall. At least the sufferings of mortals are shorter. And they seem to learn more quickly than gods, considering the brief span of time they have in which to learn.

Since my first creation walked your earth, your kind has had a role to play in history. None so important, I think, as yours."

"Your first creation?"

"You don't want to believe me the creator of humanity, because that's Jehovah's title. All right then. Perhaps I'm only being poetic. Perhaps humanity was there all along, and I merely trained, shaped and molded them to the extent that I could take credit for them realizing their potential of mastery over their world. Perhaps they were created by Jehovah. Perhaps they evolved from apes as your Mr. Darwin suggests."

"You play loosely with the truth."

"Because truth is flexible. Truth is different for each of us. The world you see through your eyes is a different one in many ways from the one I see through mine. That fact doesn't make liars of either of us. But accept as truth that you are important to us, Shep, and I needed you to know how we came to be where we are. Much of what you saw was our later history, not recorded by any man of earth. It's the story of how and why we left. When my dear Athena freed me – "

"Heracles freed you," I offered, "according to Hesiod."

"Shep, don't correct our host," said Hylas, though without much conviction.

"It's all right," said Prometheus. "Athena completed the work of freeing me," he amended. "When Heracles took me away from the mountain, and the torment of the eagle, I was still bound with shackles. They slowed my progress and kept me from leaving Olympus and interfering with man. Athena removed them because I told her the secret of Zeus's downfall."

"I thought that Thetis the Nereid was to be the mother of Zeus's overthrower. Wasn't that the prophecy?" My classical education had been some time ago, but I remembered Prometheus's story well.

"That's what I told Zeus," admitted Prometheus. "I believe you'd say that information was 'a red herring.'"

"I've... never heard that expression."

He snapped his fingers and looked sheepish. "Hasn't been invented yet! Sorry. I confuse present and future at times. I told Zeus a misleading story, both to throw him off the track and because I rather liked Thetis. She deserved better than him. Because of my prophecy, she was shipped off and married a mortal. But the true prophecy, the secret of his downfall, was one he already knew, if he had thought about it. Athena's mother – " he patted his wife's pretty knee " – was prophesied to have a male child who would overthrow Zeus. That's why he swallowed her, and Athena was born in his head."

"An unbelievable story." (Me)

"Shep!" (Hylas)

"Completely!" (Prometheus)

"Why do you perpetuate these stories if they're not true?" I asked.

"Do you believe that Jehovah created the world in exactly 168 hours?" he came back pointedly.

"I... I don't know. It's not really important, is it?"

"Exactly! The way a story is dressed up is not important. The heart of the story is what matters."

"Like telling Zeus to worry about his prospective son by one goddess when the threat was his grandson by another?"

"Just so. I don't like deception, Shep; but, knowing the truth, Zeus would have prevented the birth of Raxes, remained king of the gods, and humanity would have stagnated utterly. Zeus had to go, no matter the sacrifices," he looked sadly at Athena, "required of the rest of us."

"Are you telling me that Raxes overthrew Zeus? That he did your bidding? If he was on your side then, why does he hate you so now?"

"There is more to the story," he explained. He held out his hand to me. "If I may?"

"If you may... what?"

"If you'll allow me, I can show you the rest."

I hesitated. This... man... had sent me the dreams; the dreams I thought came from Satan; the dreams I still suspected were ungodly.

"It won't hurt," he offered gently. "I'm going to let you experience what I saw, so long ago."

I sighed and nodded. "At least maybe I'll understand what's happened to me."

"Lie back and make yourself comfortable. This won't take long."

He laid a hand on my forehead, and reality dropped out of sight.

FOURTEEN

I stood once again at the peak of Mt. Olympus, in the hidden garden that no mortal would ever find, even had he the wherewithal to climb the mountain.

Once again? Yes, for I was seeing through the eyes of Prometheus. I inhabited his body, shared his soul. I *was* him.

It had been years since we had left, my Athena and I, years in which we had discovered our love for each other, had nurtured our child, had given him over to a mortal family to raise as their own. Our hearts had swelled to the bursting point with love for each other and for him, and then, inevitably, had broken as we left him.

Our precious Raxes.

Knowing she carried a child, Zeus had, of course, remembered the old prophecy that Metis's male offspring would overthrow him. He'd wanted the child killed before it consumed nectar and ambrosia, and became immortal. My ruse that his overthrow lay with Thetis's son had fooled him, but, still, Zeus was jealous of his power. The old prophecy nagged at him. He would be certain.

STEVEN H. WILSON 213

Athena had told him that the child was a girl, and, not wanting a child by Ares, she had left it to die of exposure on a mountainside, as the mortals were wont to do. Then she took her leave of Olympus, saying she needed time away to recover from all that had happened. She played the recalcitrant daughter, letting her father believe that she had seen the error of her ways. He should have known she was too proud to do anything of the kind, but Zeus ever underestimated others. Instead of concerning himself with Athena, Zeus combed the world searching for a girl child of godly blood, but, of course, there wasn't one to be found. In time, he gave up the search, satisfied the child was dead.

Now the time was ripe for our return. Zeus would suspect nothing. He'd probably forgotten the entire matter. As we walked slowly toward the Hall of the Pantheon, I grasped my beautiful wife's hand in mine and asked, "Are you sure this is what you want?"

She squeezed my hand in hers. "It's what we must do. Your creations, the mortals, have to thrive. My father will continue to oppress them. They'll be little more than cattle. They're better than that."

"That's why I gave them fire," I agreed. "I wanted them to grow, not just be our playthings."

She pulled me close and squeezed me, breathing deeply, drawing what strength she could. Then, resolved, she pulled back. "Let's go."

We entered the Hall, back, once again, among our brother and sister gods.

Ares was laughing. I heard him before we entered. He had a braying, obnoxious laugh that I'm sure he thought was manly. I thought it sounded like the call of a moose in its death throes.

"I told you, Father," he exclaimed as we entered, "I said that young Teocoulos was every bit the hero that Achilles was! Look at the dead at his feet!"

"Let it go!" moaned his sister, Artemis. "Must every champion be measured by your precious Achilles? He died readily enough!"

"After killing thousands," maintained Ares. "Prince Hector and your unnatural Amazon queen among them!"

"There is nothing unnatural about the love of woman for woman," said Artemis, looking her brother up and down. "Especially if you are the best the male gender has to offer. But your hero's treatment of his noblest opponent, Hector – that was unnatural! Dragging his body behind his chariot for days! It's no wonder Apollo tired of him and guided the arrow of Paris to kill him."

"Paris," spat Ares with disgust. "His only use was touching off the war, truly the finest entertainment in living memory!" He turned to Zeus, "Father, we must engineer another such contest among the humans. These individual quests against monsters are simply not the stuff of legend! Men are so much more amusing when they're part of a group, fighting a war. Something about being one of a number suppresses their pesky sense of morality and lets them fight with abandon. And why shouldn't they? It's not as if their individual lives were worth anything!"

Zeus waved him off, staring intently into the distance, where he observed a hero's trials.

"I'm watching the games, Ares," he grumbled. "Leave me be!"

Ever as before, I thought. Squabbling, threatening, obsessing over the pointless tests they contrived for mortals. Not a creative thought or impulse among the lot, except for Apollo or Hephaestus. But Apollo was sex-mad and couldn't focus, and Hephaestus was held in contempt by his entire family.

Once, I reflected sadly, these creatures had built worlds.

"I'm out of nectar!" announced Ares. "Where is that damned girl? Hebe! Or Ganymede! Curse the boy!" He looked around for some servant to fill his goblet, and he spotted us.

"Well, well! Please don't tell me you've come to re-introduce 'clever' heroes who fight their battles with their minds!'"

"No," said Athena with a weary shake of her head. She said it so quietly that, over the din of Ares's demands for refreshment, and the chatter of the rest about the movements in the game down on earth, she likely couldn't be heard. Still, she added, "I'm not here to rejoin your games."

Zeus seemed to notice her for the first time. "Daughter!" he called out, motioning to her. "Come and tell me what you think of my new champion! Is he as smart as your Perseus was?"

She held her place. "It doesn't matter," she said calmly. "It doesn't matter how smart they are, or how brave, or how capable. You will let them win or lose in battle, but you will never let them change their situation. You will never let them grow."

"As usual, you're mistaken," said Hera. She sat away from the others, looking detached and disdainful. She turned up her nose as if the smell in the room offended her, but gods do not have body odor. It was merely an affectation. "I've arranged for this one to become a king when he has completed his labors. That is progress!"

"No," said Athena, "it isn't. It's a worthless prize, the latest in a series of worthless prizes given to the latest in a series of mortals who have played your games, amused you, and wasted their abilities providing entertainment, as you waste your abilities consuming it."

"Nectar, dammit!" barked Ares.

Zeus's eyebrows knitted together and his face reddened to nearly the shade of his fiery hair. "Daughter," he said slowly, "I have tolerated your liaison with this... pretender." To this he added a sneer for my benefit. "But if you think that you're going to come in here, after all this time, and start ridiculing me – "

"I do not ridicule," Athena maintained. "I state fact. You are wasting your power. Once you worked to build this world, to make it a better place.

You asked your fellow gods to populate it with diverse species and oversee its myriad aspects: its seas, its rivers, its mountains and its lowest places. All this effort led to one phenomenal success: the animal we call human. It is a superior species, almost godlike in that it can rise above base instinct and actually reason. It is capable of evolving, of ruling this world... and you distract it with empty contests. Child's play!"

Zeus stabbed an angry finger at me. "You have put these thoughts in her head! You! The fire thief!"

Athena looked as though he'd slapped her. "No one – ever! – puts thoughts in my head. My husband stole fire – stole it because you refused to give it freely! Did it ever occur to you, Father, that this – " she clasped my arm emphatically, "is the god of foresight? That he knows the future? That he wanted to help the humans because he saw their great destiny?"

"He wanted to spite me!" roared Zeus.

"I wanted to help you, Cousin," I said as evenly as I could. "Our destinies, gods' and mortals', are linked. What helps them helps us. Think about it – would I spite you, knowing what my fate would be? I knew it. Of course I knew it! Would spite be motive enough to suffer such punishment?"

"Dammit!" shrieked Ares, gesturing downward to where they'd watched the battle on earth below. "The monster has been slain, and we missed it! And for what? Father, send them away. Or let me take them from here and thrash them!"

"He has no power to send us anywhere," said Athena. "He no longer rules Olympus."

"Wha – ?" Ares stammered. He began to laugh. Zeus's face reddened even deeper. His hands shook at his sides.

Ignoring them, Athena continued, "My husband knew the name of him who would overthrow you, Father."

"He said Thetis – " Zeus began.

"I lied," I assured him.

"You deceitful cur! After I welcomed you back among us!"

"With shackles on my legs? And scars on my belly where my liver had been ripped from me, day after day for years? You expected gratitude?"

"I expected honor!"

"There was no time for honor," Athena said coldly. "Prometheus had to be free to play his part in your downfall. It was he who trained the new king of Heaven." She gestured. A door opened, and he entered.

Our son.

"This is Raxes," Athena told the assembled gods. "You no doubt remember the day he was conceived, on this very spot where we stand." She tapped a foot on the floor, as if they needed more specific indication of the location of which she spoke.

Ares swallowed and his eyes grew round. "On this very spot... but... he is... mine?"

"You impregnated me with him, Ares," Athena replied. "He is not – and never will be – yours."

The god of war proved then that he had one shred of dignity: he did not actually pout. Still, he took on the aspect of a wounded child. "How could you not tell me, Athena? How could you do that, even to an enemy?"

The charlatan! Had he not, only days ago, posed as a serpent and taunted the boy with the truth of his parentage? Had that not left poor Raxes angry and confused enough, without this show of false pain?

Raxes, who had been cool to us since the encounter in the woods with the serpent, seemed swayed by the dramatic excesses of his blood father. I saw a familiar look of compassion in the boy's eye, as I'd seen in the past when he'd witnessed the cruelty of man against man, or animal against animal.

In contrast to the feigned sadness of his son and the ill-gotten sympathy of his grandson, Zeus threw back his head and laughed. "This?" he erupted amidst guffaws, "the new king of Heaven? This slip of a boy?"

"It was foretold, Father," Athena said quietly.

"Foretold?" Zeus demanded. "Never to me!"

"Yes, to you. For was it not prophecy which caused you to trick my mother, Metis to turn herself into a fly? Was it not prophecy which caused you to swallow her, whole and live, so that I was born within your very head?"

Zeus's demeanor darkened, but still he smiled. "Metis's son was predicted to take my throne."

"The fates are not so easily thwarted, Father. For though Metis bore only a daughter to you, that daughter has born a son. You forced me to surrender my chastity, so the son of Metis's line was born of your own spite and cruelty. They are your undoing, for they fathered this child!"

As Athena spoke so forcefully, the assembled gods began to stand and cluster – some about Zeus and some about her. Ares stood with his father, Hera with her favorite son, and so with Zeus. Hephaestus, who had always admired Athena and liked mortals better than gods, though he disliked people in general, came to our side. And so with the others. Each god took a side.

Ares looked pleadingly at the boy. "Would you turn on the father you've never known? Would you stand against the just and rightful king of the gods? Has your mother's hatred so infected your heart, that you cannot see she is only using you for revenge?"

"Silence, Ares!" snapped Athena.

"No," muttered Raxes. "No, let him speak."

"He is the king of lies, my son," said Athena. He says only what is needed to foment hostility and violence."

Raxes took a step toward Ares. "He is my father." It wasn't a heartfelt declaration. It was more the statement of one trying to grasp a difficult concept. Raxes was trying to decide how he felt about having the war god for a father and what it meant to him. Nevertheless, Ares smiled proudly.

"Choose carefully, Raxes," said the War God gently. "If you make the wrong choice, we shall be forever separated, and that would break my heart."

Zeus looked pointedly at Raxes. "Well, boy? Will you be the instrument of my downfall, as planned?"

The boy looked from one to the other of us: at Athena, at Ares, at Zeus, at me. There was confusion in his eyes, with a hard edge of resentment. No doubt he resented being put in this position. Only days ago, those eyes had been wide and innocent, viewing heaven and earth only as places of great wonder.

What had we done?

Raxes set his jaw. "No," he said weakly. "No, I'll have no part of it. I won't fight a battle because you tell me to, or because fate decrees it." His voice went cold, and he added, "I'm not some mortal you can use for your entertainments."

The gods who had gathered about us began to edge away, casting their eyes sideways, to see what others were doing. They knew of the prophecy, of my fore-knowledge. They knew the power to overthrow the King lay with Raxes. Without his backing, they would not be so foolish as to stand with us.

Zeus nodded, grimacing. "It seems your champion doubts your prophecy, Fire-thief, which doubt eliminates my need to trounce him and allows me to move directly to dispensing justice. Prometheus, you and my daughter will leave this place, never to return. I banish you from Olympus and from earth. That leaves you Hades. If you think you can find a fourth

alternative, I welcome you to take it. In any event, you will leave my sight."
He stepped toward the boy. "You, Raxes..."

Our son looked up and regarded his Grandfather. Although nearly grown to full godhood, he still looked tiny next to Zeus. I must admit, I was more concerned with his welfare and emotional state than any punishment Zeus might declare for us. I had been banished, and worse, before, but I hoped Zeus would have the good grace –

"You will be imprisoned within a volcano, I think, beneath the earth. It's kept the Titans in check – "

As the gods around us gasped, Raxes protested, "Mighty Zeus, I have done nothing! I was merely included in the schemes of others!"

"Innocence does not impress me. Male child of the line of Metis, I have long known you would be a threat, if you surfaced. Ares, take him away now."

If ever a god had been loyal to Zeus, it was Ares. There was no nobility in his loyalty. He supported his father because he was treated by him with such favor; and because battles tended to erupt whenever Zeus was around. Ares lived for conflict, so, he stood by his father in all things.

Now he turned on Zeus. "Father, no! He is my son!"

Zeus waved dismissively. "You have sons aplenty. Have some more, if it'll make you feel better. But this one must go."

"No!" whined Ares. "Father, I beg you! Let him stay with me! I have just learned of his existence!"

Liar!

Ares gathered Raxes in a one-armed embrace. "He'll be a good boy, won't you, son? I'll vouch for him. If he misbehaves, you can send us both away! You'll behave, won't you, Raxes?"

Putting love ahead of his security and comfort? I never thought Ares had it in him.

Raxes was not moved. He looked witheringly at the man who had sired him and pulled out of his grasp. "I promise nothing. I want no part of any of you."

Zeus's fury reached its peak. His eyes flashed, spilling jagged lightning bolts out from them. His hands glowed, as his body prepared to manifest its dread power. "Enough! Take him and imprison him! Now!"

Father and son locked eyes while the grandson looked away. Just what was happening in Raxes's mind I could not fathom. After a long minute, Ares looked away. His voice dead to feeling, he almost whispered, "I will not lift a hand against him. Do what you will."

Enraged, Zeus hurled himself forward. The other gods fled back toward the walls, making themselves as small as they could in the eyes of their king. I thought Zeus would land on Ares, but he ignored his son. His body crackling with primal force, he seized Raxes by the throat, lifted him off his feet, and reared back to hurl him bodily from the room. He had once cast Hephaestus from Mount Olympus in this way. Athena's nails dug into my arm and she gasped aloud, seeing her child threatened. We both leaped forward.

Then everything burst into flame.

Not everything, truth be told, only Zeus and Raxes. After a moment I could see the boy was the source of the fire. It licked out from the very core of him, snaking about his opponent and swallowing Zeus. The old god shrieked in agony, for even gods feel pain when struck by god-generated forces. That is why they all ran in fear of Zeus's thunderbolts. Now, it seemed, one of his offspring had manifested a similarly frightening power.

Trembling in pain, Zeus stepped away from the boy, his skin red and raw. Smoke poured from his now-nude body. His clothing had burned away in the blast. Gritting his teeth, he raised his arm and made a throwing gesture in the boy's direction, as though tossing a shot-put. From his fingers, a bolt of lightning erupted and struck Raxes square in the chest.

The boy tripped backwards, nearly falling. He screamed. The skin of his chest was blackened and charred, but his face showed only rage, not pain. Holding out both arms, as if beckoning a paramour into an embrace, he summoned a tremendous flash of fire. It flowed forward, consuming Zeus, driving him to his knees. He opened his mouth to scream again, but Raxes did not let up. A second wash of flame cascaded over his grandfather. Zeus clutched his head in his hands and fell forward, trembling. Still, Raxes continued. He stalked forward, standing over the suffering god, and raised his hands to strike anew.

Athena rushed to place herself between her father and her son. "Raxes," she cried, taking the boy's face between her hands, "that's enough!"

Raxes looked at her blankly, in his rage not recognizing her.

"He is defeated," Athena pressed. "Your powers are too much for him."

"I thought you wanted him dead," said Raxes through his teeth.

"No," said Athena with sadness, "I wanted nothing that's happened. I only knew he had to be removed from power. By proving your ability to overcome him, you have done that. The gods will follow you, now."

Indeed, the assemblage had circled 'round the boy, their new king. They looked on him speculatively, hopefully, guardedly.

Raxes raised his eyes, scanned each face, then said quietly, defiantly, "No." He looked me, then at his mother. "I shall not take the throne. I do not want it."

The gods gasped.

"Raxes, my son, please – " my wife began, but he held up a hand to stay her words.

"You only claimed me as your son when you wanted me to carry out your plans."

"I did not claim you," Athena explained, "because Zeus would have exacted revenge on you, destroyed you if he could, imprisoned you if he could not. He could not know of your existence until the time was right."

I could see that her words did not sway him, and so I tried to reach him. The boy and I had been so close, perhaps he would listen to me. "Raxes, I know that you feel used and betrayed, but you must understand why we did what we did. The very fact that we had to deceive you shows how corrupt Zeus's reign was. That he was too powerful and too capricious is evidenced by the fact that we had to hide you from him. I came for you as soon as it was safe and raised you as my own – "

" – Raised me to act out my part in your drama," he finished bitterly.

"Raised you to be a hero, a deliverer, to your people," I corrected. "But never as a mere pawn in a game, Raxes! My affection for you – "

"Is like the affection of the fisherman for the worm!" he spat. "Do not speak to me of affection, Prometheus! You have betrayed me! You are what Zeus called you – a pretender! You pretended to be a mere advisor, while seeking the throne for yourself. You pretended to be a loving father to me, when, in fact..." He turned to regard Ares, whose arrogant face was stone as he watched these events. "I have a father."

Raxes took a step forward, held out his arms and took Ares's shoulders, moving as if he would embrace the god of war. "Ares," he choked, "you have been a victim of deceit, just as I have. They did not tell you you had a son. I did not know who was my real father. They offer me the throne of heaven, but all I want is to live honestly. I want to know the god who gave me life. I want to be a son to my father, a son he can be proud of. Come, Father. Leave this horrid place with me, and let us live as father and son should."

Athena's face was stone. I tried to keep my own so, but I believe I failed. My wife, devoted as she was to reason, was more adept than I at keeping her emotions in check. Though these events might be causing her unbearable pain, she stood proud. For my part, though I knew all this would happen, I still stood shocked, unbelieving, as this child I had raised to manhood rejected me. I would sooner have spent another thousand years chained to the mountainside, with the eagle tearing my flesh each day, than ever again live through this moment. I fought back tears of shame that Raxes should turn to the closest thing I had to an immortal enemy, and offer him the title, "Father."

But, like father like son, Ares did not want the honor offered him. After a moment's silence, he raised his arm and struck Raxes's face with the back of his hand, hard. The boy reeled from the force of the impact and clutched a hand to his cheek, his eyes wide with shock and pain.

"Coward!" spat Ares. "Fool! Who are you to deny destiny? Who are you to refuse the throne, when it is offered?"

"But, Father – " the astonished boy began.

"You are no son of mine!" hissed Ares. "I will not claim you! You have dishonored the gods! Raised your hand against our rightful leader! I curse the day your were born!"

Raxes backed away from his just-discovered father, tears in his eyes but staying there. He shook his head in the slow manner of one who simply does not believe that with which he is confronted. He held Ares's gaze until the other looked away in disgust. Then he trained his eyes on his mother, then on me.

"None of you are worthy of the title of 'god!' You care for nothing but your games of power! I..." His emotions overcame him. He couldn't speak. Instead, he turned, fled the room and left us there, three pretenders to the throne, and the huddled mass of a dethroned king on the floor.

For the first time since Raxes was born, Athena, goddess of wisdom and reason, wept.

FIFTEEN

I awoke to find myself still lying on the couch on the terrace. I was back in my own body, back in New Olympus. Athena and Prometheus watched over me with expectation, Hylas with concern.

"You had a vision?" asked Hylas.

"I suppose that's what you call it."

"As good a name as any," agreed Prometheus. "It was, in fact, a direct transfer of my memories to your mind. I showed you the final days of Olympus. The beginning of the feud between Raxes and the rest of us."

"But..." I wondered, trying to absorb it all, "how did you come to be here? On this world? With Raxes? What happened to Zeus and Ares?" I couldn't believe I was speaking of ancient, mythical gods as though they were acquaintances of mine.

But they were!

"Ares attempted to claim the throne himself," explained Athena. "He did not enjoy the support of the gods, however. They respected his prowess in battle, because it brought them exciting entertainments; but they knew he was too self-absorbed, too unstable, to rule them. My father... left."

"Where?" I asked.

I saw a goddess shrug, an odd sight. "We never knew. He ascended from Olympus toward the sky. He was a sky god, after all. I suppose he was comfortable there."

"Like Jesus, ascending to Heaven," I muttered.

"There are many parallels," observed Prometheus, "between the stories and worship of your Jehovah and those of our kind."

"Except my God is real," I maintained.

Prometheus chuckled, "And we are... what?"

I chose not to answer. I did not believe they were actually gods, but neither did I want to have that argument. I was satisfied that they had once been on earth. The primitive people of the time would have thought them gods.

"Ares went to live among the mortals," Athena went on, "where he engendered many wars. For all I know, he still exerts his influence over your people. I became queen."

Prometheus squeezed her hand. "And ushered in a new golden age."

"For half of the people of New Earth, when they're not at war."

"Why did Scorpius say that you murdered Ares?" I wondered, "if he still lives?"

"Because he is no longer alive," Athena said carefully, "in the way he once was. Without us to support him, Ares... lost his identity. Parts of his consciousness entered into mortals. Parts of theirs entered into him. He became... dispersed. Or perhaps absorbed. Though his spirit of warfare lives on, he is no longer an individual. He is not worshiped by name.

"Gods need worship, to maintain their sense of self. Like many dependencies, this one is destructive to its victim."

"That's all very... metaphysical," I observed.

"It's all too real a phenomenon, I assure you. Many of our number have been lost this way."

"But what happens to their physical bodies?" I asked. What she described sounded like the inverse of death to me, the loss of the spirit, rather than the body.

"For our kind, the link between spirit and matter is different from what you're accustomed to. A healthy spirit can restore a damaged body, even reassemble a destroyed body from its component elements."

"Create life from dust?" I asked.

A smile played about her lips. "Isn't that what gods do? What is physical life, anyway, aside from a set of chemical reactions? It simply needs the correct conditions and components to be triggered. We can easily control these conditions. When the spirit fails, however... what happens to the body is inconsequential."

I wasn't sure she had answered my question. Perhaps she couldn't. Another mystery nagged at me, though. "If Raxes wanted nothing more to do with you," I asked, "then why is he here with you? Why did you come here to begin with? Why couldn't you usher in your new golden age on earth?"

"The influence of Ares, coupled with generations of being used by Zeus as pawns in games of war, was too strong on earth. The majority of humanity was married to violence and the use of force. Reason could not hold dominion over their minds, nor could thoughts of the arts. Reason and creativity are the activities of individual minds, working independently. Minds twisted to function only as cogs in a larger machine are incapable of such pursuits. The only opening I had with most humans was as the goddess of strategic warfare. But successful campaigns in war are only of benefit if, once the land is secure, its people's thoughts turn back to building, rather than tearing down."

"The Friends believe that a nation built on war cannot be turned to gentler pursuits. If our origins lie in violence, our course is already decided."

"You may be right," said Athena. "In any event, I gathered a cadre of humans who were open to my influence – philosophers, artists, musicians – and brought them here, to build a new human world."

"And Raxes? After what had happened – "

"Shep, I know you have never been a parent, but... Could you yet conceive turning your back on someone you loved, even if they'd rejected and betrayed you? You were shocked to your very core when you learned the truth about Hylas's people, and yet he is still with you. Your friend Philip is a despicable waste of human flesh, and yet you brought him here to protect him. Would you expect me, then, to leave earth and abandon my only child?"

"No, but I'm surprised, after what I saw, that he'd accompany you." As I was surprised, after all I had put him through, that Hylas sat beside me even now.

"It wasn't easy," admitted Prometheus. "Raxes wouldn't speak to us for a human century. And when he did... well, you've seen how belligerent he is."

"He's hurt," I observed.

"And he holds onto his pain," Athena sighed. "When I promised him that he would be left alone, he agreed to accompany us here. He too saw how devoted humans were to his father. He knew he could make no place for himself on earth. We agreed that he would be allowed to foster a community of worshipers for himself – "

"The Aspar?"

"Yes. You see what kind of people he has been patron to."

"Indeed. The Aspar are obsessed with war, and I suppose Raxes's resentment of you is reflected in their sexual customs. Those are like a little boy's dream, a playground open to boys only. Filthy girls are used for gratification or reproduction and then done away with out of hand, and the only allegiances are to one's fellow boys."

Hylas winced, and I realized I had gotten caught up in my analysis and forgotten that I was talking about the only home he had ever known.

"My own world is not without its faults," I said to him. "I don't mean..." I didn't know how to finish.

He shrugged. "I left my countrymen behind when I came with you. I... I'm trying to keep an open mind."

"Always wise," offered Athena.

I wanted to say more, but what was I to say? I could tell Hylas that I didn't tar him with the same brush as I did his people, but... was that true? Although I hadn't condemned him for deceiving me into sexual congress, neither did I believe it was acceptable that he did so. I still questioned his true sense of justice, especially where women were concerned. He was not a Christian. Could he be truly just?

My thoughts were interrupted as Vintinus rushed in, concern evident on his usually elfin, mirthful face. "My Queen," he announced, "Your son, Raxes – "

She nodded. "He's arrived. I was expecting him. Do not trouble yourself, Vintinus. Let him come as he will."

From within the palace we heard the sound of slamming doors and hurried footsteps approaching. A youthful, angry voice called out, "Athena? Dammit, woman, where are you hiding?"

The goddess shook her head in exasperation and replied loudly, "I am not hiding, Raxes. I am on the terrace."

A halo of pale yellow light splashed over the entry to the building, heralding the boy-god's arrival. Pale yellow, I observed, was not the color he had radiated in our previous encounter. I wondered at the properties of his self-generated fire. Did it shift with his mood? He sounded no less angry than he had been at our first meeting.

When he appeared through the door and came among us, it also seemed to me that he looked older, still a young man by all visible evidence, but with a weariness in his eyes, a sunken appearance. He seemed to have grown thin. Was I contrasting him with the version I'd seen in my visions? That Raxes had been over a thousand years younger. At what age did a god pass his prime?

He looked at me first and with disapproval. "Getting your new pet acclimated?" he asked his mother. "Taught him any tricks?"

"Behave yourself, Raxes," said Prometheus. "You are a guest. So is Shep."

"You put me on par with a mortal?"

"A guest is a guest," replied the elder god. "You know that. I taught you manners."

"Manners!" scoffed Raxes. "Always maintaining appearances, oblivious to the truth! A pity you never took to teaching honesty, Prometheus."

"It is an old and tired argument," said Athena.

"But relevant, old woman." Raxes gestured at me. "Your consort chides me for my manners with your guest, and yet, has an honest word passed your whoring lips in his presence? You tell him he's my equal – a lie! You treat him with kindness and graciousness, only disguising your intentions to use him to your own ends! You'd take the filthy mortal to your bed, were it necessary to distract him from – "

I came to my feet, almost unaware. "Quiet, boy!" I barked out. "A man, no matter his age, does not address his mother in such a fashion!"

Prometheus gave me a look of appreciative surprise. I thought Athena was going to laugh. Hylas, on the other hand, looked as though he wanted to find a place to hide. His eyes said to me, "Now you've done it, Shep. He's going to kill you. More than once."

But Raxes, while not amused, took my rebuke in stride. "Jehovah says that we must honor our parents and obey them in all things."

"That's right," I said.

Raxes stepped closer to me and held my eye. "But what if your parents only want to use your abilities to their own selfish ends?"

"Perhaps they're wiser than you give them credit for being," I replied. "Perhaps you should try having a little faith."

He laughed harshly. "And do you have faith in the goddess Athena, Shepherd Autrey? Do you have faith in the one who snatched you from your world and brought you here to fight her battles? If you're going to defend her, you should at least know who and what she is. Tell him... Mother."

"What does he mean?" I asked Athena. "Is he referring to the Oracle's instructions?"

"Not entirely, no," said Athena. "In fact, it was I who brought you here across space, from your own world. I had watched events on earth from time to time, and I noted the coming of your Christian religion with interest. It held promise to become a philosophy which might teach humanity the peace and spiritual fulfillment I sought for them."

"You... approve... of the worship of another god?" I asked.

"Why shouldn't I? I was one of hundreds of gods on earth. Do you think I expected all mortals to pray to me only? It would be unrealistic, to say the least. But Christianity turned into one more power-grabbing establishment among your people, one more excuse to murder and torture each other. Its message of brotherhood was lost almost as soon as it began. Then your Society of Friends was formed, Shep, and I thought perhaps there was hope once again. Oh, I'd seen reason for hope before – the Enlightenment, the Renaissance, Galileo, Da Vinci, Rousseau – many advances in science and philosophy and art, but a movement which focused on peace... that was truly of interest to me.

"I can't say that your voice rose higher than those of your comrades as I observed, for most of you were far more open, spiritually, than the rest of humanity. But when you thought you were dying, and you called out to God in a prayer of harmony and acceptance... That was when I was able to truly hear you, to connect with you, and bring you here."

"So that was your doing. I had wondered."

"I hope it was not too jarring for you, this method of transport."

"Well, finding oneself suddenly on a field of battle is a little disconcerting, but when one has only a moment before been dangling from a tree with a rope about one's neck... I suppose it was far worse for those poor fools who were trying to kill me."

"How so?" she asked.

"Well, when I simply vanished – "

"You did not vanish," said Athena. "You died."

"How's that?"

"Your body died on earth. It has since been buried. I brought only your consciousness across the heavens, and placed it in a new, reconstituted body."

"I see..." I muttered. I supposed I should mourn the passing of my earthly body, yet... here I was, in a body identical to it. There was no evidence to support any claim that I had lost the body I'd been born with. "So... I was that interesting to you."

"Yes. I brought you here to see if your presence might change the course of events on New Earth."

"Like bringing in a new stud to improve the stock?"

"Hardly flattering, but an apt comparison."

"And Philip? Why him?"

"Because he was your companion, and you seemed so devoted to him. I sense that has changed. Oh well, Hylas and Xhylanna are both more fit companions for you. Higher intelligence, strong moral fiber. They can aid you in – "

"Now just a minute!" Raxes loomed over her, wagging a finger. "I frankly don't care what you do with this earth beast, or your fallen priestess; but the boy is mine!"

Athena waved a hand dismissively. "The boy is clearly far more devoted the Shep than to any of us, Raxes. Leave him alone."

Raxes, paused, swallowed, and his yellow aura paled to a sickly gray. He took a moment, as if to gather his resolve, then exclaimed, "I will not! Hylas is one of the most worthy of his generation. He would have developed into a prize warrior and leader, until you threw this... " he glared at me, "unmanly peace-lover into the mix. I will not have so promising a specimen wasted on an experiment which proves nothing, other than that even gods may become senile!"

"You'd prefer he spend his life leading armies to kill anything that walks, I suppose?" asked Athena.

"It is the game the humans play. It is no more meaningless than your games for control of Heaven, Mother." He sniffed. "I demand that Hylas be returned to me."

Athena heaved a very tired sigh. "I suppose this is to be a challenge, then?"

"Absolutely."

With no enthusiasm, she sighed, "Very well, then, for the allegiance of Hylas – "

"Just a minute," I interrupted. Hylas grabbed my arm and squeezed it painfully. I waved him off. "Has anyone thought to ask Hylas? What if he doesn't want to be returned to Raxes's service?"

"What he wants is irrelevant," said Raxes. "I can easily make him forget his time with you."

As he voiced the threat, it occurred to me how appalling it was. Hylas? Forget me? But he was so devoted and... and yes, I enjoyed his admiration.

I valued his friendship, even if it was encumbered with alien ideas, even if he had tricked me into committing a sin with him, he...

"You can't just make a human being the stakes in your battle!" I said.

"It is not 'our' battle," said Raxes. "It will be yours."

"What?" I wondered.

"Gods do not battle one another," said Athena. "It is a firm custom by which we live. Even though he does not recognize my authority, Raxes may not battle me. The other gods would not tolerate it. Until and unless he is ready to challenge me for the throne itself, Raxes will not raise a hand against a fellow god."

"I have no interest in your political games, old woman," said Raxes.

"Then whom do you expect to battle?" I asked. "For I will not."

"You will," said Raxes, "or your Hylas will be lost to you."

"This is insane!" I cried.

"It is the way such disagreements must be worked out," said Athena. "Conflict may occur only among mortals, acting on our behalf."

"So," I said sourly, "you have legislated peace in Heaven by shunting war to earth?"

"By leaving man and woman the choice to fight," said Athena. "They can refuse, if they wish."

"If they are willing to accept the consequences," said Raxes. "Most are not. You, for instance, Shepherd Autrey, are surely not willing to allow Xhylanna to be harmed, or to lose control of Hylas."

"I do not control Hylas," I said, "but I would certainly not wish to see his memory tampered with. He should be free – "

"Then you must fight for his freedom," Raxes said savagely.

I met his gaze and said slowly. "I will not fight."

"Then Hylas is mine," snapped Raxes. "And I will take him from you now."

I shrugged, and sat back down on the couch. "Do what you will, Raxes. What's the point in my resisting you?"

The war god looked puzzled. "Don't you care?"

"I do," I said. "I do care." I looked across to Hylas, reaching out to grasp his shoulder. "You are the truest friend I could imagine having, Hylas," I said to him, ignoring the others. "You are my reward for every false friendship I have ever wasted my affections on." I cast a sideways glance at Philip. "But I cannot stop Raxes. I could fight. I might win, but then what?" I turned to look at Raxes. "Would you really let him go? Give up your prize warrior?"

"I – " Raxes began.

"Of course you wouldn't," I interrupted. "You would never forgive or forget the insult of my converting one of your own to the ways of peace. You'd constantly engineer ways to hurt us, to enfold us in your idiotic wars. It's the only way you can amuse yourself. The only way you can find to have revenge on your mother for... for whatever wrong it is you imagine she's committed against you."

"Empty words," said Raxes. "His friendship with you is nothing but a string of disappointments, Hylas. For all his talk of peace, what kind of a man stands by and lets his friend be taken?"

"I cannot prevent you from taking him," I said, standing to confront Raxes. "I cannot stand against you. You claim to be a god – "

"I am a god!"

"I do not believe that, but you have great power. More power than I do. I cannot hope to resist you."

"Then you concede?"

I shook my head. "I will not lift my hand in violence to a fellow man."

"You have killed! I saw you!"

"In desperation, yes, and I begged God's forgiveness – "

"Which god?"

"The only one," I said pointedly. "The one who forgives me the sin of murder, and gives me the courage to resist sinning again. With His aid, I will not fight or kill my fellow man."

Raxes gestured with one hand, as though he were a stage magician, calling his audience's attention to some magnificent act of illusion. In the open space before us on the terrace, a ball of light flared into being. Around it the air began to whirl in a pattern like a cyclone. I could feel its disturbance on my skin as it picked up speed. Dust gathered from everywhere, caught up in the hot wind. Within the ball, shadowy forms began to take shape and appeared to move under their own power. As I watched, the light dimmed. My view of these shapes clarified.

Even before the wind died, I saw what Raxes had materialized. I exclaimed and rushed forward, for where the light had gone was my own beloved Xhylanna, whole and healthy! Beside her was Philip, now unrestrained and likewise none the worse for wear.

Raxes held up a hand to stop me. "Wait!" he commanded.

I ignored him and held out my arms to my bride. A smile engulfing her lovely face, she made to run toward me. Then she froze, just as suddenly as she had appeared, just as surely as I had frozen the guard in Aspar only a few nights ago.

"You will not be allowed near her," hissed Raxes. "I have brought her here for purposes of demonstration only."

"What – ?" I began.

"You've been told already that gods do not fight gods. We choose champions. My... mother..." his nose wrinkled with distaste at the word, "has chosen you. I choose your erstwhile friend Meigs."

"What?" I demanded again. "Philip, in the name of Christian charity, tell him you'll have no part in this!"

Philip smiled coldly. "Why would I tell him that, Shep? I volunteered to be the champion of Raxes. It seemed the only way to protect myself, given the way you've turned on me these last few days."

"Philip, you're a fool! You know I will not fight you. Indeed, you've seen the powers Athena has granted me. Were I to fight you, you'd stand no chance!"

His lip curled up, exposing teeth and changing the smile to a predator's sneer. "Perhaps, if you took a moment to think about it, you would realize that one god can as easily grant his champion special powers as can the next. Athena gave you powers – "

"The powers of peaceful restraint and healing," I reminded him.

He nodded. "As she would, wont to augment your natural proclivities. I, on the other hand, have never been as committed to peace and healing as you."

"That's painfully apparent!"

"So mine are not powers of life," he continued, "but of death."

"You propose to kill me? Then stop running your fool mouth and try!"

"I propose to defeat you, Shep, not kill you. Defeat is so much more satisfying a goal. Defeating you means forcing you to fight."

"That you will never do!"

"No? I'm well aware that you won't fight to defend yourself, but suppose I were to turn my powers of death on... others?"

A chill ran down my spine as I realized the implications of his words. "Philip – " I began.

He ignored me. He turned to Xhylanna and gestured as Raxes had. Her mobility returned and she finished a step forward, only to be caught by Philip's arm.

"Leave her alone!" I warned him.

Again, he smiled at me and said pleasantly, "No."

Gently he lifted his hand to caress Xhylanna's face. She screamed. Clutching her throat as though strangling, she writhed in pain and shrieked until her voice was raw. I stepped toward her, only to find my progress impeded as I struck an invisible barrier. It yielded enough to avoid injuring me, but held me fast in my place.

"Xhylanna!" I cried out.

She could not hear me. Her face had gone purple, and now blood began to trickle from her nose and mouth. She had stopped screaming and begun gasping for air, emitting a sickly, gurgling sound. She coughed and the blood was everywhere.

I did not have to be a physician to know... my Xhylanna was dying.

From my lungs came a scream like none I'd ever heard, much less believed I was capable of producing. Forgetting all else, I rushed at Philip, determined to rip the sneering face from his skull with my bare hands. He had killed my wife, and he would suffer the most painful death I could manage to inflict on a fellow human being. There was no God. There was no Christ. I was a follower of no one. I was a killer, and he was going to die.

I struck the invisible wall and rebounded with such force that I fell on my backside.

Raxes stepped over me, unhindered by his own barrier. His color had changed again. He was back to yellow, and it was a healthier yellow that bathed him, more like sunshine than bile.

"Good," he purred at me. "That's much better, Shep. Now you are behaving as a man should. Kill or be killed!"

I spat at him, not caring that the stream missed and landed on my own leg.

He ignored the insult. "I want you to kill him, of course, or at least try. Although he is my champion, his death would be a victory for me nonetheless, for it would mean that I'd won you to my side."

"Never!" I managed.

"You can't help it, Shep. You're only mortal. Like all your kind, if pushed hard enough, you will kill; but I don't want you to kill in a rage. No, I want you to make the rational choice to kill. I want you to make your plans carefully, end your friend's life systematically, knowing logically that only thus may you keep Hylas's allegiance and save Xhylanna."

I bit back a sob at the mention of her name. "Xhylanna is dead."

He smiled brightly. "No! She's still alive. I've frozen her at the moment of death. Kill him – " he gestured absently at Philip, " – and she can be healed and returned to you."

"No!" screamed Philip, inflamed by the lack of attention, by being treated as a mere pawn. "I will kill him, Lord Raxes! You will see!"

Raxes shrugged. "Either way, I win. If you die, Shep, Xhylanna dies. And Hylas will still be mine."

"No," came a weak but determined voice.

Raxes, surprised, looked to its source, and I raised up on my shoulder and followed his gaze.

It was Hylas who had spoken. He stood, facing his former god, frightened, yes, but resolved to speak his piece. The set of his jaw said he knew his own mind and would not be swayed. He advanced on Raxes. "I will never belong to you! I will never follow you! Kill me if you like. Torture me. Do the same to those I love. I will not follow you. Shep is right! This violence must end, and the worship of creatures like you must end with it!"

Raxes was enraged, even pained by this. I saw it in his eyes. He swallowed hard. The healthy golden glow faded again. Was it Hylas who had done that? By rejecting Raxes, had he affected the false god's power?

"You have no say in this." Raxes's voice shook. "You cannot simply break the training of a lifetime! I will push you until you follow my ways, just as I pushed him!" He pointed to me. "Mortals are easy to manipulate.

Take from them that which they love, and they fight! Your reflex is my power!" He paused, considering. "Perhaps I should make you kill Meigs, little Hylas. Or let him kill you, to sweeten the hatred of Shep's battle. I can always bring you back, if – "

I stood, grabbed the boy-god by his shoulder and shoved him. He whirled on me, shocked by the indignity. "You dare – "

"Shut up!" I commanded him. His eyes narrowed, but he was silent for the moment. I shook my head at him in disgust. "Truly you are evil," I said. "You would drive us to murder and to die for no reason but your own pleasure, and then you resurrect us at your whim? Does life mean so little?"

I turned to Athena and Prometheus, who had stood by and watched all of this. "And you! You claim to love humanity!" I gestured to where Xhylanna lay at the brink of death. "This woman has been your most ardent follower! How can you allow this? Why do you stand by while your spawn works evil? Help her, damn you!"

Before they could answer, Raxes was at my shoulder, speaking with such encouragement in his voice that you'd never know I had just condemned him.

"You can force their hands, Shep. All you have to do is worship them and they will be honor-bound to protect you – to grant you favors! Show them fealty, and you will have all you want!"

"What idiocy are you spouting? A god is not hidebound by the whims of a mortal, any more than – "

"It is true, Shepherd," interrupted Athena. "We are bound by honor, by our emotional and spiritual need for worship, to answer the prayers of our worshipers. If you swear allegiance to one of us, and crave our intervention, we must save Xhylanna and stop Raxes."

It would be so easy to mouth the words. If, unbelievable as it sounded, all I had to do was fly their colors and my wish would be granted... I looked to Xhylanna, frozen so near to death. She could be safe and warm and in my arms again... I would do it. I had only to say...

"No," I choked. "No, dammit! I love the Lord with all my heart and all my soul. I cannot betray Him."

"Then ask Jehovah to save your beloved," mocked Raxes. "Won't he do it?"

"He will save her soul, if she's willing," It echoed a hollow note in my ears, even as I said it.

"But he will not restore her to health? Not much of a god!"

"I would follow Him sooner than you, had He no power at all!"

"Shep," Prometheus coaxed gently, "we will help you, if you will let us."

He sounded so sincere. This... man... whatever he was, divine or human... he cared about humanity. That much I could not deny.

"He's tempted," said Raxes, amused. "He's really tempted, Step-Father." The boy god seized my chin in his hand and forced me to face him. He moved in close, his breath hot on my face. It was like leaning in too close to the fireplace. "But before you commit yourself, know this. You call me evil, but, human, the very Lord of Evil stands before you! The one who sent you the dreams. The one who plotted to overthrow the king of Heaven! The one who was cast out!"

The one who... yes, I'd made the connection early on. The Pretender. The Fallen Angel. I had assumed, of course, that I knew to whom such titles referred. But then I'd met Prometheus, lived his thoughts and emotions with him, seen him as a friend of Man. I'd felt dis-proven in my early assumptions. He couldn't be...

"You call me evil?" pressed Raxes. "Look at him and call him by his name!"

I looked at him, but couldn't say the words. I shook my head. "You can't be."

Prometheus looked sad. He grimaced, but nodded gently. "But I am. I cannot lie to you on that score, Shep. I assure you, I am Satan."

SIXTEEN

I am not often rendered speechless. I like to think that doesn't mean I talk to excess, but I am rarely at a loss for words, even when confronted with the unexpected or the unlikely. This statement from Prometheus, however, left me gawking in silent amazement. He seemed so inoffensive, so generous. His was a completely sympathetic presence, and yet...

I assure you, I am Satan.

He said it without shame, without apology, and yet with complete awareness, I think, of the exact effect it must have on me. And the effect was profound. I was torn to the breaking point. These creatures, these "gods"... one wanted to manipulate me into evil, the other openly admitted he was Satan! And I was somehow expected to choose sides!

I wished for silence. Had I been among Friends, I certainly might have had it. In the midst of this pathetic excuse for a divine family, however, although they were quiet at the moment, I could not depend upon it silence continuing for long. Relieved of the distractions of noise and discord, I might have sought the Lord's wisdom. How was a believer to answer such a confession? Had it been only my life on the line, I could have easily spit in all their faces and let them do what they might to me.

It was not my life on the line, however. It was Xhylanna's life, as well as Hylas's freedom.

Xhylanna... until Philip had worked his evil power against her, I had not realized the depth of my feelings for her. How could I not, you might wonder? Indeed, what sort of fool meets the perfect woman, beds her, marries her, and does not conceive all along what life might be like if she were taken away from him? My sort of fool, I suppose. In my defense, I can only say that everything had happened so fast there had not been time for reflection.

Now, as she had nearly died before me, I knew: I would die for this woman. I would kill for this woman. I would do anything – anything! – to keep her at my side.

And all I had to do was kill my detestable friend.

They would restore Xhylanna's health; Philip would no longer threaten us; and I would have played right into the hands of evil. The battle would continue. Raxes would never concede defeat, and I would be but a tainted opponent for his pawns. Or was I tainted already, no matter the decision I made now? Prometheus had placed his thoughts, his dreams inside my head. He and his bride had granted me my powers. The devil already had a hold on me.

Something struck me from behind, and I lost my balance. Arms wrapped around my midsection, dragging me to the ground. I was flipped on my back, and my assailant landed heavily on top of me.

Philip. I had allowed myself to be distracted too long, and he had grown impatient for the battle in which he would prove himself to his new god. He struck me in the face with his fist, his teeth bared in a feral snarl. All humanity was gone from him, if, indeed, he had ever possessed any.

I pressed my arms against the ground and gained leverage enough to throw him off me. I was bigger than he, and had always been stronger.

From his new, undignified position, he laughed coldly and spat, "This isn't a physical battle, you know."

He raised a hand, pointed at me. My right arm went numb. I lifted it before me to examine it, and discovered the flesh was suddenly wrinkled and aged, as though it belonged to a man a century old. The limb was withered and dying. Of course, Raxes had granted Philip the power of death. It seemed he could apply it selectively.

"Why not simply kill me, and be done with it?" I asked.

"Don't think I can't!"

Indeed, I did think he couldn't. I do still. If Athena had granted me powers of life and peace, then they should logically cancel out powers of death and hate. Indeed, if the gifted powers were dependent on the strength of one's will, then I should be more than Philip's equal.

"How does it feel to lose a piece of yourself?" taunted Raxes. "As you have robbed me of Hylas?"

"Have you considered, Raxes," asked Prometheus, "that he might not have robbed you at all? Rather, he may simply have done more to earn Hylas's admiration?"

"What difference will it make when he's dead?" Raxes demanded. "Go on, Meigs, use the power I gave you!"

But before Philip could act, I had used my own power. Almost unbidden, that ability of mine which had saved Xhylanna in battle now caused the vigor to return to my stricken limb. The numbness vanished. The skin filled out again, and smoothed. The color warmed to a normal, youthful hue.

"Sorry, old man," I said to Philip. "It seems my powers are a match for yours." He stepped toward me, goaded into action. "I wonder if the reverse is true," I continued. Gathering my will and focusing on holding him in his place, I commanded, "Stand still!"

He stopped in place, as though he'd struck an invisible wall like the one Raxes had placed before me earlier. He explored it with his hands and, frustrated, beat his palms against it. The wall being intangible, his actions made no sound.

"Why are you doing this, Philip?" I asked him. "What can you hope to gain?"

"The favor of the gods," he spat at me. "Real gods, who can be seen and touched and can directly help me!"

"And Raxes wants this battle?" I pressed on.

"I do!" responded the god. "Because I want you out of my way!"

"But you," I said to Athena and Prometheus, "do you want us to battle?"

Athena said sadly, "We want you to prosper."

"And is war the key to prosperity?" I demanded.

"Much of your race believes so," said Prometheus.

"Then teach them better!"

Philip lunged against my barrier, and the impact, though soundless, was painful to me. It was as if he had thrown his weight against my side.

"We cannot teach those who are unwilling to learn," Athena nodded at my opponent. "As you have tried to teach this one and failed, so have we tried and failed again and again. In so many ways, we are limited to being what our worshipers expect us to be."

Philip lunged again, and the pain shattered my concentration. The barrier dropped, and he was on me. His hands found my throat and his thumbs dug into my windpipe. I gasped for breath and flailed, trying to rip him from me with my hands, to wound him with my knees or feet.

He leered at me. "I'm killing you, you stupid bastard! How does it feel? Why don't you ask your mighty friends to save you, eh? Why don't you ask them to strike me dead?"

"Gods do not battle humans," said Prometheus.

Philip laughed harshly. "You're on your own, old man."

Stars filled my eyes as I lost oxygen. In this position, I could not overpower Philip. Once my mind accepted this fact, I ceased struggling. My only chance of survival lay beyond my physical capabilities. I relaxed my body and engaged my mind. My flesh grew pleasantly warm, but the sensation was not pleasant to my opponent. He screamed and ripped his hands away, as though burned. He examined them, expecting, no doubt, to find damage. There was none, but the moment I'd gained allowed me to again propel him from atop me.

Standing over him, I focused on restraining him where he was, perhaps forcing him to become unconscious. Simultaneously, he was trying his own new abilities on me again. With a snarl, he grabbed my wrists and held them tight. I felt heat radiating from him. It wasn't the pleasant heat of a moment ago, the warm glow of a mind at peace. It was the uncomfortable heat that burned and damaged. In a moment, my hands and then my arms would age and shrivel. Fear struck me. I collected my wits and laughed at it. I would not be afraid. My powers of peace and restraint were more than the equal of his hate-driven abilities.

The heat faded. I remained unaffected. Frustrated, Philip yanked his hands away, reared back and shoved me. I easily maintained my balance by back-peddling.

"That's it, Shep!" called Athena. "You're doing it! Trust in the power I gave you, and he cannot harm you!"

"And then I am free to serve you?" I asked.

"It is I who gave you the power," she reminded me.

"And it is your place to rule over us, especially those who please you."

"That is the way," she agreed.

A strangled cry rang out behind me. Damn me for allowing Athena and Prometheus to draw all my attention! Philip, unnoticed and impatient to prove himself a great killer, and crept up on Hylas, taking him by surprise. Now he had the boy in a head lock and was digging his fingers into the flesh by his throat. He wrenched Hylas's head backward, so I could be sure to see the damage he was inflicting. Blood oozed where his nails dug in, and the flesh around the wound began to fade and wrinkle as mine had earlier.

"Let him go, Philip!" I commanded. "Stop this! Your quarrel is with me!"

Hylas's breath gurgled in his throat as he tried, weakly, to claw away Philip's hands. His strength was failing him. His arms began to age now.

"I don't want to quarrel with you, you fool," snapped Philip, "I simply want you dead. You and any who stand beside you!" He lifted Hylas away from him by the hair and looked into the boy's eyes. They were watery and lifeless. His body quivered helplessly. "It seems I've about accomplished my purpose with this one." He shrugged and cast Hylas to the ground. As his body struck, I swore I heard bones snapping.

With a cry of primal rage I was on him. I did not think of any special powers. I did not think of Christ. I did not think at all. I wanted, I needed, but I only felt want and need. There was no reason behind them. I wanted – I needed! – Philip to be dead. Now.

I pummeled his face with my fists. I've said already I was no fighter. I wasn't accustomed to the sensation of my fists striking the body of another. I am ashamed to say that there was satisfaction in the sinful practice of transforming Philip's face to bloody pulp. He shrieked his protests, but I ignored him. When my knuckles grew sore from repeated impact, I seized his shoulders and beat him against the ground, letting his head flail like it was a rag doll's. Some distant part of me suggested that his neck might be about to break. I didn't care.

Correction: I cared very much. I wanted his neck to break! I wanted him dead. Yes, I decided, I wanted his death and I would have it. To punctuate my realization, I said to him, "I'm going to kill you now, Philip."

God help me!

As I moved to close my fingers about his throat, I saw a warm, red glow from the corner of my eye. I looked up to see Raxes, grinning, standing over me. Philip dimly recognized him as well, and attempted to speak.

"M – my powers," Philip breathed. "What..." His head sank and hit the ground hard.

"Your powers were meant to counter his," explained Raxes gently. "Since Shep eschewed the use of his divine powers, yours could not be brought into play. This is a truly human contest of strength and passion. You have brought two of his loved ones to the brink of death. I'm afraid he has more emotional motivation than you do."

Philip groaned, and I almost felt sorry for him. After what he'd done, though, true sympathy was not in me. I had to act, now, to save Xhylanna and Hylas. I tightened my hands against his flesh. He looked pathetically up at me, and I hesitated.

"Do it!" Raxes urged quietly in my ear. "You must do this, and break free! You cannot stay here and be a pawn of Satan! Kill Philip, and consecrate Hylas to Raxes and to war. Only I can save Hylas now!" As he spoke, his aura deepened in color, red and vibrant like a late summer sunset. It bathed me in its heat, and Raxes stood as tall and powerful as I'd yet seen him. It could be no coincidence that this change in him came at the moment I had erupted in violence.

Perhaps my next action will seem rash to you – rash, unexpected, even bizarre. At that moment in time, that hopeless moment, all that I loved was at risk – yes, indeed, all that I loved!

I realized then that I had never loved earth or any of its citizens. Oh, my family, to be sure. One always loves one's family. One feels sentiment for one's hometown and one's neighbors. A Quaker feels a general, intellectual and spiritual love for all mankind. Despite all of that, I knew, I had never truly, deeply, hopelessly loved before, as I loved my new wife and my new friend.

I dropped Philip like a stone against the hard ground and leapt, in one movement, to Raxes. Before the glowing red boy-god could react, I had a knife against his throat.

(A knife? Yes, taken from Philip. He had been wearing it in a scabbard on his belt since we'd first encountered the Aspar. Said he needed protection in this savage culture. He'd never used it, and I had taken it from him easily. As easily as I might have taken his life, had I not remembered who the real enemy was.)

"You want to see me kill, Raxes?" I asked, holding his neck and pushing him forward, so that the blade dug into his jugular. "I shall kill, then. I'll kill the real author of my suffering! Why should I bother with Philip? Look at him! He's pathetic – too weak to cause me any real harm, now or ever."

Athena gasped at the violence directed at her son, but held her place.

Raxes actually smiled. "You've learned well the sin of murder, haven't you, Jehovah worshiper?"

"Murder? Hardly. I am not tainted by sin in this, nor in anything else that's happened here, come to mention it! In killing you, I am merely doing as Christ instructed. Before attempting to make my peace with god, I must make my peace with man. I have made my peace with this man. He cannot harm me, and I do not fear him. But I cannot make peace with you as a man. Nor are you a god. All I can do with a false god who threatens me and mine is kill him! And that is not murder, for murder is the killing of man!"

He became more serious in demeanor, though not afraid. "You split hairs. Killing is a sin, still, even if you could kill a god."

"I will kill you or die – happily! – trying! And, if I die, Heaven will not be barred to me. I do not sin in protecting these innocents! I do not sin in ending your control over those I love!"

"Innocent?" wondered Raxes. "Do you not deplore Xhylanna's habits of extra-marital intercourse? Or Hylas's homosexuality? Your Bible says those are sins!"

"My Bible," I responded, wondering at my own words, "was written by men. Divinely inspired men who loved God, yes, but men. They could not understand the fullness of His laws, and thus they could not help but err in putting them into flawed, human language. God is love, the love revealed in Christ. Love, pure love, cannot sin."

There were tears in my eyes as I said it, for I was moved by the truth washing over me even as I spoke it. The others saw, I knew, for Athena said quietly, her voice shaking, "Shep?"

"He's babbling!" declared Raxes. "He's lost his mind!"

I relaxed my grip on the dagger, overwhelmed. "Babbling, yes! What I'm feeling, what I'm realizing, is too much for one man's mind! Perhaps I am losing my faculties, but... What a fool I've been! To think that my... times... with Xhylanna were sins! To think... I prayed to the Lord for forgiveness when... when all we did was love! And Hylas..."

I looked to the pathetic heap on the ground, still breathing, by some miracle.

"... All he wanted was my love, my acceptance... demonstrated in the only fashion he was accustomed to. How could that be wrong? His love was pure! Love only becomes sinful when it's motivated by a desire to control what is not ours. To take what doesn't belong to us. Like your attachment to Hylas, Raxes, and all your followers. You don't want them to prosper! You want only – "

I was interrupted by a queer sensation between my shoulder blades. It took a few moments for it to register to me as pain. By that time, the tip of the protruding blade was in my field of vision, thrusting forward through my now-splintered breast bone.

I realized that there was blood everywhere. I realized it was mine. I heard a satisfied, "Die, you son of a bitch!" and I realized that Philip had killed me.

SEVENTEEN

I choked on my own blood, which also oozed from the wound in my chest. I felt a horrid, burning sensation at the point of the sword's entry, a burning and an icy cold, which began to spread. Why was I still aware? Surely I was already dead! No one could survive such a wound as Philip had inflicted upon me, not for long.

But I was still aware – aware, for instance, that Philip, my murderer, was looking down on me. His face was unreadable. It was not compassionate or sorrowful, yet it held no joy or satisfaction at my imminent death. Should he not be happy to be my killer? It was as if he could not believe he had actually done what he had set out to do. As weak as I was, some corner of my mind found the power to think on this and propose that, perhaps, Philip had really sought only his own death in attempting to fight me. I would never know if this was true.

I tried to speak. I wanted to say goodbye to my loved ones, though Xhylanna and Hylas were neither in any shape to hear me. The blood in my mouth and throat prevented me, and I only gurgled.

As if from a hundred miles away, I heard a shuffling and sounds of a struggle by my side. It was not the struggle of battle, but the struggle of one person making a supreme effort to accomplish something far beyond his powers. What was I missing in these final moments?

Something brushed my arm – fingertips. They were wet and cold. Painfully, I turned my head to see their owner. The hilt of the sword in my back dug into me as I moved, impeding my efforts, but I managed to turn enough. A sob wracked me as I realized that it was Hylas who had fought his way, bleeding and dying, to my side. He crawled, inching forward like a cricket with its leg torn off. I met his eyes – they were sunken and aged. His blonde hair had gone white, and his ivory skin was blueish gray. It was a frail old man, the shadow of my friend, come to die at my side. I wanted to tell him to lay where he was, give in, and we would ascend to Heaven together. I could not speak. He clambered forward, coughing, spitting blood. His last act in life would be to fall beside me.

My vision began to blur, and the world darkened. I was dying. Again I tried to mouth the simple word "goodbye."

His hand found its target, seizing my shoulder. Then, thanks be to God, he stopped and rested. Good, I thought. Now we shall face the infinite together. Perhaps Xhylanna's spirit would join us as well, though I prayed she might be spared to live out her worldly life and find Christ. Of Hylas's salvation I had no doubt. He had chosen to follow me, and thus he was a Christian. Properly, he should have followed Christ, but the Lord would not dismiss a follower on a technicality. Would He?

I shut my eyes and prayed. I asked God to receive our souls. It was becoming easy, this prayer of dying. I'd had occasion to use it so often lately. I placed myself in God's hands, and found my soul at peace.

There was heat radiating through my side. Interesting sensation, dying, I thought. Heat and cold alternated. The heat was chasing away the cold, however, and seemed to be spreading through me. The light returned to my eyes, yellow and hot. I realized that the focal points of the growing heat were Hylas's hands on my flesh. (When had he found the strength to touch me with the other?) It was heat like that we had felt when we'd touched and defeated the Aspar; heat like that we had felt when we'd been in each others' arms – and now that thought was less shameful and strange to me. Of course it was. My sins were forgiven. I was dying. Jesus was reaching out to me.

But I realized I wasn't dying. I opened my eyes and saw that the golden light was not the light of Christ, come to raise my soul to heaven. It was the light of the power Hylas and I shared, bathing us as he clasped me and embraced me, pressing his head to my chest. (His head? But he had been unable to lift it!) In wonder, I found that the blood was gone from my mouth.

Looking down, I saw Hylas kneeling over me; but this was not the leprous haunt who had clasped me in a dying embrace only moments ago. He was restored! His face young and smooth again, his muscles filled once more with youthful vigor, his hair glowing like the sun and his eyes, blue, shining with laughter and joy. We were both alive and well.

I reached up and brushed my fingers across the sword, which still protruded from my very heart. Hylas turned me, seized it and, with one fierce yank, pulled it from my back. There was no pain, only a feeling of relief. I looked to the gaping, red hole it had left. To my amazement, it began to close before my eyes. In the golden light the edges of my torn flesh glimmered and seemed to melt together. Soon there was no evidence of the mortal wound I had suffered. I sat up, whole and alive.

Raxes actually smiled in appreciation as I stood and dusted myself off. "I've rarely seen a human who could wield divine power so effectively."

Philip stalked toward me. "Then let me show you how I – "

Raxes waved him off. "You've had your chance, Meigs, and failed. Remove yourself from my presence, or I'll wipe you from existence." Thus dismissing Philip, he focused his sole attention on me. "But you,

Shep. You're magnificent! Now you must swear allegiance to me! I'll give you anything you – "

I backhanded him in the face.

Surprise lit his eyes, but not anger. In fact, he grinned, and the fiery red glow behind and around his skin intensified even more. "That hurt."

"I plan to do more than hurt you, you pathetic excuse for a thinking creature! I'm going to kill you!"

"Oh, Shep, stop this!" exhorted Athena.

"No! Raxes wants battle. I'll give it to him. But I'll make him fight his own battles. He is my enemy."

For his part, Raxes was invigorated by my rage. My sudden turn to violence was feeding him. I believe – forgive me again for being indelicate – he was aroused by my challenge. More, he seemed intoxicated by it. It made sense. When he thought I had taken Hylas from him, his power had faded, visible in the depleted color of his aura. Now, though Hylas was lost to him forever, he was restored by the violence Philip had committed at his behest, and even more so by my desire to kill him.

"Fight me, Raxes!" I challenged him. "Fight me and die!"

I hadn't lost my mind. I knew I couldn't kill him, if he could even be killed. He, on the other hand, just might have been losing his mind. He bared his teeth in a feral grin and laughed, almost giggling. "Yes! Yes I'll fight you!"

As he advanced, swinging a wild punch which I ducked, his mother cried out again. "Raxes, no! Gods do not fight mortals!"

He was lost to reason. I threw myself at him bodily, tackling him and bringing us both careening to the ground. Landing on top of him, I rained blows on his face, bloodying his nose. Through it all, he laughed.

Levering his legs, he threw me from him. I landed at his feet, and he leaped to stand over me. "That round to you, Shep! Get up, and this time I'll trounce you!"

I got up. Fighting was anathema to me, but I was going to see this to the finish, whichever of us it finished, if not both. I advanced, swinging my fist, driving it into his perfect nose. It connected with a solid crunch.

Keep in mind that I had never fought before, aside from my few misadventures here. I had not learned the skills involved. What techniques I was using were those I had seen used in fights I had happened to observe. I would have expected to feel helpless, weak and incompetent. I did not. I felt strong, stronger than I ever had. Was I fueled by my rage, as many warriors were? Did the excitement of battle augment my strength? Or was it something more? I had no basis for comparison.

My limbs felt strong and sure. As I connected each punch with the boy-god, I felt confidence that my fist would find its target. Indeed, I felt an overwhelming certainty that I would win this battle, that I would prevail over my opponent. I could almost picture myself, standing triumphant, having finished him.

I could picture it. It was as if I had somehow gained what some call second sight, the ability to glimpse the future. Foresight... I glanced at Prometheus who watched us. He was supposed to be the god of Foresight, was he not? Was this sense of the future coming from him? It was certain that the feeling of power and certainty I was experiencing now was much like the feeling I'd had, the sense of self I'd possessed, in my dreams of his past.

Was Prometheus lending me his strength? Or was I somehow taking it against his will? Seeing me watching him, he nodded slightly. I was not using his prowess unbidden. He was supplementing my strength with his own. I wondered, would it weaken him? And yet he stood tall as my struggle continued. Indeed, if anything, he was invigorated by the sharing. Well, he was a Titan. He was strong. I was strong.

My next blow sent Raxes to the ground. Rubbing his bruised chin, he grinned up at me, his eyes now fully scarlet with fire. The aura about him was edged in yellow and white in places. Like a flame which gains intensity as it burns more fuel, he was getting stronger, brighter, fueled by our conflict.

"Yes!" he sang out. "That's it! Keep going!"

"You're enjoying this, aren't you?" I asked him. "No matter the pain, you're feeding off the violence!"

"Yes, yes!"

"After all, the god of war can't get enough war, can he? And you are the god of war!"

"I..." He looked uncertain for a moment, then he smiled again and said lustfully, "I am War!"

"That is all Raxes is, then?" I asked. "The desire for war?"

"War!" he shouted back at me. "I don't care about Raxes, I am War!"

Behind me, I heard a quiet moan from Athena.

"Fight me!" ordered Raxes. "You are my enemy!"

I stepped back from him. "I am Shepherd Autrey."

He shook his head like a madman. "No! You have no name! You are no one! You are the enemy!"

Slowly, I moved one step closer to him. "I am Shepherd," I said evenly.

"Shepherd," he repeated, as though in a trance. Then, petulantly, "I don't care!"

"Who are you?" I asked quietly.

"I am your enemy!"

"Who?" I asked again.

"I am Shepherd's enemy!" he screamed. "I will kill you!"

"I have no enemies," I answered him. "I love all that lives, as Christ does. So who are you?"

"I am your enemy!"

"Then you must not exist. You must be no one."

Athena whispered, "Shep... I beg you... stop."

Shrieking, Raxes charged me, and again we grappled on the ground. When he rolled on top of me, trying to get his hands about my throat, I drove my knee into his groin. He howled in pain. As he pulled away, I pressed my attack, again punching his face. He reeled, dazed.

I seized him by the shoulders and said, "I do not hate you. I do not wish to hurt you, but this is what you want, isn't it?" When he didn't answer, I shook him hard and shouted again, "Isn't it!?"

"Want... war... want hate," he panted.

"Jesus said that if a man wants your shirt, give him your coat as well. We are to give others what they want and need. That is Christian love. I'm giving you what you need. You need me to fight you. That is who you are."

"Shep," – Athena again – "don't you see what you're doing to him?"

* She still stood at a distance from our conflict, still the Queen presiding over gladiators. She wept, though. Beside her, Prometheus reached out and draped an arm around her shoulders. He seemed solemn about this conflict, but not distraught. I took comfort from that fact. He was not afraid...

My eyes scanned the Pretender again. Some detail had drawn my attention. Yes... was it my imagination, or were the scars on his abdomen fading?

"I'm giving your son what he wants, your Majesty," I replied. "Do you want more?" I asked him.

He nodded, trembling. He reminded me of dipsomaniacs I had treated, when withdrawal from alcohol was at its worst, and the delirium had set in. "More," he begged me.

I struck him again. He glowed brighter than ever, white and hot. I shoved him from me. He stumbled backwards. The fire about him grew blindingly bright and then began to fade. No... it wasn't the fire that was fading.

It was him. Raxes was fading away before my eyes.

Now Athena rushed forward, her regal sense of distance abandoned in light of her son's imminent demise. She grabbed me, her hands digging into my arms, attempting to tear me away.

"You don't know what you're doing!"

I looked at her impassively. She would never know what effort it took for me to look in a mother's terrified, tear-filled eyes and pretend I did not know of or care about her pain. "I know exactly what I'm doing. I'm killing him. I'm killing him by giving him what he wants most – my hand raised in violence. I'm feeding him the only thing he knows how to consume, and he's gorged himself on it. Like his father before him, he's allowing his ego to be absorbed by my rage. He's given up all desire to be himself any longer, as long as he's fed the energy of hatred that he so desperately craves!"

"Please," Athena wept. "If you understand the love of a mother for her son... "

"I do. At least I think I do. But your son is lost, goddess. All he knew is forgotten. All he knows is hate."

Her chin quivered and she shook her head in frantic denial. "You can't do this! Prometheus gave you this power, but he would never – "

"He would never hurt your son? I know that! Of course he wouldn't! He loves the stupid boy! That's why this insane conflict has gone on and on – neither of you is willing to raise a hand against him. Yet, that's what he's been trying to get you to do all these centuries. He wants to bring you down to his level. He wants to prove to himself that you're not better than he; because, if you are better, then you were right to reject him. He is unworthy!"

There was disbelief in Athena's eyes. "I never rejected him!"

"But you never embraced him. You only used him in your plan for a great future!"

"I wanted only the best for him!"

"He didn't care, because you didn't love him."

"I did love him! I do love him! Raxes!" She screamed at the fading image before us, "Raxes, don't do this! Don't give yourself up to this!" She turned to me. "Shep, I know how you're doing this! You're focusing all your rage, giving it to him. You're acting on your hatred in his name, and he can't help but drink it in!"

"That's right," I agreed.

"Then you can stop this!"

"I can. I won't."

She fell to her knees. Athena. The goddess. The Queen of Olympus. She fell to her knees before me. Before a mortal. "Please... I beg you... spare him."

"He won't spare my family."

"Yes," she insisted, "yes he will! I grant you my protection eternal! Look!" She pointed behind me.

I turned, and my heart stopped. Where moments ago my Xhylanna had lain a veritable corpse, unmoving, frozen in time, she now stood, healed, whole and beautiful. She looked at me in fear – her last memory was of nearly dying at Philip's hands. Then, inspecting herself, she realized she had been saved. She smiled at me and rushed forward.

"Shep!" she sang as she took my hand in hers. "What has happened?"

Athena answered. "You are free, daughter, and you are safe."

Xhylanna, focused on me, had overlooked the presence of the others. Now she dropped to her knees. "Goddess," she said, head bowed, "forgive me. I did not – "

Athena reached out and took Xhylanna's hand. "Forgive me, daughter. I have let this go too far. Shep, please. You can save Raxes."

"Raxes?" Xhylanna wondered. Her gaze followed Athena's to the fading patch of light.

I squeezed my bride's hand to reassure her, then gestured for silence. I had to concentrate. I closed my eyes, relaxed my body, allowed my fists to unclench and my jaw muscles to loosen. I searched out my inner light again – no small task, considering the external light before me was still intense enough to penetrate my eyelids. I placed myself at peace. I remembered that Xhylanna was beside me, her hand in mine, that Hylas was unharmed. My anger drained away.

"Raxes!" Athena sighed, relieved. I opened my eyes. The boy-god was substantial again, if weak. He slumped to the ground, caught by the open arms of his mother and step-father. They both hugged him. Athena kissed his forehead, and Prometheus tousled his hair. He was too weak to protest their intimacy.

After a time, Athena said, "Thank you, Shep."

"Why didn't you just do this earlier?" I asked, gesturing to Xhylanna and Hylas. "You could have extended your protection at the outset, and stopped this madness."

"I would have left you without a cause to champion. Humans must strive for a goal. The gods must represent those goals. Only thus are your people able to strengthen mine through worship. I have broken the rules to save my child. Only time will tell what price I must pay for that."

"For doing what you obviously wanted to do all along?" I asked.

"You don't understand. Nectar and ambrosia keep us immortal, but worship is our food. We need your positive energies to keep us vital, to make us want to keep living. We must therefore always be what you expect us to be. Your love is our sustenance."

"No. Our love is your opiate. You are addicted to worship. Like any other addicts, you require each dose be more powerful than the last. In your quest for more of your chosen drug, you lose interest in all else. Life becomes meaningless. Only satisfying your damnable craving for a few minutes brings you any pleasure, and that pleasure is later offset by withdrawal and suffering. You are caught in a cycle you cannot break. Or could not."

"You think I have broken it, then?"

"You can answer that better than I, your majesty. Can you back down from your ongoing war with your son? Can you see past your rivalry and love him? Can you admit that you, yourself, would rather have loved Zeus than overthrow him?"

"He was hurting so many people – !"

"Yes! But he was your father! You were his little girl! His favorite! He loved you more than anything!"

"Except power," she amended. Her eyes were wet again.

"Except power," I agreed. "If he could have seen past his need to be the powerful king, and seen how much his daughter loved him, perhaps no overthrow would have been necessary. Perhaps he would have trusted you and your peaceful, wise counsel, and led the gods to break the cycle, and men to flourish, rather than stagnate. But he didn't see past his throne. He probably couldn't. Tell me, your majesty... can you?"

"I – I did not desire the throne!"

"And yet its brilliance blinds you to your son's needs. Just as your father was blinded, though he loved you more than anything."

"And I love Raxes more than anything!"

"Then why are you enemies?"

"Because... Because he chose to stand for war."

"He chose to stand for having a kingdom of his own. He didn't want the kingdom of Zeus, because Zeus had rejected him. He didn't want to rule alongside you because you had betrayed him. The Aspar were his chance to be his own man... or his own god. It's very like the choice you forced on me: betray my beliefs by killing, or betray my god by allying myself with Satan."

"It seems you did neither," said Prometheus, "and yet, were you aware that you were tapping my power?"

"I was."

"It does not frighten you that you were accepting the power of Satan?"

"Honestly...? I suppose it did frighten me, but... when Philip tried to kill Xhylanna, I realized exactly how it would be to live without her. I realized how very much I love her."

Xhylanna wrapped one arm around my shoulders and snuggled herself close to me, oblivious, suddenly, of the presence of her gods.

"All that I did in using your power, I did out of love. Although it flew in the face of everything I've been taught – everything I believe! – I used violence to defeat Raxes. I had to. I love Xhylanna." I paused a moment, then, trying out words that would only days ago been unutterable for me, I said, "And I love Hylas as well. That love is pure. I love them only for what they are and what they can be, not for any plan or purpose I might devise for them. Where love is pure, there can be no sin. Not even in using Satan's power."

Raxes was stirring now. He had been disoriented and docile. Now he struggled in Athena's embrace, pushing away her arms and trying to sit up on his own.

I knelt to speak to him. "Your mother loves you," I told him. "Perhaps you should consider that, and put an end to these games of war."

"Love!" he snorted. "She does not love!"

"How would you know?" I asked. "Have you ever loved anyone?"

Unbidden, Raxes's eyes cast briefly and bitterly at Prometheus.

"A child or a beast recognizes no emotion but anger," I went on. "He does not consider other feelings like love, because those we love disappoint us, and that brings pain. An immature creature refuses to confront that pain. But think, Raxes, you who admire bravery, how cowardly it is to only fight in battles where we can win. To only sustain the ephemeral losses of others."

His eyes flamed with rekindled rage. "You are nothing! I could stamp you out – "

"You could," I admitted. "And yet I continue. Humanity walks ever in the Shadow of Death, and yet God has told us to fear no evil, for He is with us. I have no power, but what I am given. And yet I continue to walk through that valley."

"And if I shatter your legs?" asked Raxes.

"Then I will crawl."

"Why?"

"Because I cannot give up. My life is God-given, and precious. I must make whatever I can of it. I must not waste it. If I had your powers, I can only begin to imagine what I'd do with them. But I would never idle them away, playing games with lower orders of animals."

Above me, Prometheus heaved a sigh and smiled admiringly. "Fire," he said firmly. "It was only a matter of time until one of you brought it back to the Heavens."

"That's what you need from us, isn't it?" I asked. "Not our worship, but our ability to fight a losing battle. You don't know how."

"Why would we?"

"Jesus taught humility. Though he had all the powers of God at his disposal, he walked as a man. He accomplished, in his helplessness, more than he would have by working miracles alone. It seems to me that your difficulties with Raxes began because you were so busy engineering the future that you neglected to tend to the present. You," I said to the grey-eyed beauty kneeling beside me, "were so busy being the Mother Goddess that you forgot to be a mother. You were so convinced that all you were doing was right, and that your motives were noble... you never allowed that you might be wrong. You couldn't forgive him for not forgiving you. You waited for unconditional surrender."

Prometheus considered it. "Admitting that they're wrong. Something mortals can do."

"Not easily," I said. "But, when you're not the grandest thing in the universe, you have to learn to be wrong occasionally."

Husband and wife eyed each other for a moment, hope for a potentially better future evident in their expressions, and yet I knew that they were also thinking that I was but a mortal who had not seen three full decades' existence. They had lived millennia. How could I know anything they didn't?

Surprising, then, when Prometheus said, "Perhaps... you can teach us."

Athena reached out and tenderly grasped Raxes's head, cupping her hand behind his ear. She drew him toward her, but he stiffened.

"I do not want you touching me!" he spat.

"What do you want?" she asked sadly.

"I... I do not know. Just leave me."

Athena looked back up at me. "How am I to love someone who hates me?"

She was stepping onto ground unfamiliar to me, but I had started down this road. It would have been cowardly to withdraw now. "I have no children of my own," I said. I looked to Xhylanna and added, "Not yet." My beloved grinned at me and winked. "But mortal parents do it all the time. You... you sometimes have to step back, for a time. Let Raxes be Raxes and then meet him on his own terms – not as a pawn, not as an opponent. Love him... help him... seek the best for him... even if he doesn't acknowledge that you're doing it. He won't be able to hurt you anymore, if you don't give him the power to... if you can find it in yourself to stop being what your worshipers expect you to be, and start being the person – the god, if you must – that you want to be."

"And what will my worshipers do then?" she asked.

"Perhaps they'll follow your example, and seek the best in themselves. Perhaps they'll give up trying to invoke your name to bring them victory in battle and use it to name that to which they aspire, that pinnacle they strive to attain." I shrugged. "Or perhaps they'll fall down on their backsides and bemoan their fate, demanding to know why you have forsaken them."

"They do that anyway," Athena observed.

"Many do; but... if you can lead them to see themselves as something other than pawns to be used... if you can see yourself as something other than their queen, directing them in their games... then perhaps you'll surpass your father and truly make a difference for your people. As it is, you have been trapped in the role of leader, the mortals of this planet in the roles of pawns, and no one has been free."

"We came here out of love for humanity," said Prometheus. "To give them a better future."

"But you suppressed that love, as you suppressed your love for Raxes, beneath your determination for them to succeed. Now humanity... and Raxes... are filled with bitterness."

I suddenly felt a fool, lecturing to gods. They were gods I didn't believe in, true, yet here they were! What was I to make of them? Whatever they were, they were older, smarter, more powerful than I... who was I to preach to them?

As if to echo my thoughts, Raxes said, to no one in particular, "I have been bested by a mortal. I am no sort of god. Even my most promising follower has deserted me. Perhaps it would have been best had I simply ceased to exist. Why did you stop him?" he demanded of his mother.

"I couldn't let you go," she wept.

Hylas stepped forward and knelt, not in deference to his god, but simply to be close enough to address him comfortably. "Raxes," he said quietly, even coaxingly, "I did not abandon you. I was never given a choice in following you, so, truly, I never was your follower. I was consecrated to you by my father. It seems both of us had parents trying to determine the courses of our lives."

To his credit, Hylas did not look up to see what the reaction of Raxes's parents was to his remarks. This moment was between him and the god in whose name he had lived his few years of life. "I chose a new path... at least, I think I've chosen it. I don't really know. Until a few days ago, I didn't know there were such choices. I was like you... locked into being what other people told me to be. Now I'm going to see who I can be on my own."

"You must feel terribly deceived by me," said Raxes. "I convinced you I was a powerful god to be followed. Now look at me."

"I have been... " Hylas stopped and chose the word carefully. "... disappointed by more than one person I chose to follow."

He did not look at me. I was grateful.

Hylas went on, "You never made me any promises, Raxes. Others made many promises on your behalf. I tried to hold Shep accountable for my expectations of him; he condemned me for not following his people's moral code... at some point, we have to start judging others by what they are, not what we wish they were, or we'll be at war each with everyone else's nature until the end of time."

"I thought such a war was exactly what I wanted," said Raxes. "I suppose... I suppose I have much to think about."

Athena spoke. She had dried her eyes, and the note of certainty which seemed to be her birthright had returned to her voice. "You need to do more than think, my son. I like another part of Shep's God's behavior – the part where the gods walk as humans. My father used to do that. I have done it. But we never limited ourselves to the helplessness of humans. I think it might benefit us if we did. I plan to make a sojourn on New Earth soon, as one of the mortals. I want you to do it now. Let the Aspar take

268 PEACE LORD OF THE RED PLANET

care of themselves for a while. You can walk among them and find your way."

"Why should I listen to you?" Raxes asked, but it wasn't as spiteful a question as it might have been. He only sounded tired.

"You don't have to, of course. You could refuse, and I suppose I could attempt to confine you, as my father once wanted to. Who knows? You might be so weak that I could do it; but I think even you recognize that debts must be paid. I saved your identity just now, with Shep's help."

"To settle the debt, then. I'll do as you ask. One year?"

Athena nodded agreeably. "Come back to me in one year. We'll see then where we stand."

"Just a minute," I said quickly.

"Shep?" Athena asked.

"There's the matter of my debt to be settled. You owe your life to us both, Raxes."

Athena looked dubious, but I could see that she agreed it was my right to ask. "What payment would you have, Shep?"

I nodded at Philip, who lay in a corner, trying to be invisible.

"Take him with you."

EPILOGUE

In bed in a palace guest room that night, lying in the afterglow, Xhylanna asked me, "Would you really have killed him, Shep?"

I had related to her all that had transpired while she was under Raxes's spell. It all seemed so unreal until now, retelling it.

"Beloved," I sighed, "I did not intend to kill him. Or drive him into dissolution, as the case may be. I fervently hoped that Athena would react as she did. Still, even the pretense of that kind of violence – "

"Your bruises are not pretend, my husband."

I winced as she demonstrated. "No. And I inflicted some real pain on Raxes. I thought I would never do such a thing to any being. My claim that he was not human and thus not subject to God's law may have fooled him, but I... no. I knew that what I was proposing to do was against God's law. I knew that the violence I was committing was against everything I believe."

"Have you changed your mind about the use of violence?"

"No. I still believe that God would not raise His hand against us, and so we have no business raising our hands against each other. And had Raxes only threatened my life, I would have let him kill me and be done with it."

"Shep!"

"My love, I would have. But..." I stopped and brushed a sweaty lock from her eyes. "He didn't threaten me. He threatened to kill you. And enslave Hylas. It may be breaking the rules, but... I'm just not strong enough to let that happen, if I can stop it. Motivated by love, I don't see that failure as a sin. If it is, well, I trust God is forgiving. For if it had come to it... yes. I would have killed him."

She kissed me, deeply and for a long time.

━━━━━━━━

Sunrise came to New Olympus. It's quite a spectacle to watch sunrise from so high above a planet's surface. A whole world stretches out before you, bathed in a warm glow from the guardian of worldly life... A brilliant metaphor for a new start.

Our ship was prepared to leave as morning washed over the city. Athena, Prometheus and a contingent of their people accompanied us as we prepared to depart.

"You could stay longer," said Prometheus.

Raxes and Philip were gone, sojourning in the world below, meeting its people and learning what it was to be human. Well, Raxes was learning. Philip knew already all that he would ever know about the subject, and that was not very much. When all was said and done, I pitied Raxes having to be in Philip's company for an extended period of time. I suppose I should have pitied Philip instead. After all, Raxes was not patient. He might kill my former friend in a fit of temper. I could summon no sympathy.

Prometheus clasped my hand. "You're always welcome here, my friend."

I laughed despite myself. "Always room for one more sinner in Hell?"

The Titan grinned. "I'm pleased you see the connection between the Judeo-Christian devil and myself. Many do not." He sobered. "But I'd ask you to consider something else: Zeus tortured me for generations."

"He punished you. For giving that which belonged to the gods to man."

"Precisely. I introduced you to sin, by making you aware that it existed, and giving you the ability to even ask the question, 'what is sinful?' In so doing, I made you responsible for your sins. I left you liable to pay the price for them."

"'The wages of sin is death,'" I quoted.

"The price for making a mistake is high," he agreed. "But we can't learn without making mistakes. And I don't believe a father demands that his children pick up after themselves before they are ready. While men and women learn, they will make mistakes, they will sin. If they must be accountable for all those sins while they learn, if their souls must be destroyed because they have been subjected to impurity, then they have no hope. They cannot grow, they cannot learn, for the process of learning must surely kill them. And yet, if they are to live, to learn, to grow, someone must clean up after them. The price for their mistakes must be paid. How did your god answer this need?"

"'For God so loved the world,'" I said, "'that he gave his only begotten son, that whosoever believeth in him should not perish, but have everlasting life.'"

He nodded again. "Christ paid the price for your sins, so that you could live on and grow. Zeus tortured me as punishment... payment... for the knowledge I gave humanity."

"Are you saying... you suffered... for our sins?"

He held up his hand. "Don't get too excited. There is great power in your belief in Christ, and I have no desire to supplant or damage it."

"But you said you were Satan!" I exclaimed.

"In many ways I am. Again, you are both right and wrong. But please just remember, as much as I am he who tempted mankind to sin, I am also he who paid the price for that sin."

"You're Satan... and Christ?" I asked.

"Isn't everybody?"

Athena embraced me, having similarly bid farewell to Xhylanna and Hylas. My wife nearly had to force herself to accept so informal a gesture from her goddess, but she managed. Would I have been similarly overwhelmed, were Jesus to hold out his arms to me? I thought it likely. Peter had balked at having his feet washed, after all.

"What will you do now, Shep?" Athena asked me.

"I believe I owe my bride a honeymoon," I said.

"A what?" wondered Xhylanna.

"When two people are married," I explained, "it's customary for them to go away from family and friends for a few days, to... "

"Have a lot of sex?" she grinned wickedly.

I blushed. "That, too. My people don't talk about that."

"Your people are very backward in that way. Besides, aren't we far away from our accustomed surroundings?" She gestured at the Olympian palace behind us. "And friends and family?"

"I'm here," said Hylas, sounding vaguely offended.

"The catamite doesn't count," Xhylanna replied. "Who would go away for days of sex and not bring their catamite?"

I drummed my fingers on her knee in annoyance and stared. "You're just trying to fluster me now, aren't you?"

"Now and forever, beloved," she laughed and snuggled close to me.

"After the days of sexual excess have ended," said Athena, amused, "what then? What will be your mission, Shep? Do you want to return to Earth?"

I studied a patch of flesh on Xhylanna's belly which I'd not yet memorized. "Never," I said. "Not without what I've found here. As to mission, my mission will always be that which my God has given me: to bring a message of peace and forgiveness to others. Aside from being home to the love of my life, this world is desperately in need of that message."

"I agree," said the goddess. "I have tried to spread it myself but, I'm afraid I'm still tarred with the brush of the war goddess. What this world needs is a god of peace, something that never existed in our traditions."

"My God is a god of peace," I said.

"But your god is a god of all. Peace, war, love, anger... don't your people ascribe them all to him?"

"And more."

"Mine are accustomed to multiple gods, each fulfilling a different purpose. I think the time has come for a god of peace." She looked deliberately at me. "It would not be the first time we have elevated a mortal to the pantheon. What do you say?"

"Me? A god of peace?"

Xhylanna looked impressed, and I thought Hylas might choke on his astonishment.

"It's fitting," said Athena.

"It's blasphemous! I'm a man, not God!"

"My brother Dionysus was no more divine than was, oh, Perseus or Achilles. There were legions of half-god, half-human children, and all were considered mortal. But Dionysus was a god. It's not just about birth, Shep."

"I'm not talking about breeding, I'm talking about... God is... well... God!"

"Yes, that's a profound argument."

Xhylanna leaned in to me. "Shep, think of what you could accomplish as one of their number. Think of the leadership you could provide!"

"Jesus led as a mortal. That's good enough for me. I mean no offense, Athena, but I don't even accept that you are gods in the sense I understand divinity. If I'm not willing to give you the title, I certainly won't take it myself."

"I suppose that's fair," she admitted.

"I have seen now, Athena, how truly like Jesus a man is capable of being. I was able, by faith, to resist temptation."

"What about your sins with me?" asked Xhylanna.

"And me?" asked Hylas.

"The only sin I committed with either of you was to judge your love as shameful or wrong, to wound you out of my own misguided sense of morality. Out of pride. Can you forgive me?"

Hylas laughed, and Xhylanna kissed me tenderly. "All is forgiven, my love."

"Then we have pushed sin away, and it cannot touch us. There can't be sin where no one is harmed, can there?" I turned back to the Queen of the so-called gods. "Like Jesus, I shall roam the world I have been reborn into. I won't save its people from sin, I'll show them how to rise above it, how to keep it from ever touching them. I'll show them how to love each other, as they love themselves. And first, perhaps, I'll have to show them they are worth loving... as I have been shown.

"Perhaps that was Christ's greatest gift to us: not that he saved us from sin, but that he gave divine authority to the idea that we were worth saving."

I gestured to the ship. "Now I believe it's time we were on our way."

"Where will we go?" asked Hylas. "None of us has a home any longer."

I placed my arms around them both. "Home is where our loved ones are, Hylas. I'm home now... wherever we go."

Xhylanna smiled and kissed me.

"So let's go explore this world of yours. See what we can teach. See what we can learn. And mostly... to find out what happens next."

"But now abideth faith, hope, love, these three; and the greatest of these is love." – Saul of Tarsus (The Apostle Paul)

Steven H. Wilson has interviewed Jonathan Frakes for *Starlog* magazine, written for DC Comics *Star Trek* classic and *Warlord* series, and, most recently, served as principal writer and director for Prometheus Radio Theatre and publisher of Firebringer Press. His original science fiction series, *The Arbiter Chronicles*, currently boasting sixteen full-cast audio dramas and the novel *Taken Liberty*, has won the Mark Time Silver Award and the Parsec Award for Best Audio Drama (long form). Active in science fiction fandom since 1984, he has written, drawn, edited and published fanzines, acted and directed with a comedy troupe, and served as a gopher, a con chair or a guest at roughly a hundred conventions. Wilson, who serves as IT manager for Howard County (Maryland) Fire & Rescue, holds degrees from the University of Maryland College of Journalism and the Johns Hopkins University Whiting School of Engineering. *Peace Lord of the Red Planet* is his second novel.